THE PLUM TREE

SHE WAS AT THE STATION IN HER PHAETON TO MEET ME

THE PLUM TREE

By

DAVID GRAHAM PHILLIPS

Author of
The Cost, Golden Fleece, Etc.

ILLUSTRATED BY
E. M. ASHE

THE GREGG PRESS
UPPER SADDLE RIVER, N.J.

First published in 1905 by The Bobbs - Merrill Company
Republished in 1968 by
The Gregg Press
121 Pleasant Avenue
Upper Saddle River, New Jersey, U.S.A.

Library of Congress Catalog Card Number: 68 - 57547

Printed in United States of America

AMERICAN NOVELS OF MUCKRAKING, PROPAGANDA, AND SOCIAL PROTEST

The United States has suffered quite a few spells of sickness, if one may judge by the long and varied procession of novels dealing with the ills of its society. As each generation has sought assurances for the social hope that springs eternal in a democracy, muckraking, propagandizing, and advocating reforms have been not only implicit in partisan politics but also germane to literary production. While it has been said that Americans are readier to believe in charlatans than in utopias, there remains a sneaking feeling that maybe Oscar Wilde was right when he remarked: "Progress is the realization of utopias." Some such moral—if indeed moral it be—may be derived from the Gregg series of "American Novels of Muckraking, Propaganda, and Social Protest."

One purpose underlying the selection of the titles in the series is to provide examples of socio-economic novels which are presently out of print but which are nevertheless important in showing the history of the genre, a topic so far treated by historians only sporadically. Most of these works can rarely be found in the original editions; and many were printed on paper which is beginning to shatter. The series should prove a boon to librarians and to scholars who work in the fields of literary history and the social sciences. Its usefulness as supplementary reading for college courses in American studies and social history speaks for itself.

In turning the pages of the novels we begin with the groping 1830's and the fabulous 40's—when, as Emerson put it, every man in New England was running around with a plan for reorganizing society in his vestpocket. And we end with the "Era of the Muckrakers"—when the long-existent fervor to remake the world nearer to the mind's desire became a contagious fever, and phrases were bandied about like "frenzied finance," "conspicuous consumption," "malefactors of great wealth," "how the other half lives" and "the shame of the cities." In this series we find artifacts from the days following the panic of 1837, when Horace Greeley devoted a regular column in his *Tribune* to the kind of "associationism" that overtook Brook Farm; and we come along to the period early in the present century when the "yellow" journalism of Hearst and Pulitzer reached full flower and young Sinclair

Lewis swept the floors of Helicon Hall, the socialist community supported by Upton Sinclair with the profits of *The Jungle*. That was the epoch when the young intellectuals stormed college halls to hear Jack London expound the principles of socialism. In between, we find specimens emanating from the Gilded Age, with the ensuing clamor against business combinations eventuating in the Sherman Anti-Trust Act of 1890, and the agricultural depression that aroused Midwestern farmers to "raise less corn and more hell" or to align themselves with the People's Party. Business panics in 1873 and 1893 stirred up the coals, young preachers discovered the social gospel, bewhiskered anarchists were the chief "reds," strikes became for the first time a matter of wide public concern, and the play based on *Uncle Tom's Cabin* was the best money-maker on the stage.

One of the features of the list is a careful selection of works concerned with the Negro. The earliest is *The Slave*, by the historian Richard Hildreth. It was not only the first fully developed antislavery novel, but a pattern-maker for the many subsequent tales presenting the chief character as a light-skinned mulatto. The Russians translated it in the 1950's. Another is Harriet Beecher Stowe's *Dred*, a sequel to *Uncle Tom's Cabin* and perhaps more cogent propaganda. The idea that the Negro is constitutionally unable to cope with American society is curiously set forth in *Liberia*, by Sarah J. Hale, a staunch Yankee best known for her verses about Mary and her little lamb. Mrs. Hale was propagandizing for solving the slavery problem by returning the Negroes to Africa. Presenting the Southern side, *Aunt Phillis's Cabin*, by Mary H. Eastman, has been chosen from the batch of novels which sought in vain to counter the effect of Mrs. Stowe's world-famed classic of protest. The blasting of Northern prejudice against the Negro after the Civil War is well illustrated in two works: Rebecca Harding Davis's *Waiting for the Verdict*, a title still apt a century after it first appeared, and Albion W. Tourgée's tract for the times *Pactolus Prime*, which vitriolically scores the essential prejudice of white against black and is, apparently, the first American novel dealing with the Negro problem with a setting in Washington, D. C.

Joaquin Miller's *Life Amongst the Modocs* deals with the mistreatment of Indians. Few in number but judiciously chosen for illustrative purposes are stories exposing the white slave traffic—

from the days when the Mann Act was legislated and city slums were being muckraked both in and out of fiction to a degree probably more thorough than is the case even today. Among the other problems considered in these stories are divorce, prisons, and the criminal code, political corruption, pacificism, states rights, the social responsibilities of the churches, the plight of the Jew and the Immigrant, and even medical frauds.

But the theme governing the largest single element in this collection is the business tycoon and the battle between the capitalist power elite and the working class. The range in the picturization of "the typical American figure," as Henry James declared the captain of industry to be, runs quite a gamut in the series, from the romantic treatment in *Sevenoaks,* by the first editor of *Scribner's Magazine,* to the excoriation of corporation machinations by avowed socialists not unacquainted with Karl Marx. The tycoons pilloried range from bankers, real estate promoters, mill owners, and railroad magnates to lumber barons. One might view the development of this theme in the amazing profusion of fictional examples as a symbol of the growing unrest precipitated in a traditionally agrarian society bewildered by its confrontation with huge industrial corporations and big cities. But possibly it proves no more than the homely wisdom distilled into the humorist's wisecrack: "We have met the enemy—and the enemy is us!"

PROFESSOR CLARENCE GOHDES
Duke University
September, 1968   *Durham, North Carolina*

DAVID GRAHAM PHILLIPS

David Graham Phillips, journalist, reformer, essayist, and novelist, was born in Madison, Indiana, in 1867. His father was a banker; his mother was a descendant of "Light-Horse Harry" Lee, a hero of the Revolutionary War, whose combative spirit and audacity Phillips seemed to echo. Phillips attended school in Madison, and upon graduation took a job as a language tutor at Asbury College (now DePauw University), followed by a B. A. at Princeton, Class of 1887. That year he landed a job on the Cincinnati *Times-Star* on the strength of his coverage of a murder story. This coup was the beginning of a brilliant journalistic career. In 1890 he worked for the New York *Tribune*, and covered the Police Court beat for the *Sun*. Joseph Pulitzer, owner of the powerful *World*, recognized Phillips' genius, and sent him to London as a special correspondent, then promoted him to Editor in 1893, again largely because of a "scoop." This time Phillips was first with the story of the collision between the *Camperdown* and the *Victoria*, off the coast of Asia Minor. Pulitzer later revised his good opinion of his Editor when he recognized himself in *The Great God Success*, an attack upon yellow journalism.

In 1902, Phillips did free-lance work for the *Saturday Evening Post, McClure's, Munsey's, Everybody's, Delineator, Harper's,* and *Success*. He published an article called "Treason of the Senate" in *Cosmopolitan,* and earned the wrath of Theodore Roosevelt, who by coining the disparaging term "muckraker" gave a name to this now-famous school of literature. Phillips' exposé contributed to the movement for the popular election of senators, and earned him the hatred of the vested interests. From 1901 to 1911 he wrote twenty-three novels and a one-act play, *The Worth of a Woman,* which was performed at Madison Square Theatre in 1908. His novels were successful and averaged a sale of 100,000 copies each.

Phillips' unflattering portraits of upper-class American females cost him his life. On January 23, 1911, the mentally deranged son of a prominent doctor waited as Phillips approached the door of the New York Princeton Club, and fired six bullets into the body of this gifted, controversial writer who was only approaching the height of his career. The assassin believed that Phillips had maligned his sister in the character of Margaret Severance of *The Fashionable Adventures of Joshua Craig.* Phillips died the next evening at Bellevue Hospital.

Upper Saddle River, N. J.   F. C. S.
October, 1968

CONTENTS

THE PLUM TREE

THE PLUM TREE

I

HOW IT ALL BEGAN

"We can hold out six months longer,—at least six months." My mother's tone made the six months stretch encouragingly into six long years.

I see her now, vividly as if it were only yesterday. We were at our scant breakfast, I as blue as was ever even twenty-five, she brave and confident. And hers was no mere pretense to reassure me, no cheerless optimism of ignorance, but the through-and-through courage and strength of those who flinch for no bogey that life or death can conjure. Her tone lifted me; I glanced at her, and what shone from her eyes set me on my feet, face to the foe. The table-cloth was darned in many places, but so skilfully that you could

I

have looked closely without detecting it. Not a lump of sugar, not a slice of bread, went to waste in that house; yet even I had to think twice to realize that we were poor, desperately poor. She did not hide our poverty; she beautified it, she dignified it into Spartan simplicity. I know it is not the glamour over the past that makes me believe there are no women now like those of the race to which she belonged. The world, to-day, yields comfort too easily to the capable; hardship is the only mould for such character, and in those days, in this middle-western country, even the capable were not strangers to hardship.

"When I was young," she went on, "and things looked black, as they have a habit of looking to the young and inexperienced,"—that put in with a teasing smile for me,—"I used to say to myself, 'Well, anyhow, they can't *kill* me.' And the thought used to cheer me up wonderfully. In fact, it still does."

I no longer felt hopeless. I began to gnaw my troubles again—despair is still.

"Judge Granby is a dog," said I; "yes, a dog."

"Why 'dog'?" objected my mother. "Why

not simply 'mean man'? I've never known a dog that could equal a man who set out to be 'ornery.'"

"When I think of all the work I've done for him in these three years—"

"For yourself," she interrupted. "Work you do for others doesn't amount to much unless it's been first and best for yourself."

"But he was benefited by it, too," I urged, "and has taken life easy, and has had more clients and bigger fees than he ever had before. I'd like to give him a jolt. I'd stop nagging him to put my name in a miserable corner of the glass in his door. I'd hang out a big sign of my own over my own office door."

My mother burst into a radiant smile. "I've been waiting a year to hear that," she said.

Thereupon I had a shock of fright—inside, for I'd never have dared to show fear before my mother. There's nothing else that makes you so brave as living with some one before whom you haven't the courage to let your cowardice show its feather. If we didn't keep each other up to the mark, what a spectacle of fright and flight this

world-drama would be! Vanity, the greatest of
vices, is also the greatest of virtues, or the source
of the greatest virtues—which comes to the same
thing.

"When will you do it?" she went on, and then
I knew I was in for it, and how well-founded was
the suspicion that had been keeping my lips tight-
shut upon my dream of independence.

"I'll—I'll think about it," was my answer, in
a tone which I hoped she would see was not hesi-
tating, but reflective; "I mustn't go too far,—or
too fast."

"Better go too far and too fast than not go at
all," retorted my wise mother. "Once a tortoise
beat a hare,—*once*. It never happened again, yet
the whole timid world has been talking about it
ever since." And she fell into a study from which
she roused herself to say, "You'd better let *me*
bargain for the office and the furniture,—and the
big sign." She knew—but could not or would
not teach me—how to get a dollar's worth for a
dollar; would not, I suspect, for she despised par-
simony, declaring it to be another virtue which is
becoming only in a woman.

"Of course,—when—" I began.

"We've got to do something in the next six months," she warned. And now she made the six months seem six minutes.

I had at my tongue's end something about the danger of dragging her down into misfortune; but before speaking I looked at her, and, looking, refrained. To say it to *her* would have been too absurd,—to her who had been left a widow with nothing at all, who had educated me for college, and who had helped me through my first year there,—helped me with money, I mean. But for what she gave besides, more, immeasurably more, —but for her courage in me and round me and under me,—I'd never have got my degree or anything else, I fear. To call that courage help would be like saying the mainspring helps the watch to go. I looked at her. "They can't kill me, can they?" said I, with a laugh which sounded so brave that it straightway made me brave.

So it was settled.

But that was the first step in a fight I can't remember even now without a sinking at the heart. The farmers of Jackson County, of which Pulaski

was the county seat, found in litigation their chief
distraction from the stupefying dullness of farm
life in those days of pause, after the Indian and
nature had been conquered and before the big
world's arteries of thought and action had pene-
trated. The farmers took eagerly to litigation
to save themselves from stagnation. Still, a
new lawyer, especially if he was young, had an
agonizing time of it convincing their slow, stiff,
suspicious natures that he could be trusted in such
a crisis as "going to law."

To make matters worse I fell in love.

Once—it was years afterward, though not
many years ago—Burbank, at the time governor,
was with me, and we were going over the main
points for his annual message. One of my suggestions—my orders to all my agents, high and
low, have always been sugar-coated as "suggestions"—started a new train of thought in him,
and he took pen and paper to fix it before it had
a chance to escape. As he wrote, my glance wandered along the shelves of the book-cases. It
paused on the farthest and lowest shelf. I rose

and went there, and found my old school-books, those I used when I was in Public School Number Three, too near thirty years ago!

In the shelf one book stood higher than the others—tall and thin and ragged, its covers torn, its pages scribbled, stained and dog-eared. Looking through that old physical geography was like a first talk with a long-lost friend. It had, indeed, been my old friend. Behind its broad back I had eaten forbidden apples, I had aimed and discharged the blow-gun, I had reveled in blood-and-thunder tales that made the drowsy school-room fade before the vast wilderness, the scene of breathless struggles between Indian and settler, or open into the high seas where pirate, or worse-than-pirate Britisher, struck flag to American privateer or man-o'-war.

On an impulse shot up from the dustiest depths of memory, I turned the old geography sidewise and examined the edges of the cover. Yes, there was the *cache* I had made by splitting the paste-board with my jack-knife. I thrust in my finger-nail; out came a slip of paper. I glanced at Burbank—he was still busy. I, somewhat stealth-

ily, you may imagine, opened the paper and—
well, my heart beat much more rapidly as I saw
in a school-girl scrawl:

I was no longer master of a state; I was a boy
in school again. I could see her laboring over
this game of "friendship, love, indifference, hate."
I could see "Redney" Griggs, who sat between
her and me, in the row of desks between and
parallel to my row and hers,—could see him
swoop and snatch the paper from her, look at it,
grin maliciously, and toss it over to me. I was
in grade A, was sixteen, and was beginning to
take myself seriously. She was in grade D, was
little more than half my age, but looked older,—
and how sweet and pretty she was! She had
black hair, thick and wavy, with little tresses escaping from plaits and ribbons to float about her
forehead, ears, and neck. Her skin was darker
then, I think, than it is now, but it had the same

smoothness and glow,—certainly, it could not have had more.

I think the dart must have struck that day,— why else did I keep the bit of paper? But it did not trouble me until the first winter of my launching forth as "Harvey Sayler, Attorney and Counselor at Law." She was the daughter of the Episcopal preacher; and, as every one thought well of the prospects of my mother's son, our courtship was undisturbed. Then, in the spring, when fortune was at its coldest and love at its most feverish, her father accepted a call to a church in Boston, eight hundred miles away.

To go to see her was impossible; how could the money be spared,—fifty dollars, at the least? Once—when they had been gone about four months—my mother insisted that I must. But I refused, and I do not know whether it is to my credit or not, for my refusal gave her only pain, whereas the sacrifices she would have had to make, had I gone, would have given her only pleasure. I had no fear that Betty would change in our separation. There are some people you hope are stanch, and some people you think will be stanch, if—, and then there are those, many women and a few men, whom it is impossible to think of as false or even faltering. I did not fully appreciate that quality then, for my memory was not then dotted with the graves of false friendships and littered with the rubbish of broken promises; but I did appreciate it enough to build securely upon it.

Build? No, that is not the word. There may be those who are stimulated to achievement by being in love, though I doubt it. At any rate, I was not one of them. My love for her absorbed my thoughts, and paralyzed my courage. Of the qualities that have contributed to what success I may have had, I put in the first rank a disposition to see the gloomiest side of the future. But it has not helped to make my life happier, invaluable though it has been in preventing misadventure from catching me napping.

So another year passed. Then came hard times,—*real* hard times. I had some clients—enough to insure mother and myself a living, with the interest on mortgage and note kept down. But my clients were poor, and poor pay, and slow pay. Nobody was doing well but the note-shavers. I— How mother fought to keep the front brave and bright!—not her front, for that was bright by nature, like the sky beyond the clouds; but our front, my front,—the front of our affairs. No one must see that we were pinching,—so I must be the most obviously prosperous young lawyer in Pulaski. What that struggle cost her I did not then realize; no, could not realize until I looked at her face for the last time, looked and turned away and thought on the meaning of the lines and the hollows over which Death had spread his proclamation of eternal peace. I have heard it said of those markings in human faces, "How ugly!" But it seems to me that, to any one with eyes and imagination, line and wrinkle and hollow always have the somber grandeur of tragedy. I remember my mother when her face was smooth and had the shallow beauty that the shallow dote on. But her face whereon was written the story of fearlessness, sacrifice, and love,—that is the face beautiful of my mother for me.

In the midst of those times of trial, when she had ceased to smile,—for she had none of that hypocritical cheerfulness which depresses and is a mere vanity to make silly onlookers cry "Brave!" when there is no true bravery,—just when we were at our lowest ebb, came an offer from Bill Dominick to put me into politics.

I had been interested in politics ever since I was seven years old. I recall distinctly the beginning :—

On a November afternoon,—it must have been November, though I remember that it was summer-warm, with all the windows open and many men in the streets in shirt-sleeves,—at any rate, I was on my way home from school. As I neared the court-house I saw a crowd in the yard and was reminded that it was election day, and that my father was running for reëlection to the state senate; so, I bolted for his law office in the second story of the Masonic Temple, across the street from the court-house.

He was at the window and was looking at the polling place so intently that he took no notice of me as I stood beside him. I know now why he

was absorbed and why his face was stern and
sad. I can shut my eyes and see that court-house
yard, the long line of men going up to vote, single file, each man calling out his name as he
handed in his ballot, and Tom Weedon—who
shot an escaping prisoner when he was deputy
sheriff—repeating the name in a loud voice.
Each oncoming voter in that curiously regular
and compact file was holding out his right arm
stiff so that the hand was about a foot clear of
the thigh; and in every one of those thus conspicuous hands was a conspicuous bit of white
paper—a ballot. As each man reached the polling window and gave in his name, he swung
that hand round with a stiff-armed, circular motion that kept it clear of the body and in full
view until the bit of paper disappeared in the slit
in the ballot box.

I wished to ask my father what this strange
spectacle meant; but, as I glanced up at him to
begin my question, I knew I must not, for I felt
that I was seeing something which shocked him
so profoundly that he would take me away if I
reminded him of my presence. I know now that

I was witnessing the crude beginnings of the money-machine in politics,—the beginnings of the downfall of parties,—the beginnings of the overthrow of the people as the political power. Those stiff-armed men were the "floating voters" of that ward of Pulaski. They had been bought up by a rich candidate of the opposition party, which was less scrupulous than our party, then in the flush of devotion to "principles" and led by such old-fashioned men as my father with old-fashioned notions of honor and honesty. Those "floaters" had to keep the ballot in full view from the time they got it of the agent of their purchaser until they had deposited it beyond the possibility of substitution—he must see them "deliver the goods."

My father was defeated. He saw that, in politics, the day of the public servant of public interests was over, and that the night of the private servant of private interests had begun. He resigned the leadership into the dexterous hands of a politician. Soon afterward he died, muttering: "Prosperity has ruined my country!"

From that election day my interest in politics

grew, and but for my mother's bitter prejudice
I should have been an active politician, perhaps
before I was out of college.

Pulaski, indeed all that section of my state,
was strongly of my party. Therefore Dominick,
its local boss, was absolute. At the last county
election, four years before the time of which I
am writing, there had been a spasmodic attempt
to oust him. He had grown so insolent, and had
put his prices for political and political-commercial "favors" to our leading citizens so high,
that the "best element" in our party reluctantly
broke from its allegiance. To save himself he
had been forced to order flagrant cheating on the
tally sheets; his ally and fellow conspirator,
M'Coskrey, the opposition boss, was caught and
was indicted by the grand jury. The Reformers
made such a stir that Ben Cass, the county prosecutor, though a Dominick man, disobeyed his
master and tried and convicted M'Coskrey. Of
course, following the custom in cases of yielding
to pressure from public sentiment, he made the
trial-errors necessary to insure reversal in the
higher court; and he finally gave Dominick's

judge the opportunity to quash the indictment. But the boss was relentless,—Cass had been disobedient, and had put upon "my friend M'Coskrey" the disgrace of making a sorry figure in court. "Ben can look to his swell reform friends for a renomination," said he; "he'll not get it from me."

Thus it came to pass that Dominick's lieutenant, Buck Fessenden, appeared in my office one afternoon in July, and, after a brief parley, asked me how I'd like to be prosecuting attorney of Jackson County. Four thousand a year for four years, and a reëlection if I should give satisfaction; and afterward, the bench or a seat in Congress! I could pay off everything; I could marry!

It was my first distinct vision of the plum tree. To how many thousands of our brightest, most promising young Americans it is shown each year in just such circumstances!

II

That evening after supper I went to see Dominick.

In the lower end of Pulaski there was a large beer-garden, known as Dominick's headquarters. He received half the profits in return for making it his loafing-place, the seat of the source of all political honor, preferment and privilege in the third, sixth and seventh congressional districts. I found him enthroned at the end of a long table in the farthest corner of the garden. On one side of him sat James Spencer, judge of the circuit court,—"Dominick's judge"; on the other side Henry De Forest, principal owner of the Pulaski Gas and Street Railway Company. There were several minor celebrities in politics, the law, and business down either side of the table, then Fessenden, talking with Cowley, our lieutenant governor. As soon as I appeared Fessenden nodded

to me, rose, and said to the others generally:
"Come on, boys, let's adjourn to the next table.
Mr. Dominick wants to talk to this young fel-
low."

I knew something of politics, but I was not
prepared to see that distinguished company rise
and, with not a shadow of resentment on any
man's face, with only a respectful, envious glance
at me, who was to deprive them of sunshine for
a few minutes, remove themselves and their
glasses to another table. When I knew Dominick better, and other bosses in this republic of
ours, I knew that the boss is never above the
weaknesses of the monarch class for a rigid and
servile court etiquette. My own lack of this
weakness has been a mistake which might have
been serious had my political power been based
upon men. It is a blunder to treat men without
self-respect as if they were your equals. They
expect to cringe; if they are not compelled to do
so, they are very likely to forget their place. At
the court of a boss are seen only those who have
lost self-respect and those who never had it. The

first are the lower though they rank themselves,
and are ranked, above the "just naturally low."

But—Dominick was alone, his eternal glass of
sarsaparilla before him. He used the left corner
of his mouth both for his cigar and for speech.
To bid me draw near and seat myself, he had to
shift his cigar. When the few words necessary
were half-spoken, half-grunted, he rolled his
cigar back to the corner which it rarely left. He
nodded condescendingly, and, as I took the indicated chair at his right, gave me a hand that was
fat and firm, not unlike the flabby yet tenacious
sucker of a moist sea-creature.

He was a huge, tall man, enormously muscu-
lar, with a high head like a block, straight in
front, behind and on either side; keen, shifty, pig
eyes, pompous cheeks, a raw, wide mouth; slov-
enly dress, with a big diamond as a collar button
and another on his puffy little finger. He was
about forty years old, had graduated from black-
smith too lazy to work into prize-fighter, thence
into saloon-keeper. It was as a saloon-keeper that
he founded and built his power, made himself the

local middleman between our two great political factors, those who buy and break laws and those who aid and abet the lawlessness by selling themselves as voters or as office-holders.

Dominick had fixed his eyes upon his sarsaparilla. He frowned savagely into its pale brown foam when he realized that I purposed to force him to speak first. His voice was ominously surly as he shifted his cigar to say: "Well, young fellow, what can I do for you?"

"Mr. Fessenden told me you wanted to see me," said I.

"He didn't say nothing of the sort," growled Dominick. "I've knowed Buck seventeen years, and he ain't no liar."

I flushed and glanced at the distinguished company silently waiting to return to the royal presence. Surely, if these eminent fellow citizens of mine endured this insulting monarch, I could,— I, the youthful, the obscure, the despondent. Said I: "Perhaps I did not express myself quite accurately. Fessenden told me you were considering making me your candidate for county prosecutor, and suggested that I call and see you."

HE SHIFTED HIS CIGAR TO SAY: "WELL, YOUNG FELLOW, WHAT
CAN I DO FOR YOU?" *p. 20*

Dominick gave a gleam and a grunt like a hog that has been flattered with a rough scratching of its hide. But he answered: "I don't give no nominations. That's the province of the party, young man."

"But *you* are the party," was my reply. At the time I was not conscious that I had thus easily dropped down among the hide-scratchers. I assured myself that I was simply stating the truth, and ignored the fact that telling the truth can be the most degrading sycophancy, and the subtlest and for that reason the most shameless, lying.

"Well, I guess I've got a little something to say about the party," he conceded. "Us young fellows that are active in politics like to see young fellows pushed to the front. A good many of the boys ain't stuck on Ben Cass,—he's too stuck on himself. He's getting out of touch with the common people, and is boot-licking in with the swells up town. So, when I heard you wanted the nomination for prosecutor, I told Buck to trot you round and let us look you over. Good party man?"

"Yes—and my father and grandfather before me."

"No reform germs in your system?"

I laughed—I was really amused, such a relief was it to see a gleam of pleasantry in that menacing mass. "I'm no better than my party," said I, "and I don't desert it just because it doesn't happen to do everything according to my notions."

"That's right," approved Dominick, falling naturally into the rôle of political schoolmaster. "There ain't no government without responsibility, and there ain't no responsibility without organization, and there ain't no organization without men willing to sink their differences." He paused.

I looked my admiration,—I was most grateful to him for this chance to think him an intellect. Who likes to admit that he bows before a mere brute? The compulsory courtiers of a despot may possibly and in part tell the truth about him, after they are safe; but was there ever a voluntary courtier whose opinion of his monarch could be believed? The more distinguished the courtier the greater his necessity to exaggerate his royal master—or mistress—to others and to himself.

Dominick forged on: "Somebody's got to lead, and the leader's got to be obeyed. Otherwise what becomes of the party? Why, it goes to hell, and we've got anarchy."

This was terse, pointed, plausible—the stereotyped "machine" argument. I nodded emphatically.

"Ben Cass," he proceeded, "believes in discipline and organization and leadership only when they're to elect him to a fat job. He wants to use the party, but when the party wants service in return, up goes Mr. Cass' snout and tail, and off he lopes. He's what I call a cast iron—" I shall omit the vigorous phrase wherein he summarized Cass. His vocabulary was not large; he therefore frequently resorted to the garbage barrel and the muck heap for missiles.

I showed in my face my scorn for the Cass sort of selfishness and insubordination. "The leader has all the strings in his hand," said I. "He's the only one who can judge what must be done. He must be trusted and obeyed."

"I see you've got the right stuff in you, young man," said Dominick heartily. "So you want the job?"

I hesitated,—I was thinking of him, of his bestial tyranny, and of my self-respect, unsullied, but also untempted, theretofore.

He scowled. "Do you, or don't you?"

"Yes," said I,—I was thinking of the debts and mother and Betty. "Yes, indeed; I'd esteem it a great honor, and I'd be grateful to you." If I had thrust myself over-head into a sewer I should have felt less vile than I did as my fears and longings uttered those degrading words.

He grunted. "Well, we'll see. Tell the boys at the other table to come back." He nodded a dismissal and gave me that moist, strong grip again.

As I went toward the other table each man there had a hand round his glass in readiness for the message of recall. I mentally called the roll —wealth, respectability, honor, all on their knees before Dominick, each with his eye upon the branch of the plum tree that bore the kind of fruit he fancied. And I wondered how they felt inside,—for I was then ignorant of the great foundation truth of practical ethics, that a man's conscience is not the producer but the product of his career.

Fessenden accompanied me to the door. "The old man's in a hell of a humor to-night," said he. "His wife's caught on to a little game he's been up to, and she's the only human being he's afraid of. She came in here, one night, and led him out by the ear. What a fool a man is to marry when there's a chance of running into a mess like that! But—you made a hit with him. Besides, he needs you. Your family—" Buck checked himself, feeling that drink was making him voluble.

"He's a strong man, isn't he?" said I; "a born leader."

"Middle-weight champion in his day," replied Fessenden. "He can still knock out anybody in the organization in one round."

"Good night and thank you," said I. So I went my way, not elated but utterly depressed,— more depressed than when I won the first case in which I knew my client's opponent was in the right and had lost only because I outgeneraled his stupid lawyer. I was, like most of the sons and daughters of the vigorous families of the earnest, deeply religious early-West, an idealist by inheritance and by training; but I suppose any young man, however practical, must feel a shock when he begins those compromises between theoretical and practical right which are part of the daily routine of active life, and without which active life is impossible.

I had said nothing to my mother, because I did not wish to raise her hopes—or her objections. I now decided to be silent until the matter should be settled. The next day but one Fessenden came, bad news in his face. "The old man liked you," he began, "but—"

I had not then learned to control my expression. I could not help showing what ruins of lofty castles that ominous "but" dropped upon my head.

"You'll soon be used to getting it in the neck if you stay in politics," said Fessenden. "There's not much else. But you ain't so bad off as you think. The old man has decided that he can afford to run one of his reliable hacks for the place.

He's suddenly found a way of sinking his hooks
in the head devil of the Reformers and Ben Cass'
chief backer, Singer,—you know him,—the lawyer."

Singer was one of the leaders of the state bar
and superintendent of our Sunday-school.

"Dominick has made De Forest give Singer
the law business of the Gas and Street Railway
Company, so Singer is coming over to us." Buck
grinned. "He has found that 'local interests must
be subordinated to the broader interests of the
party in state and nation.' "

I had been reading in our party's morning paper what a wise and patriotic move Singer had
made in advising the putting off of a Reform
campaign,—and I had believed in the sincerity of
his motive!

Fessenden echoed my sneer, and went on:
"He's a rotten hypocrite; but then, we can always
pull the bung out of these Reform movements
that way."

"You said it isn't as bad for me as it seems,"
I interrupted.

"Oh, yes. You're to be on the ticket. The old

man's going to send you to the legislature,—
lower house, of course."

I did not cheer up. An assemblyman got only
a thousand a year.

"The pay ain't much," confessed Buck, "but
there ain't nothing to do except vote according to
order. Then there's a great deal to be picked
up on the side,—the old man understands that
others have got to live besides him. Salaries in
politics don't cut no figure nowadays, anyhow.
It's the chance the place gives for pick-ups."

At first I flatly refused, but Buck pointed out
that I was foolish to throw away the benefits sure
to come through the "old man's" liking for me.
"He'll take care of you," he assured me. "He's
got you booked for a quick rise." My poverty
was so pressing that I had not the courage to refuse,—the year and a half of ferocious struggle
and the longing to marry Betty Crosby had combined to break my spirit. I believe it is Johnson
who says the worst feature of genteel poverty is
its power to make one ridiculous. I don't think
so. No; its worst feature is its power to make
one afraid.

That night I told my mother of my impending
"honors." We were in the dark on our little
front porch. She was silent, and presently I
thought I heard her suppressing a sigh. "You
don't like it, mother?" said I.

"No, Harvey, but—I see no light ahead in
any other direction, and I guess one should always steer toward what light there is." She
stood behind my chair, put her hands on my
shoulders, and rested her chin lightly on the top
of my head. "Besides, I can trust you. Whatever direction you take, you're sure to win in the
end."

I was glad it was dark. An hour after I went
to bed I heard some one stirring in the house,—
it seemed to me there was a voice, too. I rose
and went into the hall, and so, softly to my mother's room. Her door was ajar. She was near the
window, kneeling there in the moonlight, pray-
ing—for me.

I had not been long in the legislature before I
saw that my position was even more contemptible than I anticipated. So contemptible, indeed,

was it that, had I not been away from home and among those as basely situated as myself, it would have been intolerable,—a convict infinitely prefers the penitentiary to the chain gang. Then, too, there was consolation in the fact that the people, my fellow citizens, in their stupidity and ignorance about political conditions, did not realize what public office had come to mean. At home they believed what the machine-controlled newspapers said of me—that I was a "manly, independent young man," that I was "making a vigorous stand for what was honest in public affairs," that I was the "honorable and distinguished son of an honorable and distinguished father." How often I read those and similar eulogies of young men just starting in public life! And is it not really amazing that the people believe, that they never say to themselves: "But, if he were actually what he so loudly professes to be, how could he have got public office from a boss and a machine?"

I soon gave up trying to fool myself into imagining I was the servant of the people by introducing or speaking for petty little popular measures. I saw clearly that graft was the backbone, the whole skeleton of legislative business, and that its fleshly cover of pretended public service could be seen only by the blind. I saw, also, that no one in the machine of either party had any real power. The state boss of our party, United States Senator Dunkirk, was a creature and servant of corporations. Silliman, the state boss of the opposition party, was the same, but got less for his services because his party was hopelessly in the minority and its machine could be useful only as a sort of supplement and scapegoat.

With the men at the top, Dunkirk and Silliman, mere lackeys, I saw my own future plainly enough. I saw myself crawling on year after year,—crawling one of two roads. Either I should become a political scullion, a wretched party hack, despising myself and despised by those who used me, or I should develop into a lackey's lackey or a plain lackey, lieutenant of a boss or a boss, so-called—a derisive name, really, when the only kind of boss-ship open was head political procurer to one or more rich corporations or groups of corporations. I felt I should probably become a scullion, as I thought I had no taste or instinct for business, and as I was developing some talent for "mixing," and for dispensing "hot air" from the stump.

I turned these things over and over in my mind with an energy that sprang from shame, from the knowledge of what my mother would think if she knew the truth about her son, and from a realization that I was no nearer marrying Betty Crosby than before. At last I wrought myself into a sullen fury beneath a calm surface. The lessons in self-restraint and self-hiding I learned in that first of my two years as assemblyman have been invaluable.

When I entered upon my second and last winter, I was outwardly as serene as—as a volcano on the verge of eruption.

III

SAYLER "DRAWS THE LINE"

In February the railways traversing our state sent to the capitol a bill that had been drawn by our ablest lawyers and reviewed by the craftiest of the great corporation lawyers of New York City. Its purpose, most shrewdly and slyly concealed, was to exempt the railways from practically all taxation. It was so subtly worded that this would be disclosed only when the companies should be brought to court for refusing to pay their usual share of the taxes. Such measures are usually "straddled" through a legislature,—that is, neither party takes the responsibility, but the boss of each machine assigns to vote for them all the men whose seats are secure beyond any ordinary assault of public indignation. In this case, of the ninety-one members of the lower house, thirty-two were assigned by Dunkirk and seventeen by Silliman to make up a majority with three to spare.

My boss, Dominick, got wind that Dunkirk and Silliman were cutting an extra melon of uncommon size. He descended upon the capitol and served notice on Dunkirk that the eleven Dominick men assigned to vote for the bill would vote against it unless he got seven thousand dollars apiece for them,—seventy-seven thousand dollars. Dunkirk needed every one of Dominick's men to make up his portion of the majority; he yielded after trying in vain to reduce the price. All Dominick would say to him on that point, so I heard afterward, was:

"Every day you put me off, I go up a thousand dollars a head."

We who were to be voted so profitably for Dunkirk, Silliman, Dominick, and the railroads, learned what was going on,—Silliman went on a "tear" and talked too much. Nine of us, *not* including myself, got together and sent Cassidy, member from the second Jackson County district, to Dominick to plead for a share. I happened to be with him in the Capital City Hotel bar when Cassidy came up, and, hemming and hawing, explained how he and his fellow insurgents felt.

Dominick's veins seemed cords straining to bind down a demon struggling to escape. "It's back to the bench you go, Pat Cassidy,—back to the bench where I found you," he snarled, with a volley of profanity and sewage. "I don't know nothing about this here bill except that it's for the good of the party. Go back to that gang of damned wharf rats, and tell 'em, if I hear another squeak, I'll put 'em where I got 'em."

Cassidy shrank away with a furtive glance of envy and hate at me, whom Dominick treated with peculiar consideration,—I think it was because I was the only man of education and of any pretensions to "family" in official position in his machine. He used to like to class himself and me together as "us gentlemen," in contrast to "them muckers," meaning my colleagues.

Next day, just before the voting began, Dominick seated himself at the front of the governor's gallery,—the only person in it. I see him now as he looked that day,—black and heavy-jawed and scowling, leaning forward with both forearms on the railing, and his big, flat chin resting on his upturned, stubby thumbs. He was there to see that each of us, his creatures, dependent absolutely upon him for our political lives, should vote as he had sold us in block. There was no chance to shirk or even to squirm. As the roll-call proceeded, one after another, seven of us, obeyed that will frowning from the gallery,— jumped through the hoop of fire under the quivering lash. I was eighth on the roll.

"Sayler!" How my name echoed through that horrible silence!

I could not answer. Gradually every face turned toward me,—I could see them, could feel them, and, to make bad enough worse, I yielded to an imperious fascination, the fascination of that incarnation of brute-power,—power of muscle and power of will. I turned my eyes upon the amazed, furious eyes of my master. It seemed to me that his lips must give passage to the oaths and filth swelling beneath his chest, and seething behind his eyes.

"Sayler!" repeated the clerk in a voice that exploded within me.

"No!" I shouted,—not in answer to the clerk,

but in denial of that insolent master-to-dog command from the beast in the gallery.

The look in his eyes changed to relief and contemptuous approval. There was a murmur of derision from my fellow members. Then I remembered that a negative was, at that stage of the bill, a vote for it,—I had done just the reverse of what I intended. The roll-call went on, and I sat debating with myself. Prudence, inclination, the natural timidity of youth, the utter futility of opposition, fear, above all else, fear,—these joined in bidding me let my vote stand as cast. On the other side stood my notion of self-respect. I felt I must then and there and for ever decide whether I was a thing or a man. Yet, again and again I had voted for measures just as corrupt, —had voted for them with no protest beyond a cynical shrug and a wry look. Every man, even the laxest, if he is to continue to "count as one," must have a point where he draws the line beyond which he will not go. The liar must have things he will not lie about, the thief things he will not steal, the compromiser things he will not compromise, the practical man in the pulpit, in politics, in business, in the professor's chair, or editorial tribune, things he will not sacrifice, whatever the cost. That is "practical honor." I had reached my line of practical honor, my line between possible compromise and certain demoralization. And I realized it.

When the roll-call ended I rose, and, in a voice that I knew was firm and clear, said: "Mr. Speaker, I voted in the negative by mistake. I wish my vote recorded in the affirmative. I am against the bill."

Amid a fearful silence I took my seat. With a suddenness that made me leap, a wild and crazy assemblyman, noted as the crank of that session, emitted a fantastic yell of enthusiastic approval. Again there was that silence; then the tension of the assembly, floor and crowded galleries, burst in a storm of hysterical laughter.

I wish I could boast how brave I felt as I reversed my vote, how indifferent to that tempest of mockery, and how strong as I went forth to meet my master and hear my death-warrant. But I can't, in honesty,—I'm only a human being, not a hero, and these are my *con*fessions, not my *pro-*

fessions. So I must relate that, though the voice that requested the change of vote was calm and courageous, the man behind it was agitated and sick with dread. There may be those who have the absolute courage some men boast,—if not directly, then by implication in despising him who shows that he has it not. For myself, I must say that I never made a venture,—and my life has been a succession of ventures, often with my whole stake upon the table,—I never made a venture that I did not have a sickening sensation at the heart. My courage, if it can be called by so sounding a name, has been in daring to make the throw when every atom of me was shrieking, "You'll lose! You'll be ruined!"

I did not see Dominick until after supper. I had nerved myself for a scene,—indeed, I had been hoping he would insult me. When one lacks the courage boldly to advance along the perilous course his intelligence counsels, he is lucky if he can and will goad some one into kicking him along it past the point where retreat is possible. Such methods of advance are not dignified, but then, is life dignified? To my sur-

prise and alarm, Dominick refused to kick me
into manhood. He had been paid, and the
seventy-seven thousand dollars, in bills of large
denomination, were warming his heart from the
inner pocket of his waistcoat. So he came up to
me, scowling, but friendly.

"Why didn't you tell me you wanted to be let
off, Harvey?" he said reproachfully. "I'd 'a' done
it. Now, damn you, you've put me in a place
where I've got to give you the whip."

To flush at this expression from Dominick
was a hypocritical refinement of sensitiveness.
To draw myself up haughtily, to turn on my
heel and walk away,—that was the silliness of a
boy. Still, I am glad I did both those absurd
things. When I told my mother how I had
ruined myself in politics she began to cry,—and
tears were not her habit. Then she got my
father's picture and kissed it and talked to it
about me, just as if he were there with us; and
for a time I felt that I was of heroic stature.

But, as the days passed, with no laurels in the
form of cases and fees, and as clients left me
through fear of Dominick's power, I shriveled

back to human size, and descended from my ped-
estal. From the ground-level I began again to
look about the matter-of-fact world.

I saw I was making only a first small pay-
ment on the heavy price for the right to say
no, for the right to be free to break with any man
or any enterprise that menaced my self-ownership. That right I felt I must keep, whatever its
cost. Some men can, or think they can, lend
their self-ownership and take it back at conve-
nience; I knew I was not of them—and let none
of them judge me. Especially let none judge me
who only deludes himself that he owns himself,
who has sold himself all his life long for salaries
and positions or for wealth, or for the empty
reputation of power he wields only on another's
sufferance.

A glance about me was enough to disclose the
chief reason why so many men had surrendered
the inner citadel of self-respect. In the crucial
hour, when they had had to choose between subservience and a hard battle with adversity, forth
from their hearts had issued a traitor weakness,
the feeling of responsibility to wife and children,

and this traitor had easily delivered them captive to some master or masters. More, or less, than human, it seemed to me, was the courage that could make successful resistance to this traitor, and could strike down and drag down wife and children. "I must give up Elizabeth," I said to myself, "for her own sake as well as for mine. Marry her I must not until I am established securely in freedom. And when will that be?" In my mood of darkness and despair, the answer to that question was a relentless, "Never, especially if you are weighted with the sense of obligation to her, of her wasting her youth in waiting for you."

I wrote her all that was in my mind. "You must forget me," I said, "and I shall forget you —for I see that you are not for me."

The answer came by telegraph—"Please don't ever again hurt me in that way." And of the letter which came two days later I remember clearly this sentence: "If you will not let me go on with you, I will make the journey alone."

This shook me, but I knew only too well how the bright and beautiful legions of the romantic

and the ideal could be put to flight, could be
hurled headlong into the abyss of oblivion by the
phalanxes of fact.

"I see what I must do," was my answer to her
letter. "And I shall do it. Be merciful to me,
Elizabeth. Do not tempt me to a worse cowardice than giving you up. I shall not write
again."

And I did not. Every one of her letters was
answered—sometimes, I remember, I wrote to
her the whole night through, shading my window
so that mother could not from her window see
the reflection of my lamp's light on the ground
and become anxious. But I destroyed those long
and often agonized answers. And I can not say
whether my heart was the heavier in the months
when I was getting her letters, to which I dared
not reply, or in those succeeding months when
her small, clear handwriting first ceased to greet
me from the mail.

IV

THE SCHOOL OF LIFE-AS-IT-IS

A day or so after I lost the only case of conse-
quence I had had in more than a year, Buck
Fessenden came into my office, and, after dosing
me liberally with those friendly protestations
and assurances which please even when they do
not convince, said: "I know you won't give me
away, Sayler, and I can't stand it any longer to
watch you going on this way. Don't you see the
old man's after you hammer and tongs? He'll
never let up. You won't get no clients, and, if
you do, *you won't win no cases.*"

Those last five words, spoken in Buck's most
significant manner, revealed what my modesty
—or, if you prefer, my stupidity—had hidden
from me. I had known all along that Dominick
was keeping away and driving away clients; but
I had not suspected his creatures on the bench.
To this day, after all these years of use, only
with the greatest reluctance and with a mor-

al uneasiness which would doubtless amuse
most political managers, do I send "suggestions"
or "intimations" to my men in judicial office—
and I always do it, and always have done it, in-
directly. And I feel relieved and grateful when
my judges, eager to "serve the party," anticipate
me by sending me a reassuring hint.

I did not let Buck see into my mind. "Nonsense!" I pooh-poohed; "I've no cause to complain of lack of business; but even if I had, I'd
not blame Dominick or any one else but myself."
Then I gave him a straight but good-humored
look. "Drop it, Buck," said I. "What did the
old man send you to me for? What does he
want?"

He was too crafty to defend an indefensible
position. "I'll admit he did send me," said he
with a grin, "but I came on my own account,
too. Do you want to make it up with him?
You can get back under the plum tree if you'll
say the word."

I could see my mother, as I had seen her two
hours before at our poor midday meal,—an old,
old woman, so broken, so worn! And all through

the misery this Dominick had brought upon us. Before I could control myself to speak, Buck burst out, a look of alarm in his face, "Don't say it, Mr. Sayler,—I know,—I know. I told him it'd be no use. Honest, he ain't as bad as you think,—he don't know no better, and it's because he liked and still likes you that he wants you back." He leaned across the desk toward me, in his earnestness,—and I could not doubt his sincerity. "Sayler," he went on, "take my advice, get out of the state. You ain't the sort that gives in, and no more is he. You've got more nerve than any other man I know, bar none, but don't waste it on a fool fight. You know enough about politics to know what you're up against."

"Thank you," said I, "but I'll stay on."

He gave over trying to persuade me. "I hope," said he, "you've got a card up your sleeve that the old man don't know about."

I made some vague reply, and he soon went away. I felt that I had confirmed his belief in my fearlessness. Yet, if he could have looked into my mind, how he would have laughed at his credulity! Probably he would have pitied me, too, for it is one of the curious facts of human nature that men are amazed and even disgusted whenever they see—in others—the weaknesses that are universal. I doubt not, many who read these memoirs will be quite honestly Pharisaical, thanking Heaven that they are not touched with any of my infirmities.

It may have been coincidence, though I think not, that, a few days after Fessenden's call, a Reform movement against Dominick appeared upon the surface of Jackson County politics. I thought, at the time, that it was the first streak of the dawn I had been watching for,—the awakening of the sluggish moral sentiment of the rank and file of the voters. I know now that it was merely the result of a quarrel among the corporations that employed Dominick. He had been giving the largest of them, Roebuck's Universal Gas and Electric Company, called the Power Trust, more than its proportional share of the privileges and spoils. The others had protested in vain, and as a last resort had ordered their lawyers to organize a movement to "purify" Jackson County, Dominick's stronghold.

I did not then know it, but I got the nomination for county prosecutor chiefly because none of the other lawyers, not even those secretly directing the Reform campaign, was brave enough publicly to provoke the Power Trust. I made a house to house, farm to farm, man to man, canvass. We had the secret ballot, and I was elected. The people rarely fail to respond to that kind of appeal if they are convinced that response can not possibly hurt, and may help, their pockets. And, by the way, those occasional responses, significant neither of morality nor of intelligence, lead political theorists far astray. As if honor or honesty could win other than sporadic and more or less hypocritical homage—practical homage, I mean—among a people whose permanent ideal is wealth, no matter how got or how used. That is another way of saying that the chief characteristic of Americans is that we are human and, whatever we may profess, cherish the human ideal universal in a world where want is man's wickedest enemy and wealth his most winning friend. But as I was relating, I was elected, and my majority, on the face of the returns, was between ten and eleven hundred. It must actually have been many thousands, for never before had Dominick "doctored" the tally sheets so recklessly.

Financially I was now on my way to the surface. I supposed that I had become a political personage also. Was I not in possession of the most powerful office in the county? I was astonished that neither Dominick nor any other member of his gang made the slightest effort to conciliate me between election day and the date of my taking office. I did succeed in forcing from reluctant grand juries indictments against a few of the most notorious, but least important, members of the gang; and I got one conviction—which was reversed on trial-errors by the higher court.

The truth was that my power had no existence. Dominick still ruled, through the judges and the newspapers. The press was silent when it could not venture to deprecate or to condemn me.

But I fought on almost alone. I did not fail to make it clear to the people why I was not succeeding, and what a sweep there must be before

Jackson County could have any real reform. I
made an even more vigorous campaign for re-
election than I had made four years before.
The farmers stood by me fairly well, but the
town went overwhelmingly against me. Why?
Because I was "bad for business" and, if re-
elected, would be still worse. The corporations
with whose · law-breaking I interfered were
threatening to remove their plants from Pulaski,
—that would have meant the departure of thousands of the merchants' best customers, and the
destruction of the town's prosperity. I think the
election was fairly honest. Dominick's man beat
me by about the same majority by which I had
been elected.

"Bad for business!"—the most potent of political slogans. And it will inevitably result some
day in the concentration of absolute power, political and all other kinds, in the hands of the few
who are strongest and cleverest. For they can
make the people bitterly regret and speedily re-
pent having tried to correct abuses; and the people, to save their dollars, will sacrifice their liberty. I doubt if they will, in our time at least, learn

to see far enough to realize that who captures their liberty captures them and, therefore, their dollars too.

By my defeat in that typical contest I was disheartened, embittered,—and ruined. For, in my enthusiasm and confidence I had gone deeply into debt for the expenses of the Reform campaign. At midnight of election day I descended into the black cave of despair. For three weeks I explored it. When I returned to the surface, I was a man, ready to deal with men on the terms of human nature. I had learned my lesson.

For woman the cost of the attainment of womanhood's maturity is the beautiful, the divine freshness of girlhood. For man, the cost of the attainment of manhood's full strength and power is equally great, and equally sad,—his divine faith in human nature, his divine belief that abstract justice and right and truth rule the world.

Even now, when life is redeeming some of those large promises to pay which I had long ago given up as hopeless bad debts; even now, it gives me a wrench to remember the cruelest chapter in that bitter lesson. So certain had I been of re-election that I had arranged to go to Boston the day after my triumph at the polls. For I knew from friends of the Crosbys in Pulaski that Elizabeth was still unmarried, was not engaged, and upon that I had built high a romantic hope.

I made up my mind that mother and I must leave Pulaski, that I must give up the law and must, in Chicago or Cleveland, get something to do that would bring in a living at once. Before I found courage to tell her that which would blast hopes wrapped round and rooted in her very heart, and, fortunately, before I had to confess to her the debts I had made, Edward Ramsay threw me a life-line.

He came bustling into my office one afternoon, big and broad, and obviously pleased with himself, and, therefore, with the world. He had hardly changed in the years since we were at Ann Arbor together. He had kept up our friendship, and had insisted on visiting me several times, though not in the past four years, which had been as busy for him as for me. Latterly his

letters urging me to visit him at their great country place, away at the other end of the state, had
set me a hard task of inventing excuses.

"Well, well!" he exclaimed, shaking my hand
violently in both his. "You wouldn't come to see
me, so I've come to you."

I tried not to show the nervousness this announcement stirred. "I'm afraid you'll find our
hospitality rather uncomfortable," was all I said.
Mother and I had not spread much sail to our
temporary gust of prosperity; and when the
storm began to gather, she straightway close-
reefed.

"Thanks, but I can't stop with you this time,"
said he. "I'm making an inspection of the Power
Trust's properties, and I've got mother and sister
along. We're living in the private car the company gives me for the tour." He went on to tell
how, since his father's death, he had been forced
into responsibilities, and was, among many other
things, a member of the Power Trust's executive
committee.

Soon came the inevitable question, "And how
are you getting on?"

"So so," replied I; "not too well, just at the present. I was beaten, you know, and have to go back to my practice in January."

"Wish you lived in my part of the state," said he. "But the Ramsay Company hasn't anything down here." He reflected a moment, then beamed. "I can get you the legal business of the Power Trust if you want it," he said. "Their lawyer down here goes on the bench, you know —he was on the ticket that won. Roebuck wanted a good, safe, first-class man on the bench in this circuit."

But he added nothing more about the Power Trust vacancy at Pulaski. True, my first impulse was that I couldn't and wouldn't accept; also, I told myself it was absurd to imagine they would consider me. Still, I wished to hear, and his failure to return to the subject settled once more the clouds his coming had lifted somewhat.

Mother was not well enough to have the Ramsays at the house that evening, so I dined with them in the car. Mrs. Ramsay was the same simple, silent, ill-at-ease person I had first met at the Ann Arbor commencement,—probably the

same that she had been ever since her husband's
wealth and her children's infection with new-
fangled ideas had forced her from the plain ways
of her youth. I liked her, but I was not so well
pleased with her daughter. Carlotta was then
twenty-two, had abundant, noticeably nice brown
hair, an indifferent skin, pettish lips, and restless
eyes, a little too close together,—a spoiled wilful
young woman, taking to herself the deference
that had been paid chiefly to her wealth. She
treated me as if I were a candidate for her favor
whom she was testing so that she might decide
whether she would be graciously pleased to tolerate him.

Usually, superciliousness has not disturbed
me. It is a cheap and harmless pleasure of cheap
and harmless people. But just at that time my
nerves were out of order, and Miss Ramsay's
airs of patronage "got" on me. I proceeded politely to convey to her the impression that she
did not attract me, that I did not think her worth
while—this, not through artful design of interesting by piquing, but simply in the hope of
rasping upon her as she was rasping upon me.

When I saw that I had gained my point, I ignored her. I tried to talk with Ed, then with his mother, but neither would interfere between me and Carlotta. I had to talk to her until she voluntarily lapsed into offended silence. Then Ed, to save the evening from disaster, began discussing with me the fate of our class-mates. I saw that Carlotta was studying me curiously,— even resentfully, I thought; and she was coldly polite when I said good night.

She and her mother called on my mother the next morning. "And what a nice girl Miss Ramsay is,—so sensible, so intelligent, and so friendly!" said my mother, relating the incidents of the visit in minute detail when I went home at noon.

"I didn't find her especially friendly," said I. Whereat I saw, or fancied I saw, a smile deep down in her eyes,—and it set me to thinking.

In the afternoon Ed looked in at my office in the court-house to say good-by. "But first, old man, I want to tell you I got that place for you. I thought I had better use the wire. Old Roebuck is delighted,—telegraphed me to close the ar-

rangement at once,—congratulated me on being
able to get you. I knew it'd be so. He has his
eyes skinned for bright young men,—all those
big men have. Whenever a fellow, especially a
bright young lawyer, shows signs of ability, they
scoop him in."

"I can't believe it," said I, dazed. "I've been
fighting him for four years—hard."

"That's it!" said he. "And don't you fret
about its being a case of trying to heap coals of
fire on your head. Roebuck don't use the fire-
shovel for that sort of thing. He's snapping you
up because you've shown him what you can do.
That's the way to get on nowadays, they tell me.
Whenever the fellows on top find the chap, especially one in public office, who makes it hot for
them, they hire him. Good business all around."

Thus, so suddenly that it giddied me, I was
translated from failure to success, from poverty to affluence, from the most harassing anxiety to ease and security. Two months before I
should have rejected the Power Trust's offer
with scorn, and should have gloried in my act
as proof of superior virtue. But in those crucial

two months I had been apprentice to the master
whom all men that ever come to anything in this
world must first serve. I had reformed my line
of battle, had adjusted it to the lines laid down
in the tactics of Life-as-it-is.

Before I was able to convince myself that my
fortunes had really changed, Ed Ramsay telegraphed me to call on him in Fredonia on business of his own. It proved to be such a trifle that
I began to puzzle at his real reason for sending
for me. When he spun that trifle out over ten
days, on each of which I was alone with Carlotta
at least half my waking hours, I thought I had
the clue to the mystery. I saw how I could in-
crease the energy of his new enthusiasm for me,
and, also, how I could cool it, if I wished to be
rash and foolish and to tempt fate again.

"Oh, the business didn't amount to much,"
was my answer to one of my mother's first questions, on my return. She smiled peculiarly. In
spite of my efforts, the red came—at least I felt
red.

"How did you like his sister?" she went on,
again with that fluttering smile in the eyes only.

"A very nice girl," said I, in anything but a natural manner. My mother's expression teased me into adding: "Don't be silly. Nothing of *that* sort. You are always imagining that every one shares your opinion of me. She isn't likely to fall in love with me. Certainly I shan't with her."

Mother's silence somehow seemed argumentative.

"I couldn't marry a girl for her money," I retorted to it.

"Of course not," rejoined mother. "But there are other things to marry for besides money, or love,—other things more sensible than either. For instance, there are the principal things,— home and children."

I was listening with an open mind.

"The glamour of courtship and honeymoon passes," she went on. "Then comes the sober business of living,—your career and your home. The woman's part in both is better played if there isn't the sort of love that is exacting, always interfering with the career, and making the home-life a succession of ups and downs, mostly downs."

"Carlotta is very ambitious," said I.

"Ambitious for her husband," replied my mother, "as a sensible woman should be. She appreciates that a woman's best chance for big dividends in marriage is by being the silent partner in her husband's career. She'll be very domestic when she has children. I saw it the instant I looked at her. She has the true maternal instinct. What a man who's going to amount to something needs isn't a woman to be taken care of, but a woman to take care of him."

She said no more,—she had made her point; and, when she had done that, she always stopped.

Within a month Ed Ramsay sent for me again, but this time it was business alone. I found him in a panic, like a man facing an avalanche and armed only with a shovel. Dunkirk, the senior United States senator for our state, lived at Fredonia. He had seen that, by tunneling the Mesaba Range, a profitable railroad between Fredonia and Chicago could be built that would shorten the time at least three hours. But it would take away about half the carrying business of the Ramsay Company, besides seriously depreciating the Ramsay interest in the existing road. "And," continued Ed, "the old scoundrel has got the capital practically subscribed in New York. The people here are hot for the new road. It'll be sure to carry at the special election, next month. He has the governor and legislature in his vest pocket, so they'll put through the charter next winter."

"I don't see that anything can be done," said Ed's lawyer, old Judge Barclay, who was at the consultation. "It means a big rake-off for Dunkirk. Politics is on a money basis nowadays. That's natural enough, since there is money to be made out of it. I don't see how those in politics that don't graft, as they call it, are any better than those that do. Would they get office if they didn't help on the jobs of the grafters? I suppose we might buy Dunkirk off."

"What do you think, Harvey?" asked Ed, looking anxiously at me. "We've got to fight the devil with fire, you know."

I shook my head. "Buying him off isn't fighting,—it's surrender. We must fight him,—with fire."

I let them talk themselves out, and then said, "Well, I'll take it to bed with me. Perhaps something will occur to me that can be worked up into a scheme."

In fact, I had already thought of a scheme, but before suggesting it I wished to be sure it was as good as it seemed. Also, there was a fundamental moral obstacle,—the road would be a public benefit; it ought to be built. That moral problem caused most of my wakefulness that night, simple though the solution was when it finally came. The first thing Ed said to me, as we faced each other alone at breakfast, showed me how well spent those hours were.

"About this business of the new road," said he. "If I were the only party at interest, I'd let Dunkirk go ahead, for it's undoubtedly a good thing from the public standpoint. But I've got to consider the interests of all those I'm trustee for,— the other share-holders in the Ramsay Company and in our other concerns here."

"Yes," replied I, "but why do you say Dunkirk intends to build the road? Why do you take that for granted?"

"He's all ready to do it, and it'd be a money-maker from the start."

"But," I went on, "you must assume that he has no intention of building, that he is only making an elaborate bluff. How do you know but that he wants to get this right of way and charter so that he can blackmail you and your concerns, not merely once, but year after year? You'd gladly pay him several hundred thousand a year not to use his charter and right of way, wouldn't you?"

"I never thought of that!" exclaimed Ed. "I believe you're right, Harvey, and you've taken a weight off my conscience. There's nothing like a good lawyer to make a man see straight. What an infernal hound old Dunkirk is!"

"And," I went on, "if he should build the road, what would he do with it? Why, the easiest and biggest source of profit would be to run big excursions every Saturday and Sunday, especially Sunday, into Fredonia. He'd fill the place every Sunday, from May till November, with roistering roughs from the slums of Chicago. How'd the people like that?"

"He wouldn't dare," objected Ramsay, stupidly insisting on leaning backward in his determination to stand straight. "He's a religious hypocrite. He'd be afraid."

"As Deacon Dunkirk he wouldn't dare," I replied. "But as the Chicago and Fredonia Short Line he'd dare anything, and nobody would blame him personally. You know how that is."

Ed was looking at me in dazed admiration. "Then," I went on, "there are the retail merchants of Fredonia. Has it ever occurred to them, in their excitement in favor of this road, that it'll ruin them? Where will the shopping be done if the women can get to Chicago in two hours and a half?"

"You're right, you're right!" exclaimed Ed, rising to pace the floor in his agitation. "Bully for you, Harvey! We'll show the people that the road'll ruin the town morally and financially."

"But you must come out in favor of it," said I. "We mustn't give Dunkirk the argument that you're fighting it because you'd be injured by it. No, you must be hot for the road. Perhaps you might give out that you were considering selling

your property on the lake front to a company that
was going to change it into a brewery and huge
pleasure park. As the lake's only a few hundred
yards wide, with the town along one bank and
your place along the other, why, I think that'd
rouse the people to their peril."

"That's the kind of fire to fight the devil with,"
said he, laughing. "I don't think Mister Senator
Dunkirk will get the consent of Fredonia."

"But there's the legislature," said I.

His face fell. "I'm afraid he'll do us in the
end, old man."

I thought not, but I only said, "Well, we've
got until next winter,—if we can beat him here."

Ed insisted that I must stay on and help him at
the delicate task of reversing the current of Fredonia sentiment. My share of the work was important enough, but, as it was confined entirely
to making suggestions, it took little of my time.
I had no leisure, however, for there was Carlotta
to look after.

When it was all over and she had told Ed and
he had shaken hands with her and had kissed me

and had otherwise shown the chaotic condition of his mind, and she and I were alone again, she said, "How did it happen? I don't remember that you really proposed to me. Yet we certainly are engaged."

"We certainly are," said I, "and that's the essential point, isn't it?"

"Yes," she admitted, "but,—" and she looked mystified.

"We drifted," I suggested.

She glanced at me with a smile that was an enigma. "Yes—we just drifted. Why do you look at me so queerly?"

"I was just going to ask you that same question," said I by way of evasion.

Then we both fell to thinking, and after a long time she roused herself to say, "But we shall be very happy. I am so fond of you. And you are going to be a great man and you do so look it, even if you aren't tall and fair, as I always thought the man I married would be. Don't look at me like that. Your eyes are strange enough when you are smiling; but when you—I often wonder what you're so sad about."

"Have you ever seen a grown person's face that wasn't sad in repose?" I asked, eager to shift from the particular to the general.

"A few idiots or near idiots," she replied with a laugh. Thereafter we talked of the future and let the past sleep in its uncovered coffin.

V

After Ed and I had carried the Fredonia election against Dunkirk's road, we went fishing with Roebuck in the northern Wisconsin woods. I had two weeks, two uninterrupted weeks, in which to impress myself upon him; besides, there was Ed, who related in tedious but effective detail, on the slightest provocation, the achievements that had made him my devoted admirer. So, when I went to visit Roebuck, in June, at his house near Chicago, he was ready to listen to me in the proper spirit.

I soon drew him on to tell of his troubles with Dunkirk—how the Senator was gouging him and every big corporation doing business in the state. "I've been loyal to the party for forty years," said he bitterly, "yet, if I had been on the other side it couldn't cost me more to do business. I have to pay enough here, heaven knows. But it costs me more in your state,—with your man

68

Dunkirk." His white face grew pink with anger.
"It's monstrous! Yet you should have heard him
address my Sunday-school scholars at the last annual outing I gave them. What an evidence of
the power of religion it is that such wretches as
he pay the tribute of hypocrisy to it!"

His business and his religion were Roebuck's
two absorbing passions,—religion rapidly pre-
dominating as he drew further away from sixty.

"Why do you endure this blackmailing, Mr.
Roebuck?" I asked. "He is growing steadily
worse."

"He is certainly more rapacious than he was
ten years ago," Roebuck admitted. "Our virtues
or our vices, whichever we give the stronger
hold on us, become more marked as we approach
Judgment. When we finally go, we are prepared
for the place that has been prepared for us."

"But why do you put up with his impudence?"

"What can we do? He has political power and
is our only protection against the people. They
have been inflamed with absurd notions about
their rights. They are filled with envy and suspicion of the rich. They have passed laws to ham-

per us in developing the country, and want to pass more and worse laws. So we must either go out of business and let the talents God has given us lie idle in a napkin, or pay the Dunkirks to prevent the people from having their ignorant wicked way, and destroying us and themselves. For how would they get work if we didn't provide it for them?"

"A miserable makeshift system," said I, harking back to Dunkirk and his blackmailing, for I was not just then in the mood to amuse myself with the contortions of Roebuck's flexible and fantastic "moral sense."

"I've been troubled in conscience a great deal, Harvey, a great deal, about the morality of what we business men are forced to do. I hope—indeed I feel—that we are justified in protecting our property in the only way open to us. The devil must be fought with fire, you know."

"How much did Dunkirk rob you of last year?" I asked.

"Nearly three hundred thousand dollars," he said, and his expression suggested that each dollar had been separated from him with as great

agony as if it had been so much flesh pinched
from his body. "There was Dominick, besides,
and a lot of infamous strike-bills to be quieted.
It cost five hundred thousand dollars in all—in
your state alone. And we didn't ask a single bit
of new legislation. All the money was paid just
to escape persecution under those alleged laws!
Yet they call this a free country! When I think
of the martyrdom—yes, the mental and moral
martyrdom, of the men who have made this country— What are the few millions a man may
amass, in compensation for what he has to endure? Why, Sayler, I've not the slightest doubt
you could find well-meaning, yes, really honest,
God-fearing people, who would tell you I am a
scoundrel! I have read *sermons,* delivered from
pulpits against me! *Sermons* from *pulpits!*"

"I have thought out a plan," said I, after a moment's silent and shocked contemplation of this
deplorable state of affairs, "a plan to end Dunkirk and cheapen the cost of political business."

At "cheapen the cost" his big ears twitched as
if they had been tickled.

"You can't expect to get what you need for

nothing," I continued, "in the present state of public opinion. But I'm sure I could reduce expenses by half—at least half."

I had his undivided attention.

"It is patently absurd," I went on, "that you who finance politics and keep in funds these fellows of both machines should let them treat you as if you were their servants. Why don't you put them in their place, servants at servants' wages?"

"But I've no time to go into politics,—and I don't know anything about it—don't want to know. It's a low business,—ignorance, corruption, filthiness."

"Take Dunkirk, for example," I pushed on. "His lieutenants and heelers hate him because he doesn't divide squarely. The only factor in his power is the rank and file of the voters of our party. They, I'm convinced, are pretty well aware of his hypocrisy,—but it doesn't matter much what they think. They vote like sheep and accept whatever leaders and candidates our machine gives them. They are almost stone-blind in their partizanship and they can always be fooled

up to the necessary point. And we can fool them
ourselves, if we go about it right, just as well as
Dunkirk does it for hire."

"But Dunkirk is *their* man, isn't he?" he suggested.

"Any man is their man whom you choose to
give them," replied I. "And don't *you* give them
Dunkirk? He takes the money from the big business interests, and with it hires the men to sit in
the legislature and finances the machine throughout the state. It takes big money to run a political machine. His power belongs to you people,
to a dozen of you, and you can take it away from
him; his popularity belongs to the party, and it
would cheer just as loudly for any other man who
wore the party uniform."

"I see," he said reflectively; "the machine rules
the party, and money rules the machine, and
we supply the money and don't get the benefit.
It's as if I let my wife or one of my employés
run my property."

"Much like that," I answered. "Now, why
shouldn't you finance the machine directly and do
away with Dunkirk, who takes as his own wages

about half what you give him? He takes it and wastes it in stock speculations,—gambling with your hard-earned wealth, gambling it away cheerfully, because he feels that you people will always give him more."

"What do you propose?" he asked; and I could see that his acute business mind was ready to pounce upon my scheme and search it hopefully if mercilessly.

"A secret, absolutely secret, combine of a dozen of the big corporations of my state,—those that make the bulk of the political business,—the combine to be under the management of some man whom they trust and whose interests are business, not political."

"He would have enormous power," said Roebuck.

I knew that he would point first and straight at that phase of my scheme, no matter how subtly I might disguise it. So I had pushed it into his face and had all but pointed at it myself so that I might explain it away. "Power?" said I. "How do you make that out? Any member of the combine that is dissatisfied can withdraw at any time

and go back to the old way of doing business. Besides, the manager won't dare appear in it at all,
—he'll have to hide himself from the people and from the politicians, behind some popular figurehead. There's another advantage that mustn't be overlooked. Dunkirk and these other demagogues who bleed you are inflaming public sentiment more and more against you big corporations,—that's their way of frightening you into yielding to their demands. Under the new plan their demagoguery would cease. Don't you think it's high time for the leaders of commerce and industry to combine intelligently against demagoguery? Don't you think they have cringed before it, and have financed and fostered it too long?"

This argument, which I had reserved for the last, had all the effect I anticipated. He sat rubbing his broad, bald forehead, twisting his white whiskers and muttering to himself. Presently he asked, "When are you and Lottie Ramsay going to be married?"

"In the fall," said I. "In about three months."

"Well, we'll talk this over again—after you

are married and settled. If you had the substantial interests to give you the steadiness and ballast, I think you'd be the very man for your scheme. Yes, something—some such thing as you suggest—must be done to stop the poisoning of public opinion against the country's best and strongest men. The political department of the business interests ought to be as thoroughly organized as the other departments are. Come to me again after you're married."

I saw that his mind was fixed, that he would be unable to trust me until I was of his class, of the aristocracy of corpulent corporate persons. I went away much downcast; but, two weeks afterward he telegraphed for me, and when I came he at once brought up the subject of the combine.

"Go ahead with it," he said. "I've been thinking it over and talking it over. We shall need only nine others besides myself and you. You represent the Ramsay interest."

He equipped me with the necessary letters of introduction and sent me forth on a tour of my state. When it was ended, my "combine" was formed. And *I* was the combine,—was master of this political blind pool. I had taken the first, the hardest step, toward the realization of my dream of real political power,—to become an unbossed boss, not the agent and servant of Plutocracy or Partizanship, but using both to further my own purposes and plans.

I had thus laid out for myself the difficult feat of controlling two fiery steeds. Difficult, but not impossible, if I should develop skill as a driver— for the skilful driver has a hand so light that his horses fancy they are going their own road at their own gait.

VI

MISS RAMSAY REVOLTS

The last remark Roebuck had made to me—
on his doorstep, as I was starting on my mission
—was: "Can't you and Lottie hurry up that marriage of yours? You ought to get it over and out
of the way." When I returned home with my
mission accomplished, the first remark my mother
made after our greeting was: "Harvey, I wish
you and Lottie were going to marry a little
sooner."

A note in her voice made me look swiftly at
her, and then, without a word, I was on my knees,
my face in her lap and she stroking my head. "I
feel that I'm going to—to your father, dear," she
said.

I heard and I thought I realized; but I did not.
Who, feeling upon him the living hand of love,
was ever able to imagine that hand other than
alive? But her look of illness, of utter exhaus-
tion,—*that* I understood and suffered for. "You

must rest," said I; "you must sit quiet and be waited on until you are strong again."

"Yes, I will rest," she answered, "as soon as my boy is settled."

That very day I wrote Carlotta telling her about mother's health and asking her to change the date of our wedding to the first week in August, then just under a month away. She telegraphed me to come and talk it over.

She was at the station in her phaeton to meet me. We had not driven far before I felt and saw that she was intensely irritated against me. As I unburdened my mind of my anxieties about mother, she listened coldly. And I had to wait a long time before I got her answer, in a strained voice and with averted eyes: "Of course, I'm sorry your mother isn't well, but I can't get ready that soon."

It was not her words that exasperated me; the lightning of speech from the storm-clouds of anger tends to clear the air. It was her expression.

Never have I known any one who could concentrate into brows and eyes and chin and lips

more of that sullen and aggressive obstinacy
which is the climax of provocativeness. Patience, in thought at least, with refusal has not
been one of my virtues. This refusal of hers, this
denial of happiness to one who had deserved so
much and had received so little, set temper to
working in me like a quick poison. But I was
silent, not so much from prudence as from ina-
bility to find adequate words.

"I can't do it," repeated Carlotta, "and I
won't." She made it clear that she meant the
"won't,"—that she was bent upon a quarrel.

But in my struggle to train those stanchest of
servants and maddest of masters, the passions, I
had got at least far enough always to choose both
the time and the ground of a quarrel. So I said:
"Very well, Carlotta. Then, that is settled." And
with an air sufficiently deceptive to pass muster
before angry eyes, I proceeded to talk of indifferent matters.

As I sat beside her, my temper glowering in
the straining leash, I revolved her conduct and
tried to puzzle out its meaning. It is clear,
thought I, that she does not care for me as people

about to marry usually profess to care. Then, does she wish to break the engagement?

That tamed my anger instantly.

Yes, I thought on, she wishes to be free—to free me. And, as my combine is formed and my career well advanced in the way to being established, what reason is there for trying to prevent her from freeing herself? None—for I can easily explain the situation to mother. "Yes," I concluded, "you can avoid a quarrel, can remain friends with Carlotta, can give and get freedom." What had changed her? I did not know; I did not waste time in puzzling; I did not tempt fate by asking. "You are poor, she is rich," I reminded myself. "That makes it impossible for you to hesitate. You must give her no excuse for thinking you lack pride."

Thus I reasoned and planned, my temper back in its kennel and peaceful as a sheep. That evening I avoided being alone with her; just as I was debating how to announce that I must be leaving by the first train in the morning a telegram came from Roebuck calling me to Chicago at once. When we were all going to bed, I said to Mrs.

Ramsay: "I shall see you and Ed in the morning, but"—to Carlotta—"you don't get up so early. I'll say good-by now,"—this in the friendliest possible way.

I was conscious of Mrs. Ramsay's look of wonder and anxiety; of Ed's wild stare from Carlotta to me and back again at her. She bit her lip and her voice was unsteady as she said: "Oh, no, Harvey. I'll be up." There was a certain meekness in her tone which would probably have delighted me had I been what is usually called "masterful."

When I came down at seven o'clock after an unquiet night, Carlotta was lying in wait for me, took me into the parlor and shut the door. "What do you mean?" she demanded, facing me with something of her wonted imperiousness.

"Mean?" said I, for once feeling no resentment at her manner.

"By leaving—this way," she explained with impatience.

"You heard Mr. Roebuck's telegram," said I.

"You are angry with me," she persisted.

"No, Carlotta," said I. "I was, but I am not.

As soon as I saw what you wished, I was grateful, not angry."

"What did I wish?"

"To let me know as gently and kindly as you could that you purposed to end our engagement. And I guess you are right. We do not seem to care for each other as we ought if we—"

"You misunderstood me," she said, pale and with flashing eyes, and in such a struggle with her emotions that she could say no more.

If I had not seen that only her pride and her vanity were engaged in the struggle, and her heart not at all, I think I should have abandoned my comfortable self-deception that my own pride forbade discussion with her. As it was, I was able to say: "Don't try to spare me, Carlotta, I'm glad you had the courage and the good sense not to let us both drift into irrevocable folly. I thank you." I opened the door into the hall. "Let us talk no more about it. We could say to each other only the things that sting or the things that stab. Let us be friends. You must give me your friendship, at least." I took her hand.

She looked strangely at me. "You want me

to humble myself, to crawl at your feet and beg your pardon," said she between her teeth. "But I shan't." She snatched away her hand and threw back her head.

"I wish nothing but what is best for us both," said I. "But let us not talk of it now—when neither of us is calm."

"You don't care for me!" she cried.

"Do *you* love *me?*" I rejoined.

Her eyes shifted. I waited for her reply and, when it did not come, I said: "Let us go to breakfast."

"I'll not go in just now," she answered, in a quiet tone, a sudden and strange shift from that of the moment before. And she let me take her hand, echoed my good-by, and made no further attempt to detain me.

That was a gloomy breakfast despite my efforts to make my own seeming of good-humor permeate to the others. Mrs. Ramsay hid a somber face behind the coffee-urn; Ed ate furiously, noisily, choking every now and then. He drove me to the station; his whole body was probably as damp from his emotions as were his eyes and

his big friendly hand. The train got under way;
I drew a long breath. I was free.

But somehow freedom did not taste as I had
anticipated. Though I reminded myself that I
had acted as any man with pride and self-respect
would have acted in such delicate circumstances,
and though I knew that Carlotta was no more in
love with me than I was with her, this end to our
engagement seemed even more humiliating to me
than its beginning had seemed. It was one more
instance of that wretched fatality which has pursued me through life, which has made every one
of my triumphs come to me in mourning robes
and with a gruesome face. In the glittering array
of "prizes" that tempts man to make a beast and
a fool of himself in the gladiatorial show called
Life, the sorriest, the most ironic, is the grand
prize, Victory.

The parlor car was crowded; its only untaken
seat was in the smoking compartment, which
had four other occupants, deep in a game of
poker. Three of them were types of commonplace, prosperous Americans; the fourth could

not be so easily classed and, therefore, interested me—especially as I was in the mood to welcome anything that would crowd to the background my far from agreeable thoughts.

The others called him "Doc," or Woodruff. As they played, they drank from flasks produced by each in turn. Doc drank with the others, and deeper than any of them. They talked more and more, he less and less, until finally he interrupted their noisy volubility only when the game compelled. I saw that he was one of those rare men upon whom amiable conversation or liquor or any other relaxing force has the reverse of the usual effect. Instead of relaxing, he drew himself together and concentrated more obstinately upon his game. Luck, so far as the cards controlled it, was rather against him, and the other three players took turns at audacious and by no means unskilful play. I was soon admiring the way he "sized up" and met each in turn. Prudence did not make him timid. He advanced and retreated, "bluffed" and held aloof, with acuteness and daring.

At a station perhaps fifty miles from Chicago,

the other three left,—and Doc had four hundred-odd dollars of their money.

I dropped into the seat opposite him—it was by the window—and amused myself watching him, while waiting for a chance to talk with him; for I saw that he was a superior person, and, in those days, when I was inconspicuous and so was not compelled constantly to be on guard, I never missed a chance to benefit by such exchanges of ideas.

He was apparently about forty years old, to strike a balance between the youth of eyes, mouth, and contour, and the age of deep lines and gray-ish, thinning hair. He had large, frank, blue eyes, a large nose, a strong forehead and chin, a grossly self-indulgent mouth,—there was the weakness, there, as usual! Evidently, the strength his mind and character gave him went in pandering to physical appetites. In confirmation of this, there were two curious marks on him,—a nick in the rim of his left ear, a souvenir of a bullet or a knife, and a scar just under the edge of his chin to the right. When he compressed his lips, this scar, not especially noticeable at other times, lifted up into his face, became of a sickly, bluish white, and transformed a careless, good-humored cynic into a man of danger, of terror.

His reverie began, as I gathered from his unguarded face, in cynical amusement, probably at his triumph over his friends. It passed on to still more agreeable things,—something in the expression of the mouth suggested thoughts of how he was going to enjoy himself as he "blew in" his winnings. Then his features shadowed, darkened, and I had my first view of the scar terrible. He shook his big head and big shoulders, roused himself, made ready to take a drink, noticed me, and said, "Won't you join me?" His look was most engaging.

I accepted and we were soon sociable, each taking an instinctive liking to the other. We talked of the business situation, of the news in the papers, and then of political affairs. Each of us saw that there he was at the other's keenest interest in life. He knew the game,—practical politics as distinguished from the politics talked by and to the public. But he evaded, without seeming to do so, all the ingenious traps I laid for drawing from him some admission that would give me a clue to where he "fitted in." I learned no more about him than I thought he learned about me.

"I hope we shall meet again," said I cordially, as we parted at the cab-stand.

"Thank you," he answered, and afterward I remembered the faint smile in his eyes.

I, of course, knew that Roebuck was greatly interested in my project for putting political business on a business basis; but not until he had explained why he sent for me did I see how it had fascinated and absorbed his mind. "You showed me," he began, "that you must have under you a practical man to handle the money and do the arranging with the heelers and all that sort of thing."

"Yes," said I; "it's a vital part of the plan. We must find a man who is perfectly trustworthy and discreet. Necessarily he'll know or suspect something—not much, but still something—of the inside workings of the combine."

"Well, I've found him," went on Roebuck, in a triumphant tone. "He's a godless person, with no character to lose, and no conception of what character means. But he's straight as a string. Providence seems to have provided such men for just such situations as these, where the devil must be fought with fire. I've been testing him for nearly fifteen years. But you can judge for yourself."

I was the reverse of pleased. It was not in my calculations to have a creature of Roebuck's foisted upon me, perhaps—indeed, probably—a spy. I purposed to choose my own man; and I decided while he was talking, that I would accept the Roebuck selection only to drop him on some plausible pretext before we began operations. I was to meet the man at dinner,—Roebuck had engaged a suite at the Auditorium. "It wouldn't do to have him at my house or club," said he; "neither do we want to be seen with him."

Coincidence is so familiar a part of the daily routine that I was not much surprised when my acquaintance, the astute poker player with the scar, walked in upon us at the Auditorium. But Roebuck was both astonished and chagrined when we shook hands and greeted each other like old friends.

"How do you do, Mr. Sayler?" said Woodruff.

"Glad to see you, Doctor Woodruff," I replied.

"Then you knew me all the time? Why didn't you speak out? We might have had an hour's business talk in the train."

"If I'd shown myself as leaky as all that, I guess there'd have been no business to talk about," he replied. "Anyhow, I didn't know you till you took out your watch with the monogram on the back, just as we were pulling in. Then I remembered where I'd seen your face before. I was up at your state house the day that you threw old Dominick down. That's been a good many years ago."

That chance, easy, smoking-compartment meeting, at which each had studied the other dispassionately, was most fortunate for us both.

The relation that was to exist between us— more, much more, than that of mere employer and employé—made fidelity, personal fidelity, imperative; and accident had laid the foundation for the mutual attachment without which there is certain to be, sooner or later, suspicion on both sides, and cause for it.

The two hours and a half with Woodruff, at and after dinner, served to reinforce my first impression. I saw that he was a thorough man of the world, that he knew politics from end to end, and that he understood the main weaknesses of human nature and how to play upon them for the advantage of his employers and for his own huge amusement. He gave a small exhibition of that skill at the expense of Roebuck. He appreciated that Roebuck was one of those unconscious hypocrites who put conscience out of court in advance by assuming that whatever they wish to do is right or *they* could not wish to do it. He led Roebuck on to show off this peculiarity of his, —a jumbling, often in the same breath, of the most sonorous piety and the most shameless business perfidy. All the time Woodruff's face was perfectly grave,—there are some men who refuse to waste any of their internal enjoyment in external show.

Before he left us I arranged to meet him the next morning for the settlement of the details of his employment. When Roebuck and I were alone, I said: "What do you know about him? Who is he?"

"He comes of a good family here in Chicago, —one of the best. Perhaps you recall the Bowker murder?"

"Vaguely," I answered.

"It was Woodruff who did it. We had a hard time getting him off. Bowker and Woodruff's younger brother were playing cards one day, and Bowker accused him of cheating. Young Woodruff drew,—perhaps they both drew at the same time. At any rate, Bowker shot first and killed his man,—he got off on the plea of self-defense. It was two years before Bowker and Doc met,—in the lobby of the Palmer House,—I happened to be there. I was talking to a friend when suddenly I felt as if something awful was about to happen. I started up, and saw Bowker just rising from a table at the far end of the room. I shan't ever forget his look,—like a bird charmed by a snake. His lips were ajar and wrinkled as if his blood had fled away inside of him, and his throat was expanding and contracting."

Roebuck wiped beads of sweat from his forehead. "It was Doc Woodruff walking slowly
toward him, with a wicked smile on his face, and
that scar—you noticed the scar?"

I nodded.

"Well, you can imagine how that scar stood
out. He came slowly on, nobody able to move a
muscle to stop him. When he was about ten feet
from Bowker and as near me as you are now,
Bowker gave a kind of shudder and scream of
fright, drew his pistol, and fired. The bullet
clipped Woodruff's ear. Quick as that—" Roebuck snapped his fingers—"Doc drew, and sent
a bullet into his heart. He fell forward across the
table and his pistol crashed on the marble floor.
Doc looked at him, gave a cold sort of laugh,
like a jeer and a curse, and walked out into the
street. When he met a policeman he said, 'I've
killed Dick Bowker. Here's my gun. Lock me
up'—perfectly cool, just as he talked to us to-
night."

"And you got him off?"

"Yes. I hated to do it, too, for Dick was one

of my best friends. But Doc was too useful to us. In his line he's without an equal."

"How did he get that scar?" said I.

"Nobody knows. He left here when he was a boy,—to avoid being sent to the reformatory. When he turned up, after a dozen years, he said he had been a doctor, but didn't say where or how. And he had that scar. One day a man asked him how he got it. He picked up a bottle, and, with his pleasant laugh, broke it over the fellow's jaw. 'About like that,' said he. People don't ask him questions."

"He's my man," said I.

VII

BYGONES

A telegram had been thrust under my door—
"I must see you. Don't fail to stop off here on
your way back. Answer. Carlotta."

Again she was at the station in her phaeton.
Her first look, long before I was near enough
for speech, showed me how her mood had
changed; but she waited until we were clear of
the town. "Forgive me," she then said in the abrupt, direct manner which was the expression of
her greatest charm, her absolute honesty. "I've
got the meanest temper in the world, but it don't
last, and as soon as you were gone I was ashamed
of myself."

"I don't understand why you are making these
apologies," said I, "and I don't understand why
you were angry."

"That's what it means to be a man," she replied. "Your letter about your mother made me
furious. You hadn't ever urged me to hurry up

the wedding on your own account. And your letter made me feel as if, while you personally didn't care whether we ever married or not, still for your mother's sake you were willing to—to sacrifice yourself."

"Let me see my letter," said I.

"I tore it into a thousand pieces," said she. "But I don't mean that you really wrote just that. You didn't. But you made me jealous of your mother, and my temper got hold of me, and then I read the meanest kind of things into and under and all round every word. And—I'm sorry."

I could find nothing to say. I saw my freedom slipping from me. I watched it, sick at heart; yet, on the other hand, I neither tried nor wished to detain it, though I could easily have made a renewal of our engagement impossible. I have no explanation for this conflict of emotions and motives.

"Don't make it so hard for me," she went on. "I never before in my life told anybody I was sorry for anything, and I thought I never would. But I *am* sorry, and—we'll have the wedding the first day of August."

Still I found nothing to say. It was so painfully obvious that, true to her training, she had not given and was not giving a thought to the state of my mind and feelings. What *she* wished, that she would do—the rest did not interest her.

"Are you satisfied, my lord?" she demanded. "Have I humbled myself sufficiently?"

"You haven't humbled yourself at all," said I. "You have only humbled me."

She did not pause on my remark long enough to see what it meant. "Now that it's all settled," she said gaily, "I don't mind telling you that I began to make my preparations to be married on the first of August—when, do you think?"

."When?" I said.

"The very day I got your nasty letter, putting me second to your mother." And she laughed, and was still laughing, when she added: "So, you see, I was determined to marry you."

"I do," said I dryly. "I suppose I ought to feel flattered."

"No, you oughtn't," she retorted. "I simply made up my mind to marry you. And I'd do it, no matter what it cost. I get *that* from father.

But I've got mother's disposition, too—and that makes me far too good for such a cold, unsentimental, ambitious person as you."

"Don't you think you're rather rash to confess so frankly—when I could still escape?"

"Not at all," was her confident answer. "I know you, and so I know nothing could make you break your word."

"There's some truth in that,"—and I hope that I do not deceive myself in thinking I was honest there. "More truth, perhaps, than you guess."

She looked shrewdly at me—and friendlily. "Don't be too sure I haven't guessed," said she. "Nobody's ever so blind as he lets others think. It's funny, isn't it? There are things in your mind that you'd never tell me, and things in my mind that I'd never tell you. And each of us guesses most of them, without ever letting on." She laughed queerly, and struck the horse smartly so that he leaped into a gait at which conversation was impossible.

When we resumed, the subject was the details of our wedding.

At home again, I found my mother too ill to

leave her bed. She had been ill before,—many
times when she wouldn't confess it, several times
when she was forced to admit it, but never before
so ill that she could not dress and come down
stairs. "I shall be up to-morrow," she assured
me, and I almost believed her. She drew a letter
from under her pillow. "This came while you
were away," she went on. "I kept it here, because—" a look of shame flitted across her face,
and then her eyes were steady and proud again,
—"why should I be ashamed of it? I had the
impulse to destroy the letter, and I'm not sure
but that I'm failing in my duty."

I took it,—yes, it was from Boston, from
Betty. I opened it and fortunately had nerved
myself against showing myself to my mother.
There was neither beginning nor end, just a single sentence:

"From the bottom of my broken heart I am
thankful that I have been spared the horror of
discovering I had bound myself for life to a
coward."

The shot went straight to the center of the target. But— There lay my mother—did *she* not

have the right to determine my destiny—she who had given me my life and her own? I tore up Betty's letter, and I looked at mother and said, "There's nothing in that to make me waver—or regret." It was the only lie I ever told her. I told it well, thank God, for she was convinced, and the look in her face repaid me a thousand-fold. It repays me once more as I write.

Carlotta and I were married at her bedside, and she lived only until the next day but one. When the doctor told me of the long concealed mortal disease that was the cause of her going, he ended with: "And, Mr. Sayler, it passes belief that she managed to keep alive for five years. I can't understand it." But *I* understood. She simply refused to go until she felt that her mission was accomplished.

"We must never forget her," said Carlotta, trying to console me by grieving with me.

I did not answer,—how could I explain? Never forget her! On the contrary, I knew that I must forget, and that I must work and grow and so heal the wound and cover its scar. I lost not a day in beginning.

To those few succeeding months I owe the power I have had all these years to concentrate my mind upon whatever I will to think about; for in those months I fought the fight I dared not lose—fought it and won. Let those who have never loved talk of remembering the dead.

I turned away from her grave with the resolve that my first act of power would be to stamp out Dominick. But for him she would not have gone for many a year. It was his persecutions that involved us in the miseries which wasted her and made her fall a victim to the mortal disease. It was his malignity that poisoned her last years, which, but for him, would have been happy.

As my plans for ousting Dunkirk took shape, I saw clearly that, if he were to be overthrown at once, I must use part of the existing control of the machine of the party,—it would take several years, at least three, to build up an entirely new control. To work quickly, I must use Croffut, Dunkirk's colleague in the Senate. And Croffut was the creature of Dominick.

Early in September Woodruff came to me, at Fredonia, his manner jubilant. "I can get Dominick," he exclaimed. "He is furious against Dunkirk because he's just discovered that Dunkirk cheated him out of a hundred thousand dollars on that perpetual street railway franchise, last winter."

"But we don't want Dominick," said I.

My face must have reflected my mind, for Woodruff merely replied, "Oh, very well. Of course that alters the case."

"We must get Croffut without him," I went on.

Woodruff shook his head. "Can't get him," he said. "Dominick controls the two southern ranges of counties. He finances his own machine from what he collects from vice and crime in those cities. He gives that branch of the plum tree to the boys. He keeps the bigger one, the corporations, for himself."

"He can be destroyed," said I, waving aside these significant reminders.

"Yes, in five years or so of hard work. Meanwhile, Dunkirk will run things at the capital to

suit himself. Anyhow, you're taking on a good
deal more than's necessary—starting with two
big fights, one of 'em against a man you ought to
use to do up the other. It's like breaking your
own sword at the beginning of the duel."

"Go back to the capital," said I, after a moment's thought; "I'll telegraph you up there what
to do."

It was my first test—my first chance to show
whether I had learned at the savage school at
which I had been a pupil. Scores, hundreds of
men, can plan, and plan wisely,—at almost any
cross-roads' general store you hear in the conversation round the stove as good plans as ever
moved the world to admiration. But execution,
—there's the rub! And the first essential of an
executive is freedom from partialities and hatreds,—not to say, "Do I like him? Do I hate
him? Was he my enemy a year or a week or a
moment ago?" but only to ask oneself the one
question, "Can he be useful to me *now?*"

"I will use Dominick to destroy Dunkirk, and
then I will destroy him," I said to myself. But
that did not satisfy me. I saw that I was tem-

porizing with the weakness that has wrecked more careers than misjudgment. I felt that I must decide then and there whether or not I would eliminate personal hatred from my life. After a long and bitter struggle, I did decide once and for all.

I telegraphed Woodruff to go ahead. When I went back to Pulaski to settle my affairs there, Dominick came to see me. Not that he dreamed of the existence of my combine or of my connection with the new political deal, but simply because I had married into the Ramsay family and was therefore now in the Olympus of corporate power before which he was on his knees,—for a price, like a wise devotee, untroubled by any such qualmishness as self-respect. I was ready for him. I put out my hand.

"I'm glad you're willing to let bygones be bygones, Mr. Sayler," said he, so moved that the tears stood in his eyes.

Then it flashed on me that, after all, he was only a big brute, driven blindly by his appetites. How silly to plot revenges upon the creatures of circumstance—how like a child beating the chair it happens to strike against! Hatreds and revenges are for the small mind with small matters to occupy it. Of the stones I have quarried to build my career, not one has been, or could have been, spared to waste as a missile.

I went down to the Cedar Grove cemetery, where my mother lay beside my father. My two sisters who died before I was born were at their feet; her parents and his on either side. And I said to her, "Mother, I am going to climb up to a place where I can use my life as you would have me use it. To rise in such a world as this I shall have to do many things you would not approve. I shall do them. But when I reach the height, I shall justify myself and you. I know how many have started with the same pledge and have been so defiled by what they had to handle that when they arrived they were past cleansing; and they neither kept nor cared to keep their pledge. But I, mother, shall not break this pledge to you."

VIII

About a month after the Chicago and Fredonia bill was smothered in committee there appeared upon the threshold of my office, in the administration building of the Ramsay Company, a man whom at first glance you might have taken for an exhorter or a collector for some pious enterprise. But if you had made a study of faces, your second glance would have cut through that gloze of oily, apologetic appeal. Behind a thin screen of short gray beard lay a heavy loose mouth, cruel and strong; above it, a great beak and a pair of pale green eyes, intensely alive. They were in startling contrast to the apparent decrepitude of the stooped shambling body, far too small for its covering of decent but somewhat rusty black.

"Senator Dunkirk," said I, rising and advancing to greet the justly feared leader of my party. I knew there was an intimate connection between this visit and the death of his pet project. I

107

thought it safe to assume that he had somehow
stumbled upon Woodruff's tunnelings, and with
that well-trained nose of his had smelled out their
origin. But I need not have disquieted myself; I
did not then know how softly Woodruff moved,
sending no warnings ahead, and leaving no trail
behind.

For several minutes the Senator and I felt for
each other in the dark in which we both straightway hid. He was the first to give up and reveal
himself in the open. "But I do not wish to waste
your time and my own, Mr. Sayler," he said; "I
have come to see you about the threatened split
in the party. You are, perhaps, surprised that I
should have come to you, when you have been so
many years out of politics, but I think you will
understand, as I explain myself. You know Mr.
Roebuck?"

"I can't say that I *know* him," I replied. "He
is not an easy man to know—indeed, who is?"

"A very able man; in some respects a great
man," Dunkirk went on. "But, like so many of
our great men of business, he can not appreciate
politics,—the difficulties of the man in public life

where persuasion and compromise must be used,
authority almost never. And, because I have re-
sisted some of his impossible demands, he has
declared war on the party. He has raised up in
it a faction headed by your old enemy, Dominick.
I need not tell you what a brute, what a beast he
is, the representative of all that is abhorrent in
politics."

"A faction headed by Dominick couldn't be
very formidable," I suggested.

"But Dominick isn't the nominal leader," replied Dunkirk. "Roebuck is far too shrewd for
that. No, he has put forward as the decoy my
colleague, Croffut,—perhaps you know him? If
so, I needn't tell you what a vain, shallow, venal
fellow he is, with his gift of gab that fools the
people."

"I know him," said I, in a tone which did not
deny the accuracy of Dunkirk's description.

"Their object," continued the Senator, "is to
buy the control of the party machinery away
from those who now manage it in the interests of
conservatism and fair dealing. If they succeed,
the only business interest that will be considered

in this state will be the Power Trust. And we
shall have Dominick, the ignorant brute, lashed
on by Roebuck's appetites, until the people will
rise in fury and elect the opposition,—and you
know what *it* is."

"What you say is most interesting," said I,
"but I confess I haven't imagination enough to
conceive a condition of affairs in which anybody
with 'the price' couldn't get what he wanted by
paying for it. Perhaps the business interests
would gain by a change,—the other crowd might
be less expensive. Certainly the demands of our
party's machine have become intolerable."

"It astonishes me, Mr. Sayler, to hear you say
that,—you, who have been in politics," he protested, taken aback by my hardly disguised attack upon him,—for he was in reality "party"
and "machine." "Surely, you understand the situation. We must have money to maintain our
organization, and to run our campaign. Our
workers can't live on air; and, to speak of only
one other factor, there are thousands and thousands of our voters, honest fellows, too, who
must be paid to come to the polls. They wouldn't

vote against us for any sum; but, unless we pay them for the day lost in the fields, they stay at home. Now, where does our money come from? The big corporations are the only source,—who else could or would give largely enough? And it is necessary and just that they should be repaid. But they are no longer content with moderate and prudent rewards for their patriotism. They make bigger and bigger, and more and more unreasonable, demands on us, and so undermine our popularity,—for the people can't be blinded wholly to what's going on. And thus, year by year, it takes more and more money to keep us in control."

"You seem to have forgotten my point," said I, smiling. "Why should *you* be kept in control? If you go out, the others come in. They bluster and threaten, in order to get themselves in; but, once they're elected, they discover that it wasn't the people's woes they were shouting about, but their own. And soon they are docile 'conservatives' lapping away at the trough, with nothing dangerous in them but their appetites."

"Precisely,—their appetites," said he.

"A starved man has to practise eating a long, long time before he can equal the performances of a trained glutton," I suggested.

His facial response to my good-humored raillery was feeble indeed. And it soon died in a look of depression that made him seem even older and more decrepit than was his wont. "The same story, wherever I go," said he sadly. "The business interests refuse to see their peril. And when I, in my zeal, persist, they,—several of them, Sayler, have grinned at me and reminded me that the legislature to be elected next fall will choose my successor! As if my own selfish interests were all I have in mind! I am old and feeble, on the verge of the grave. Do you think, Mr. Sayler, that I would continue in public life if it were not for what I conceive to be my duty to my party? I have toiled too long for it—"

"Your record speaks for itself, Senator," I put in, politely but pointedly.

"You are very discouraging, Sayler," he said forlornly. "But I refuse to be discouraged. The party needs you, and I have come to do my duty, and I won't leave without doing it."

"I have nothing to do with the company's political contributions," said I. "You will have to see Mr. Ramsay, as usual."

He waved his hand. "Let me explain, please. Roover is about to resign,—as you probably know, he's been chairman of the party's state committee for seventeen years. I've come to ask you to take his place."

It was impossible wholly to hide my amazement, my stupefaction. Had he had the shadowiest suspicion of my plans, of the true inwardness of the Croffut-Dominick movement, he would as readily have offered me his own head. In fact, he was offering me his own head; for, with the money and the other resources at my command, I needed only this place of official executive of the party to make me master. And here he was, giving me the place, under the delusion that he could use me as he had been using Roover.

He must have misread my expression, for he went on: "Don't refuse on impulse, Sayler. I and the others will do everything to make your duties as light as possible."

"I should not be content to be a mere figurehead, as Roover has been," I warned him. He had come, in his desperation, to try to get the man who combined the advantages of being, as he supposed, Dominick's enemy and a member of one of the state's financially influential families. He had come to cozen me into letting him use me in return for a mockery of an honor. And I was simply tumbling him, or, rather, permitting him to tumble himself, into the pit he had dug for me. Still, I felt that I owed it to my self-respect to give him a chance. "If I take the place, I shall fill it *to the best of my ability.*"

"Certainly, certainly,—we want your ability." Behind his bland, cordial mask I saw the spider eyes gleaming and the spider claws twitching as he felt his net quiver under hovering wings. "We want you—we need you, Sayler. We expect you to do your best."

My best! What would my "best" have been, had I been only what he thought,—dependent upon him for supplies, surrounded by his lieutenants, hearing nothing but what he chose to tell me, and able to execute only such orders as he gave or approved!

"I am sure we can count on you," he urged.

"I will try it," said I, after a further hesitation that was not altogether show.

He did not linger,—he wished to give me no chance to change my mind and fly his net. I was soon alone, staring dazedly at my windfall and wondering if fortune would ever give me anything without attaching to it that which would make me doubt whether my gift had more of bitter or more of sweet in it.

Dunkirk announced the selection of a new chairman that very afternoon,—as a forecast, of course, for there was the formality of my "election" by the sixty-three members of the state committee to be gone through. His proposition was well received. The old-line politicians remembered my father; the Reformers recalled my fight against Dominick; the business men liked my connection with the Ramsay Company, assuring stability and regard for "conservatism"; the "boys" were glad because I had a rich wife and a rich brother-in-law. The "boys" always cheer when a man with money develops political aspirations.

I did not see Woodruff until I went down to the capital to begin my initiation. I came upon him there, in the lobby of the Capital City Hotel. As we talked for a moment like barely-acquainted strangers, saying nothing that might not have been repeated broadcast, his look was asking: "How did you manage to trap Dunkirk into doing it?" I never told him the secret, and so never tore out the foundation of his belief in me as a political wizard. It is by such judicious use of their few strokes of good luck that successful men get their glamour of the superhuman. In the eyes of the average man, who is lazy or intermittent, the result of plain, incessant, unintermittent work is amazing enough. All that is needed to make him cry, "Genius!" is a little luck adroitly exploited.

I left Woodruff, to join Dunkirk. "Who is that chap over there,—Doctor Woodruff?" I asked him.

"Woodruff?" replied the Senator. "Oh, a lobbyist. He does a good deal for Roebuck, I believe. An honest fellow,—for that kind,—they tell me. It's always well to be civil to them."

Dunkirk's "initiation" of me into the duties of my office wiped away my last lingering sense of double, or, at least, doubtful, dealing. He told me nothing that was not calculated to mislead me. And he was so glib and so frank and so sympathetic that, had I not known the whole machine from the inside, I should have been his dupe.

It is not pleasant to suspect that, in some particular instance, one of your fellow men takes you for a simple-minded fool. To know you are being so regarded, not in one instance, but in general, is in the highest degree exasperating, no matter how well your vanity is under control.

Perhaps I should not have been able to play my part and deceive my deceiver had I been steadily at headquarters. As it was, I went there little and then gave no orders, apparently contenting myself with the credit for what other men were doing in my name. In fact, so obvious did I make my neglect as chairman that the party press commented on it and covertly criticized me. Dunkirk mildly reproached me for lack of interest. He did not know—indeed, he never knew—that his chief lieutenant, Thurston, in charge at headquarters, had gone over to "the enemy," and was Woodruff's right-hand man. And it is not necessary for me to say where Woodruff got the orders he transmitted to Thurston.

My excuse for keeping aloof was that I was about to be transformed into a man of family. As I was fond of children I had looked forward to this with more eagerness than I ventured to show to my wife. She might not have liked it, eager though she was also. As soon as she knew that her longings were to be satisfied, she entered upon a course of preparation so elaborate that I was secretly much amused, though I thoroughly approved and encouraged her. Every moment of her days was laid out in some duty imposed upon her by the regimen she had arranged after a study of all that science says on the subject.

As perfect tranquillity was a fundamental of the *régime,* she permitted nothing to ruffle her. But Ed more than made up for her calm. Two weeks before the event, she forbade him to enter her presence—"or any part of the grounds where I'm likely to see you," said she. "The very sight of you, looking so flustered, unnerves me."

While he and I were waiting in the sitting-room for the news, he turned his heart inside out.

"I want to tell you, Harvey," said he, "that the—boy or girl—whichever it is—is to be my heir."

"I shan't hold you to that," I replied with a laugh.

"No,—I'll never marry," he went on. "There was an—an angel. You know the Shaker settlement?—well, out there."

I looked at him in wonder. If ever there was a man who seemed unromantic, it was he, heavy and prosaic and so shy that he was visibly agitated even in bowing to a woman acquaintance.

"I met her," he was saying, "when I was driving that way,—the horse ran, I was thrown out, and her parents had to take me in and let her nurse me. You've seen her face,—or faces like it. Most of those Madonnas over on the other side in all the galleries suggest her. Well,—her parents were furious,—wouldn't hear of it,—you know Shakers think marriage and love and all those things are wicked. And she thought so, too. How she used to suffer! It wore her to a shadow. She wouldn't marry me,—wouldn't let me so much as touch her hand. But we used to meet and—then she caught a cold—waiting hours for me, one winter night, when there'd been a misunderstanding about the place—I was in one place, she in another. And the cold,—you see, she couldn't fight against it. And—and— there won't be another, Harvey. All women are sacred to me for her sake, but I couldn't any more marry than I could—could stop feeling her sitting beside me, just a little way off, wrapped in her drab shawl, with her face—like a glimpse through the gates of Heaven."

Within me up-started the memories that I kept battened down.

"Your children are mine, too, Harvey," he ended.

I took from Carlotta's work-basket an unfinished bit of baby clothing. I went to him and held it up and pointed to the monogram she had embroidered on it.

"E. R. S.," he read aloud. Then he looked at me with a queer expression beginning to form in his eyes.

"Edward Ramsay Sayler, if it's a boy," said I. "Edwina Ramsay Sayler, if it's a girl."

He snatched the bit of linen from me and buried his face in it.

The baby was a boy,—fortunately, for I don't admire the name Edwina, and I shouldn't have liked to handicap a child with it. Carlotta and Ed were delighted, but I felt a momentary keen disappointment. I had wanted a girl. Girls never leave their parents completely, as boys do. Also I should rather have looked forward to my child's having a sheltered life, one in which the fine and beautiful ideals do not have to be molded into the gross, ugly forms of the practical. I may say, in passing, that I deplore the entrance of women into the world of struggle. Women are the natural and only custodians of the ideals. We men are compelled to wander, often to wander far, from the ideal. Unless our women remain aloof from action, how are the ideals to be preserved? Man for action; woman to purify man, when he returns stained with the blood and sin of battle.

But—with the birth of the first child I began to appreciate how profoundly right my mother had been about marriage and its source of happiness. There are other flowers than the rose,— other flowers, and beautiful, the more beautiful for its absence.

IX

TO THE SEATS OF THE MIGHTY

We, our party, carried the state, as usual. Our
legislative majority was increased by eleven, to
thirty-seven on joint ballot. It was certain that
Dunkirk's successor would be of the same political faith; but would he be Dunkirk? At first that
venerable custodian of the plum tree hadn't a
doubt. He had come to look on it as his personal
property. But, after he had talked to legislators-
elect from various parts of the state, he became
uneasy. He found that the party's members were
dangerously evenly divided between himself and
the "Dominick-Croffut" faction. And soon he
was at me to declare for him.

I evaded as long as I could,—which did not
decrease his nervousness. When he put it to me
point-blank, I said: "I can't do it, Senator. I
will not mix in quarrels within the party."

"But they are saying you are against me," he
pleaded.

"And your people are saying I am for you," I retorted.

"But surely you are not against *me* and for Schoolcraft? What has he done for you?"

"And what have *you* done for me?" I replied, —a mere interrogation, without any feeling in it. "Tell me. I try to pay my debts."

His eyes shifted. "Nothing, Sayler, nothing," he said. "I didn't mean to insinuate that you owed me anything. Still, I thought—you wouldn't have been state chairman, except—"

As he halted, I said, "Except that you needed me. And you will recall that I took it only on condition that I should be free."

"Then you are opposed to me," he said. "Nobody can be on the fence in this fight."

"I do not think you can be elected," I replied.

As he sat silent, the puffs under his eyes swelled into bags and the pallor of his skin changed to the gray which makes the face look as if a haze or a cloud lay upon it. I pitied him so profoundly that, had I ventured to speak, I should have uttered impulsive generosities that would have cost me dear. How rarely are our

impulses of generosity anything but impulses to
folly, injustice, and wrong!

"We shall see," was all he said, and he rose and
shambled away.

They told me he made a pitiful sight, wheed-
ling and whining among the legislators. But he
degraded himself to some purpose. He succeeded
in rallying round him enough members to deadlock the party caucus for a month,—members
from the purely rural districts, where the sentiment of loyalty is strongest, where his piety and
unselfish devotion to the party were believed in,
and his significance as a "statesman." I let this
deadlock continue—forty-one for Dunkirk, forty-
one for Schoolcraft—until I felt that the party
throughout the state was heartily sick of the
struggle. Then Woodruff bought, at twelve
thousand dollars apiece, two Dunkirk men to
vote to transfer the contest to the floor of a joint
session of the two houses.

After four days of balloting there, seven Dominick-Croffut men voted for me—my first appearance as a candidate. On the seventy-seventh ballot Schoolcraft withdrew, and all the Domi-

nick-Croffut men voted for me. On the seventy-
ninth ballot I got, in addition, two opposition
votes Woodruff had bought for me at eight hundred dollars apiece. The ballot was: Dunkirk,
forty-one; Grassmere, (who was receiving the
opposition's complimentary vote) thirty-six;
Sayler, forty-three. I was a Senator of the
United States.

There was a wild scene. Threats, insults, blows
even, were exchanged. And down at the Capital
City Hotel Dunkirk crawled upon a table and denounced me as an infamous ingrate, a traitor, a
serpent he had warmed in his bosom. But the
people of the state accepted it as natural and satisfactory that "the vigorous and fearless young
chairman of the party's state committee" should
be agreed on as a compromise. An hour after that
last ballot, he hadn't a friend left except some
galling sympathizers from whom he hid himself. Those who had been his firmest supporters
were paying court to the new custodian of the
plum tree.

The governor was mine, and the legislature.
Mine was the Federal patronage, also—all of it,

if I chose, for Croffut was my dependent, though
he did not realize it; mine also were the indefinitely vast resources of the members of my combine. Without my consent no man could get office anywhere in my state, from governorship and
judgeship down as far as I cared to reach. Subject only to the check of public sentiment,—so
easily defeated if it be not defied,—I was master
of the making and execution of laws. Why? Not
because I was leader of the dominant party. Not
because I was a Senator of the United States.
Solely because I controlled the sources of the
money that maintained the political machinery of
both parties. The hand that holds the purse
strings is the hand that rules,—if it knows how
to rule; for rule is power *plus* ability.

I was not master because I had the plum tree.
I had the plum tree because I was master.

The legislature attended to such of the demands of my combine and such of the demands of
the public as I thought it expedient to grant, and
then adjourned. Woodruff asked a three months'
leave. I did not hear from or of him until mid-

summer, when he sent me a cablegram from London. He was in a hospital there, out of money and out of health. I cabled him a thousand dollars and asked him to come home as soon as he could. It was my first personal experience with that far from uncommon American type, the periodic drunkard. I had to cable him money three times before he started.

When he came to me at Washington, in December, he looked just as before,—calm, robust, cool, cynical, and dressed in the very extreme of the extreme fashion. I received him as if nothing had happened. It was not until the current of mutual liking was again flowing freely between us that I said: "Doc, may I impose on your friendship to the extent of an intrusion into your private affairs?"

He started, and gave me a quick look, his color mounting. "Yes," he said after a moment.

"When I heard from you," I went on, "I made some inquiries. I owe you no apology. You had given me a shock,—one of the severest of my life. But they told me that you never let—that—that peculiarity of yours interfere with business."

His head was hanging. "I always go away," he said. "Nobody that knows me ever sees me when—at that time."

I laid my hand on his arm. "Doc, why do you do—that sort of thing?"

The scar came up into his face to put agony into the reckless despair that looked from his eyes. For an instant I stood on the threshold of *his* Chamber of Remorse and Vain Regret,—and well I knew where I was. "Why not?" he asked bitterly. "There's always a—sort of horror—inside me. And it grows until I can't bear it. And then—I drown it—why shouldn't I?"

"That's very stupid for a man of your brains," said I. "There's nothing—nothing in the world, except death—that can not be wiped out or set right. Play the game, Doc. Play it with me for five years. Play it for all there is in it. Then— go back, if you want to."

He thought a long time, and I did not try to hurry him. At length he said, in his old off-hand manner: "Well, I'll go you, Senator; I'll not touch a drop."

And he didn't. Whenever I thought I saw

signs of the savage internal battle against the weakness, I gave him something important and absorbing to do, and I kept him busy until I knew the temptation had lost its power for the time.

This is the proper place to put it on the record that he was the most scrupulously honest man I have ever known. He dealt with the shadiest and least scrupulous of men—those who train their consciences to be the eager servants of their appetites; he handled hundreds of thousands of dollars, millions, first and last, all of it money for which he could never have been forced to account. He has had at one time as much as half a million dollars in checks payable to bearer. I am not confiding by nature or training, but I am confident that he kept not a penny for himself beyond his salary and his fixed commission. I put his salary at the outset, at ten thousand a year; afterward, at fifteen; finally, at twenty. His commissions, perhaps, doubled it.

There are many kinds of honesty nowadays. There is "corporate honesty," not unlike that proverbial "honor among thieves," which secures a fair or fairly fair division of the spoils. Then there is "personal honesty," which subdivides into three kinds—legal, moral, and instinctive. Legal honesty needs no definition. Moral honesty defies definition—how untangle its intertwinings of motives of fear, pride, insufficient temptation, sacrifice of the smaller chance in the hope of a larger? Finally, there is instinctive honesty—the rarest, the only bed-rock, unassailable kind. Give me the man who is honest simply because it never occurs to him, and never could occur to him, to be anything else. That is Woodruff.

There is, to be sure, another kind of instinctively honest man—he who disregards loyalty as well as self-interest in his uprightness. But there are so few of these in practical life that they may be disregarded.

Perhaps I should say something here as to the finances of my combine, though it was managed in the main precisely like all these political-commercial machines that control both parties in all the states, except a few in the South.

My assessments upon the various members of my combine were sent, for several years, to me, afterward to Woodruff directly, in one thousand, five thousand, and ten thousand dollar checks, sometimes by mail, and at other times by express or messenger.

These checks were always payable to bearer; and I made through Woodruff, for I kept to the far background in all my combine's affairs, an arrangement with several large banks in different parts of the state, including one at the capital, that these checks were to be cashed without question, no matter who presented them, provided there was a certain flourish under the line where the amount was written in figures. Sometimes these checks were signed by the corporation, and sometimes they were the personal checks of the president or some other high official. Often the signature was that of a person wholly disconnected, so far as the public knew. Once, I remember, Roebuck sent me a thousand dollar check signed by a distinguished Chicago lawyer who was just then counsel to his opponent in a case involving millions, a case which Roebuck afterward won!

Who presented these checks? I could more easily say who did not.

From the very beginning of my control I kept

my promise to reduce the cost of the political business to my clients. When I got the machine thoroughly in hand, I saw I could make it cost them less than a third of what they had been paying, on the average, for ten years. I cut off, almost at a stroke, a horde of lobbyists, lawyers, threateners without influence, and hangers-on of various kinds. I reduced the payments for legislation to a system, instead of the shameless, scandal-creating and wasteful auctioneering that had been going on for years.

In fact, so cheaply did I run the machine that I saw it would be most imprudent to let my clients have the full benefit. Cheapness would have made them uncontrollably greedy and exacting, and would have given them a wholly false idea of my value as soon as it had slipped their short memories how dearly they used to pay.

So I continued to make heavy assessments, and put by the surplus in a reserve fund for emergencies. I thought, for example, that I might some day have trouble with one or more members of my combine; my reserve would sup-

ply me with the munitions for forcing insurgents
to return to their agreements.

This fund was in no sense part of my private
fortune. Nowhere else, I think, do the eccentrici-
ties of conscience show themselves more interest-
ingly than in the various attitudes of the various
political leaders toward the large sums which the
exigencies of commercialized politics place absolutely and secretly under their control. I have
no criticism for any of these attitudes.

I have lived long enough and practically
enough to learn not to criticize the morals of
men, any more than I criticize their facial contour or their physical build. "As many men, so
many minds,"—and morals. Wrong, for practical purposes, is that which a man can not cajole
or compel his conscience to approve.

It so happened that I had a sense that to use
my assessments for my private financial profits
would be wrong. Therefore, my private fortune
has been wholly the result of the opportunities
which came through my intimacy with Roebuck
and such others of the members of my combine
as were personally agreeable,—or, perhaps it

would be more accurate to say, not disagreeable, for, in the circumstances, I naturally saw a side of those men which a friend must never see in a friend. I could not help having toward most of these distinguished clients of mine much the feeling his lawyer has for the guilty criminal he is defending.

X

Except the time given to the children,—there were presently three,—my life, in all its thoughts and associations, was now politics: at Washington, from December until Congress adjourned, chiefly national politics, the long and elaborate arrangements preliminary to the campaign for the conquest of the national fields; at home, chiefly state politics,—strengthening my hold upon the combine, strengthening my hold upon the two political machines. As the days and the weeks, the months and the years, rushed by, as the interval between breakfast and bedtime, between Sunday and Sunday, between election day and election day again, grew shorter and shorter, I played the game more and more furiously. What I won, once it was mine, seemed worthless in itself, and worth while only if I could gain the next point; and, when that was gained, the same story was repeated. Whenever I paused to reflect, it was to throttle reflection half-born, and hasten on again.

"A silly business, this living, isn't it?" said Woodruff to me.

"Yes,—but—" replied I. "You remember the hare and the hatter in *Alice in Wonderland*. 'Why?' said the hare. 'Why not?' said the hatter. A sensible man does not interrogate life; he lives it."

"H'm," retorted Woodruff.

And we went on with the game,—shuffling, dealing, staking. But more and more frequently there came hours, when, against my will, I would pause, drop my cards, watch the others; and I would wonder at them, and at myself, the maddest of these madmen,—and the saddest, because I had moments in which I was conscious of my own derangement.

I have often thought on the cause of this dissatisfaction which has never ceased to gird me, and which I have learned girds all men of intelligence who lead an active life. I think it is that such men are like a civilized man who has to live among a savage tribe. To keep alive, to have in-

fluence, he must pretend to accept the savage
point of view, must pretend to disregard his own
knowledge and intelligent methods, must play
the game of life with the crude, clumsy counters
of caste and custom and creed and thought which
the savages regard as fit and proper. Intelligent
men of action do see as clearly as the philosophers; but they have to pretend to adapt their
mental vision to that of the mass of their fellow
men or, like the philosophers, they would lead
lives of profitless inaction, enunciating truths
which are of no value to mankind until it redis-
covers them for itself. No man of trained reasoning power could fail to see that the Golden Rule
is not a piece of visionary altruism, but a sound
principle of practical self-interest. Or, could anything be clearer, to one who takes the trouble
really to think about it, than that he who ad-
vances himself at the expense of his fellow men
does not advance, but sinks down into the class
of murderers for gain, thieves, and all those who
seek to advance themselves by injustice? Yet, so
feeble is man's reason, so near to the brute is he,
so under the rule of brute appetites, that he can

not think beyond the immediate apparent good,
beyond to-day's meal.

I once said to Scarborough: "Politics is the
science and art of fooling the people."

"That is true, as far as it goes," he said. "If
that were all, justice, which is only another name
for common sense, would soon be established.
But, unfortunately, politics is the art of playing
upon cupidity, the art of fooling the people into
thinking they are helping to despoil the other fellow and will get a share of the swag."

And he was right. It is by subtle appeal to the
secret and shamefaced, but controlling, appetites
of men that the clever manipulate them. To get
a man to vote for the right you must show him
that he is voting for the personally profitable.
And very slow he is to believe that what is right
can be practically profitable. Have not the
preachers been preaching the reverse all these
years; have they not been insisting that to do
right means treasure in Heaven only?

It was in my second term as Senator, toward
the middle of it. I was speaking, one afternoon,

in defense of a measure for the big contributors,
which the party was forcing through the Senate
in face of fire from the whole country. Personally, I did not approve the measure. It was a
frontal attack upon public opinion, and frontal
attacks are as unwise and as unnecessary in politics as in war. But the party leaders in the nation
insisted, and, as the move would weaken their
hold upon the party and so improve my own
chances, I was not deeply aggrieved that my advice had been rejected. Toward the end of my
speech, aroused by applause from the visitors'
gallery, I forgot myself and began to look up
there as I talked, instead of addressing myself to
my fellow Senators. The eyes of a speaker always
wander over his audience in search of eyes that
respond. My glance wandered, unconsciously,
until it found an answering glance that fixed it.

This answering glance was not responsive, nor
even approving. It was the reverse,—and, in
spite of me, it held me. At first it was just a pair
of eyes, in the shadow of the brim of a woman's
hat, the rest of the face, the rest of the woman,
hid by those in front and on either side. There

was a movement among them, and the whole face appeared,—and I stopped short in my speech. I saw only the face, really only the mouth and the eyes,—the lips and the eyes of Elizabeth Crosby, —an expression of pain, and of pity.

I drank from the glass of water on my desk, and went on. When I ventured to look up there again, the face was gone. Had I seen or imagined? Was it she or was it only memory suddenly awakening and silhouetting her upon that background of massed humanity? I tried to convince myself that I had only imagined, but I *knew* that I had seen.

Within me—and, I suppose, within every one else—there is a dual personality: not a good and a bad, as is so often shallowly said; but one that does, and another that watches. The doer seems to me to be myself; the watcher, he who stands, like an idler at the rail of a bridge, carelessly, even indifferently, observing the tide of my thought and action that flows beneath,—who is he? I do not know. But I do know that I have no control over him,—over his cynical smile, or his lip curling in good-natured contempt of me, or his shrug at self-excuse, or his moods when he stares down at the fretting stream with a look of weariness so profound that it is tragic. It was he who was more interested in the thoughts,—the passion, the protest, the defiance, and the dread,—which the sight of that face set to boiling within me. Sometimes he smiled cynically at the turmoil, and at other times he watched it with what seemed to me bitter disgust and disappointment and regret.

While this tempest was struggling to boil over into action, Carlotta appeared. She had never stayed long at Washington after the first winter; she preferred, for the children and perhaps for herself, the quiet and the greater simplicity of Fredonia. But—"I got to thinking about it," said she, "and it seemed to me a bad idea for a man to be separated so long from his wife and children—and home influences."

That last phrase was accompanied by one of her queer shrewd looks.

"Your idea is not without merit," replied I judicially.

"What are you smiling at?" she demanded sharply.

I SAW ONLY THE LIPS AND EYES OF ELIZABETH CROSBY *p. 141*

"If it was a smile," said I, "it was at myself."

"No, you were laughing at me. You think I am jealous."

"Of what? Of whom?"

She looked fixedly at me and finally said: "I want to tell you two things about myself and you. The first is that I am afraid of you."

"Why?" said I.

"I don't know," she answered.

"And the second confession?"

"That I never trust you."

"Why?"

"I don't know."

"Yet you are always telling me I am cold."

She laughed shortly. "So is a stick of dynamite," said she.

She stayed on at Washington.

XI

It was through Carlotta that I came to know
Burbank well.

He was in the House, representing the eastern-
most district of our state. I had disliked him
when we were boys in the state assembly together,
and, when I met him again in Washington, he
seemed to me to have all his faults of fifteen years
before aggravated by persistence in them. Finally, I needed his place in Congress for a useful
lieutenant of Woodruff's and ordered him beaten
for the renomination. He made a bitter fight
against decapitation, and, as he was popular with
the people of his district, we had some difficulty
in defeating him. But when he was beaten, he
was of course helpless and hopelessly discredited,
—the people soon forget a fallen politician. He
"took off his coat" and worked hard and well
for the election of the man who had euchred him
out of the nomination. When he returned to

144

Washington to finish his term, he began a double,
desperate assault upon my friendship. The direct
assault was unsuccessful,—I understood it, and
I was in no need of lieutenants. More than I
could easily take care of were already striving to
serve me, scores of the brightest, most ambitious
young men of the state eager to do my bidding,
whatever it might be, in the hope that in return
I would "take care of" them, would admit them
to the coveted inclosure round the plum tree.
The plum tree! Is there any kind of fruit which
gladdens the eyes of ambitious man, that does not
glisten upon some one of its many boughs, heavy-
laden with corporate and public honors and
wealth?

Burbank's indirect attack, through his wife and
Carlotta, fared better.

The first of it I distinctly recall was after a
children's party at our house. Carlotta singled
out Mrs. Burbank for enthusiastic commendation.
"The other women sent nurses with their children," said she, "but Mrs. Burbank came herself.
She was so sweet in apologizing for coming. She
said she hadn't any nurse, and that she was so

timid about her children that she never could
bring herself to trust them to nurses. And really,
Harvey, you don't know how nice she was all the
afternoon. She's the kind of mother I approve of,
the kind I try to be. Don't you admire her?"

"I don't know her," said I. "The only time I
met her she struck me as being—well, rather silent."

"That's it," she exclaimed triumphantly. "She
doesn't care a rap for men. She's absorbed in her
children and her husband. " Then, after a pause,
she added: "Well, she's welcome to him. I can't
see what she finds to care for."

"Why?" said I.

"Oh, he's distinguished-looking, and polite,
offensively polite to women—he doesn't understand them at all—thinks they like deference and
flattery, the low-grade molasses kind of flattery.
He has a very nice smile. But he's so stilted
and tiresome, always serious,—and such a pose!
It's what I call the presidential pose. No doubt
he'll be President some day."

"Why?" said I. It is amusing to watch a woman fumble about for reasons for her intuitions.

Carlotta did uncommonly well. "Oh, I don't know. He's the sort of high-average American that the people go crazy about. He—he—*looks* like a President, that sort of—solemn—no-sense-of-humor, *Sunday* look,—you know what I mean. Anyhow, he's going to be President."

I thought not. A few days later, while what Carlotta had said was fresh in my mind, he overtook me walking to the capitol. As we went on together, I was smiling to myself. He certainly did look and talk like a President. He was of the average height, of the average build, and of a sort of average facial mold; he had hair that was a compromise among the average shades of brown, gray, and black, with a bald spot just where most men have it.

His pose—I saw that Carlotta was shrewdly right. He was acutely self-conscious, and was acting his pose every instant. He had selected it early in life; he would wear it, even in his nightshirt, until death. He said nothing brilliant, but neither did he say anything that would not have been generally regarded as sound and sensible. His impressive manner of delivering his words made one overvalue the freight they carried. But I soon found, for I studied him with increasing interest, thanks to my new point of view upon him,—I soon found that he had one quality the reverse of commonplace. He had magnetism.

Whenever a new candidate was proposed for Mazarin's service, he used to ask, first of all, "Has he luck?" My first question has been, "Has he magnetism?" and I think mine is the better measure. Such of one's luck as is not the blundering blindness of one's opponents is usually the result of one's magnetism. However, it is about the most dangerous of the free gifts of nature,—which are all dangerous. Burbank's merit lay in his discreet use of it. It compelled men to center upon him; he turned this to his advantage by making them feel, not how he shone, but how they shone. They went away liking him because they had new reasons for being in love with themselves.

I found only two serious weaknesses. The first was that he lacked the moral courage boldly to do either right or wrong. That explained why, in spite of his talents for impressing people both

privately and from the platform, he was at the
end of his political career. The second weakness
was that he was ashamed of his very obscure and
humble origin. He knew that his being "wholly
self-made" was a matchless political asset, and he
used it accordingly. But he looked on it somewhat as the beggar looks on the deformity he ex-
hibits to get alms.

Neither weakness made him less valuable to my
purpose,—the first one, if anything, increased his
value. I wanted an instrument that was capable,
but strong only when I used it.

I wanted a man suitable for development first
into governor of my state, and then into a President. I could not have got the presidency for
myself, but neither did I want it. My longings
were all for power,—the reality, not the shadow.
In a republic the man who has the real power
must be out of view. If he is within view, a million hands stretch to drag him from the throne.
He *must* be out of view, putting forward his pup-
pets and changing them when the people grow
bored or angry with them. And the President—
in all important matters he must obey his party,

which is, after all, simply the "interests" that finance it; in unimportant matters, his so-called power is whittled down by the party's leaders and workers, whose requirements may not be disregarded. He shakes the plum tree, but he does it under orders; others gather the fruit, and he gets only the exercise and the "honor."

I had no yearning for puppetship, however exalted the title or sonorous the fame; but to be the power that selects the king-puppet of the political puppet-hierarchy, to be the power that selects and rules him,—that was the logical development of my career.

In Burbank I thought I had found a man worthy to wear the puppet robes,—one who would glory in them. He, like most of the other ambitious men I have known, cared little who was behind the throne, provided he himself was seated upon it, the crown on his head and the crowds tossing the hats that shelter their dim-thinking brains. Also, in addition to magnetism and presence, he had dexterity and distinction and as much docility as can be expected in a man big enough to use for important work.

In September I gave him our party nomination for governor. In our one-sided state that meant his election.

As I had put him into the governorship not so much for use there as for use thereafter, it was necessary to protect him from my combine, which had destroyed his two immediate predecessors by over-use,—they had become so unpopular that their political careers ended with their terms. Protect him I must, though the task would be neither easy nor pleasant. It involved a collision with my clients,—a square test of strength between us. What was to me far more repellent, it involved my personally taking a hand in that part of my political work which I had hitherto left to Woodruff and his lieutenants.

One does not in person chase and catch and kill and dress and serve the chicken he has for dinner; he orders chicken, and hears and thinks no more about it until it is served. Thus, all the highly disagreeable part of my political work was done by others; Woodruff, admirably capable and most careful to spare my feelings, received the demands of my clients from their lawyers and trans-

mitted them to the party leaders in the legislature
with the instructions how the machinery was to
be used in making them into law. As I was
financing the machines of both parties, his task
was not difficult, though delicate.

But now that I began to look over Woodruff's
legislative program in advance, I was amazed at
the rapacity of my clients, rapacious though I
knew them to be. I had been thinking that the
independent newspapers—there were a few such,
but of small circulation and influence—were ma-
lignant in their attacks upon my "friends." In
fact, as I soon saw, they had told only a small
part of the truth. They had not found out the
worst things that were done; nor had they
grasped how little the legislature and the governor were doing other than the business of the big
corporations, most of it of doubtful public benefit, to speak temperately. An hour's study of the
facts and I realized as never before why we are
so rapidly developing a breed of multi-millionaires in this country with all the opportunities to
wealth in their hands. I had only to remember
that the system which ruled my own state was in

full blast in every one of the states of the Union. Everywhere, no sooner do the people open or propose to open a new road into a source of wealth, than men like these clients of mine hurry to the politicians and buy the rights to set up toll-gates and to fix their own schedule of tolls.

However, the time had now come when I must assert myself. I made no radical changes in that first program of Burbank's term. I contented myself with cutting off the worst items, those it would have ruined Burbank to indorse. My clients were soon grumbling, but Woodruff handled them well, placating them with excuses that soothed their annoyance to discontented silence. So ably did he manage it that not until Burbank's third year did they begin to come directly to me and complain of the way they were being "thrown down" at the capitol.

Roebuck, knowing me most intimately and feeling that he was my author and protector, was frankly insistent. "We got almost nothing at the last session," he protested, "and this winter— Woodruff tells me we may not get the only thing we're asking."

I was ready for him, as I was for each of the ten. I took out the list of measures passed or killed at the last session in the interest of the Power Trust. It contained seventy-eight items, thirty-four of them passed. I handed it to him.

"Yes,—a few things," he admitted, "but all trifles!"

"That little amendment to the Waterways law must alone have netted you three or four millions already."

"Nothing like that. Nothing like that."

"I can organize a company within twenty-four hours that will pay you four millions in cash for the right, and stock besides."

He did not take up my offer.

"You have already had thirteen matters attended to this winter," I pursued. "The one that can't be done—Really, Mr. Roebuck, the whole state knows that the trustees of the Waukeegan Christian University are your dummies. It would be insanity for the party to turn over a hundred thousand acres of valuable public land gratis to them, so that they can presently sell it to you for a song."

He reddened. "Newspaper scandal!" he blustered, but changed the subject as soon as he had shown me and re-shown himself that his motives were pure.

I saw that Burbank's last winter was to be crucial. My clients were clamorous, and were hinting at all sorts of dire doings if they were not treated better. Roebuck was questioning, in the most malignantly friendly manner, "whether, after all, Harvey, the combine isn't a mistake, and the old way wasn't the best." On the other hand Burbank was becoming restless. He had so cleverly taken advantage of the chances to do popular things, which I had either made for him or pointed out to him, that he had become something of a national figure. When he got eighty-one votes for the presidential nomination in our party's national convention his brain was dizzied. Now he was in a tremor lest my clients should demand of him things that would diminish or destroy this sapling popularity which, in his dreams, he already saw grown into a mighty tree obscuring the national heavens.

I gave many and many an hour to anxious

thought and careful planning that summer and fall. It was only a few days before Doc Woodruff appeared at Fredonia with the winter's legislative program that I saw my way straight to what I hoped was broad day. The program he brought was so outrageous that it was funny. There was nothing in it for the Ramsay interests, but each of the other ten had apparently exhausted the ingenuity of its lawyers in concocting demands that would have wrecked for ever the party granting them.

"Our friends are modest," said I.

"They've gone clean crazy," replied Woodruff. "And if you could have heard them talk! It's impossible to make them see that anybody has any rights but themselves."

"Well, let me have the details," said I. "Explain every item on this list; tell me just what it means, and just how the lawyers propose to disguise it so the people won't catch on."

When he finished, I divided the demands into three classes,—the impossible, the possible, and the practicable. "Strike out all the impossible," I directed. "Cut down the possible to the ten that are least outrageous. Those ten and the practicable must be passed."

He read off the ten which were beyond the limits of prudence, but not mob-and-hanging matters. "We can pass them, of course," was his comment. "We could pass a law ordering the state house burned, but—"

"Precisely," said I. "I think the consequences will be interesting." I cross-marked the five worst of the ten possibilities. "Save those until the last weeks of the session."

Early in the session Woodruff began to push the five least bad of the bad measures on to the calendar of the legislature, one by one. When the third was introduced, Burbank took the Limited for Washington. He arrived in time to join my wife and my little daughter Frances and me at breakfast. He was so white and sunken-eyed and his hands were so unsteady that Frances tried in vain to take her solemn, wondering, pitying gaze from his face. As soon as my study door closed behind us, he burst out, striding up and down.

"I don't know *what* to think, Sayler," he

cried, "I don't *know* what to think! The demands of these corporations have been growing,
growing, growing! And now—You have seen
the calendar?"

"Yes," said I. "Some of the bills are pretty
stiff, aren't they? But the boys tell me they're
for our best friends, and that they're all necessary."

"No doubt, no doubt," he replied, "but it will
be impossible to reconcile the people." Suddenly
he turned on me, his eyes full of fear and suspicion. "Have *you* laid a plot to ruin me, Sayler?
It certainly looks that way. Have you a secret
ambition for the presidency—"

"Don't talk rubbish, James," I interrupted.
Those few meaningless votes in the national convention had addled his common sense. "Sit
down,—calm yourself,—tell me all about it."

He seated himself and ran his fingers up and
down his temples and through his wet hair that
was being so rapidly thinned and whitened by the
struggles and anxieties of his ambition. "My
God!" he cried out, "how I am punished! When
I started in my public career, I looked forward

and saw just this time,—when I should be the
helpless tool in the hands of the power I sold
myself to. Governor!" He almost shouted the
word, rising and pacing the floor again. "Governor!"—and he laughed in wild derision.

I watched him, fascinated. I, too, at the outset of my career, had looked forward, and had
seen the same peril, but I had avoided it.
Wretched figure that he was!—what more
wretched, more pitiable than a man groveling and
moaning in the mire of his own self-contempt?
"Governor!" I said to myself, as I saw awful
thoughts flitting like demons of despair across his
face. And I shuddered, and pitied, and rejoiced,
—shuddered at the narrowness of my own
escape; pitied the man who seemed myself as I
might have been; and rejoiced that I had had my
mother with me and in me to impel me into another course.

"Come, come, Burbank," said I, "you're not
yourself; you've lost sleep—"

"Sleep!" he interrupted, "I have not closed my
eyes since I read those cursed bills."

"Tell me what you want done," was my suggestion. "I'll help in any way I can,—any way that's practicable."

"Oh, I understand your position, Sayler," he answered, when he had got control of himself again, "but I see plainly that the time has come when the power that rules me,—that rules us both,—has decided to use me to my own destruction. If I refuse to do these things, it will destroy me,—and a hundred are eager to come forward and take my place. If I do these things, the people will destroy me,—and neither is that of the smallest importance to our master."

His phrases, "the power that rules us both," and "our master," jarred on me. So far as he knew, indeed, so far as "our master" knew, were not he and I in the same class? But that was no time for personal vanity. All I said was: "The bills must go through. This is one of those crises that test a man's loyalty to the party."

"For the good of the party!" he muttered with a bitter sneer. "Crime upon crime—yes, crime, I say—that the party may keep the favor of the powers! And to what end? to what good? Why, that the party may continue in control and so may be of further use to its rulers." He rested his elbows on the table and held his face between his hands. He looked terribly old, and weary beyond the power ever to be rested again. "I stand with the party,—what am I without it?" he went on in a dull voice. "The people may forget, but, if I offend the master,—he never forgives or forgets. I'll sign the bills, Sayler,—*if* they come to me as party measures."

Burbank had responded to the test.

A baser man would have acted as scores of governors, mayors, and judges have acted in the same situation—would have accepted popular ruin and would have compelled the powers to make him rich in compensation. A braver man would have defied it and the powers, would have appealed to the people—with one chance of winning out against ten thousand chances of being disbelieved and laughed at as a "man who thinks he's too good for his party." Burbank was neither too base nor too brave; clearly, I assured myself, he is the man I want. I felt that I might safely relieve his mind, so far as I could do so without letting him too far into my secret plans.

I had not spent five minutes in explanation before he was up, his face radiant, and both hands stretched out to me.

"Forgive me, Harvey!" he cried. "I shall never distrust you again. I put my future in your hands."

XII

That was, indeed, a wild winter at the state capital,—a "carnival of corruption," the newspapers of other states called it. One of the first of the "black bills" to go through was a disguised street railway grab, out of which Senator Croffut got a handsome "counsel fee" of fifty-odd thousand dollars. But as the rout went on, ever more audaciously and recklessly, he became uneasy. In mid-February he was urging me to go West and try to do something to "curb those infernal grabbers." I refused to interfere. He went himself, and Woodruff reported to me that he was running round the state house and the hotels like a crazy man; for when he got into the thick of it, he realized that it was much worse than it seemed from Washington. In a few days he was back and at me again.

"It's very strange," said he suspiciously. "The boys say they're getting nothing out of it. They declare they're simply obeying orders."

"Whose orders?" I asked.

"I don't know," he answered, his eyes sharply upon me. "But I do know that, unless something is done, I'll not be returned to the Senate. We'll lose the legislature, sure, next fall."

"It does look that way," I said with a touch of melancholy. "That street railway grab was the beginning of our rake's progress. We've been going it, hell bent, ever since."

He tossed his handsome head and was about to launch into an angry defense of himself. But my manner checked him. He began to plead. "*You* can stop it, Sayler. Everybody out there says you can. And, if I am reëlected, I've got a good chance for the presidential nomination. Should I get it and be elected, we could form a combination that would interest you, I think."

It was a beautiful irony that in his conceit he should give as his reason why I should help him the very reason why I was not sorry he was to be beaten. For, although he was not dangerous, still he was a rival public figure to Burbank in our state, and,—well, accidents sometimes happen, unless they're guarded against.

"What shall I do?" I asked him.

"Stop them from passing any more black bills. Why, they've got half a dozen ready, some of them worse even than the two they passed over Burbank's veto, a week ago."

"For instance?"

He cited three Power Trust bills.

"But why don't *you* stop those three?" said I. "They're under the special patronage of Dominick. You have influence with him."

"Dominick!" he groaned. "Are you sure?" And when I nodded emphatically, he went on: "I'll do what I can, but—" He threw up his hands.

He was off for the West that night. When he returned, his face wore the look of doom. He had always posed for the benefit of the galleries, especially the women in the galleries. But now he became sloven in dress, often issued forth unshaven, and sat sprawled at his desk in the Senate, his chin on his shirt bosom, looking vague and starting when any one spoke to him.

Following my advice on the day when I sent him away happy, Burbank left the capital and the state just before the five worst bills left the committees. He was called to the bedside of his wife who, so all the newspapers announced, was at the point of death at Colorado Springs.

While he was there nursing her as she "hovered between life and death," the bills were jammed through the senate and the assembly.

He telegraphed the lieutenant governor not to sign them, as he was returning and wished to deal with them himself. He reached the capital on a Thursday morning, sent the bills back with a "ringing" veto message, and took the late afternoon train for Colorado Springs. It was as good a political "grand-stand play" as ever thrilled a people.

The legislature passed the bills over his veto and adjourned that night.

Press and people, without regard to party lines, were loud in their execrations of the "abandoned and shameless wretches" who had "betrayed the state and had covered themselves with eternal infamy." I quote from an editorial in the newspaper that was regarded as my personal organ. But there was only praise for Burbank; his

enemies, and those who had doubted his independence and had suspected him of willingness
to do anything to further his personal ambitions,
admitted that he had shown "fearless courage,
inflexible honesty, and the highest ideals of
private sacrifice to public duty." And they
eagerly exaggerated him, to make his white contrast more vividly with the black of the "satanic
spawn" in the legislature. His fame spread, carried far and wide by the sentimentality in that
supposed struggle between heart and conscience,
between love for the wife of his bosom and duty
to the people.

Carlotta, who like most women took no interest in politics because it lacks "heart-interest,"
came to me with eyes swimming and cheeks
aglow. She had just been reading about Burbank's heroism.

"Isn't he splendid!" she cried. "I always told
you he'd be President. And you didn't believe
me."

"Be patient with me, my dear," said I. "I am
not a woman with seven-league boots of intui-
tion. I'm only a heavy-footed man."

XIII

And now the stage had been reached at which my ten mutinous clients could be, and must be, disciplined.

As a first step, I resigned the chairmanship of the state committee and ordered the election of Woodruff to the vacancy. I should soon have substituted Woodruff for myself, in any event. I had never wanted the place, and had taken it only because to refuse it would have been to throw away the golden opportunity Dunkirk so unexpectedly thrust at me. Holding that position, or any other officially connecting me with my party's machine, made me a target; and I wished to be completely hidden, for I wished the people of my state to think me merely one of the party servants, in sympathy with the rank and file rather than with the machine. Yet, in the chairmanship, in the targetship, I must have a man whom I could trust through and through;

and, save Woodruff, who was there for the place?

When my resignation was announced, the independent and the opposition press congratulated me on my high principle in refusing to have any official connection with the machine responsible for such infamies. When Woodruff's election was announced it came as a complete surprise. Such of the newspapers as dared, and they were few, denounced it as infamy's crown of infamy; and the rank and file of the party was shocked, —as I had known it would be. He made not a murmur, but I knew what must be in his mind. I said nothing until six weeks or two months had passed; then I went straight at him.

"You are feeling bitter against me," said I. "You think I dropped out when there was danger of heavy firing, and put you up to take it."

"No, indeed, Senator," he protested, "nothing like that. Honestly, I have not had a bitter thought against you. I'm depressed simply because, just as I had a chance to get on my feet again, they won't let me."

"But," I rejoined, "I did resign and put you

in my place because I didn't want to take the fire and thought you could."

"And so I can," said he. "I haven't any reputation to lose. I'm no worse off than I was before. Let 'em do their damnedest."

"Your first campaign will probably be a failure," I went on, "and, the day after election, there'll be a shout for your head."

He shrugged his shoulders. "I'm enlisted for the war," said he. "You're my general. I go where you order."

I hope the feelings that surged up in me showed in my face, as I stretched out my hand. "Thank you, Doc," said I. "And—there's another side to it. It isn't all black."

"It isn't black at all," he replied stoutly.

I explained: "I've wanted you to have the place from the outset. But I shouldn't dare give it to you except at a time like this, when our party has done so many unpopular things that one more won't count; and there's so much to be said against us, so much worse things than they can possibly make out your election to be, that it'll soon be almost neglected."

"They're beginning to drop me already and go back to harrying those poor devils of ours in the legislature," said Woodruff.

"A few weeks more," I went on, "and you'll be safe and you are to stay chairman, no matter what happens. When they have leisure to attack you, there'll be nothing to attack. The people will have dismissed the matter from their minds. They don't care to watch the threshing of old straw."

I saw that I had lifted a weight from him, though he said nothing.

So much for my first move toward the chastening of my clients. Further and even more effective in the same direction, I cut down our campaign fund for the legislative ticket to one-fifth what it usually was; and, without even Woodruff's knowing it, I heavily subsidized the opposition machine. Wherever it could be done with safety I arranged for the trading off of our legislative ticket for our candidate for governor. "The legislature is hopelessly lost," I told Woodruff; "we must concentrate on the governorship. We must save what we can." In fact, so over-

whelmingly was our party in the majority, and
so loyal were its rank and file, that it was only
by the most careful arrangement of weak candidates and of insufficient campaign funds that
I was able to throw the legislature to the opposition. Our candidate for governor, Walbrook—
Burbank was ineligible to a second successive
term—was elected by a comfortable plurality.
And, by the way, I saw to it that the party organs
gave Woodruff enthusiastic praise for rescuing so
much from what had looked like utter ruin.

My clients had been uneasy ever since the
furious popular outburst which had followed
their breaking away from my direction and re-
straint. When they saw an opposition legislature, they readily believed what they read in the
newspapers about the "impending reign of radicalism." Silliman, the opposition leader, had accepted John Markham's offer of one hundred and
fifty thousand dollars for Croffut's seat in the
Senate; but I directed him to send Veerhoft, one
of the wildest and cleverest of the opposition
radicals. He dared not disobey me. Veerhoft
went, and Markham never saw again the seven-

ty-five thousand he had paid Silliman as a "retainer."

Veerhoft in the United States Senate gave my
clients the chills; but I was preparing the fever
for them also. I had Silliman introduce bills in
both houses of the legislature that reached for
the privileges of the big corporations and in-
itiated proceedings to expose their corruption. I
had Woodruff suggest to Governor Walbrook
that, in view of the popular clamor, he ought to
recommend measures for equalizing taxation and
readjusting the prices of franchises. As my
clients were bonded and capitalized on the basis
of no expense either for taxes or for franchises,
the governor's suggestion, eagerly adopted by
Silliman's "horde," foreshadowed ruin. If the
measures should be passed, all the dividends and
interest they were paying on "water" would go
into the public treasury.

My clients came to me, singly and in pairs,
to grovel and to implore. An interesting study
these arrogant gentlemen made as they cringed,
utterly indifferent to the appearance of self-respect, in their agony for their imperiled millions.

A mother would shrink from abasing herself to save the life of her child as these men abased themselves in the hope of saving their dollars. How they fawned and flattered! They begged my pardon for having disregarded my advice; they assured me that, if I would only exert that same genius of mine which had conceived the combine, I could devise some way of saving them from this tidal wave of popular clamor,—for they hadn't a suspicion of my part in making that tidal wave.

Reluctantly I consented to "see what I can do."

The instant change in the atmosphere of the capital, the instant outcry from the organs of both parties that "the people had voted for reform, not for confiscatory revolution," completed my demonstration. My clients realized who was master of the machines. The threatening storm rapidly scattered; the people, relieved that the Silliman program of upheaval was not to be carried out, were glad enough to see the old "conservative" order restored,—our people always reason that it is better to rot slowly by corruption than to be frightened to death by revolution.

"Hereafter, we must trust to your judgment in these political matters, Harvey," said Roebuck. "The manager must be permitted to manage."

I smiled at the ingenuousness of this speech. It did not ruffle me. Roebuck was one of those men who say their prayers in a patronizing tone.

Yes, I was master. But it is only now, in the retrospect of years, that I have any sense of triumph; for I had won the supremacy with small effort, comparatively,—with the small effort required of him who sees the conditions of a situation clearly, and, instead of trying to combat or to change them, intelligently uses them to his ends. Nor do I now regard my achievement as marvelous. Everything was in my favor; against me, there was nothing,—no organization, no plan, no knowledge of my aim. I wonder how much of their supernal glory would be left to the world's men of action, from its Alexanders and Napoleons down to its successful bandits and ward-bosses, if mankind were in the habit of

looking at what the winner had opposed to him,
—Alexander faced only by flocks of sheep-like
Asiatic slaves; Napoleon routing the badly
trained, wretchedly officered soldiers of decadent
monarchies; and the bandit or ward-boss over-
coming peaceful and unprepared and unorganized
citizens. Who would erect statues or write eulogies to a man for mowing a field of corn-stalks
with a scythe? Mankind is never more amusing
than in its hero-worship.

No, I should simply have been stupid had I
failed.

But—even had I been disposed to rein in and
congratulate myself at the quarter-stretch, I
could not have done it. A man has, perhaps, some
choice as to his mount before he enters the race
for success. But once in the saddle and off, he
must let the reins go; his control is confined to
whip and spur.

XIV

In the early autumn of that last year of his as governor, Burbank's wife died—a grim and unexpected fulfilment of their pretended anxieties of six months before.

It was, in some respects, as great a loss to me as to him—how great to us both I did not—indeed, could not—measure until several years passed. She was what I regard as a typical American wife—devoted to her husband, jealously guarding his interests, yet as keen to see his shortcomings as she was to see her own. And how much more persistent and intelligent in correcting her faults than he in correcting his! Like most men, he was vain—that is, while he would probably have admitted in a large, vague way that he wasn't perfect, when it came to details he would defend his worst fault against any and all criticism. Like most women, she, too, was vain—but an intelligent woman's vanity, instead of mak-

177

ing her self-complacent, somehow spurs her on to hide her weak points and to show her best points in the best light. For example, Mrs. Burbank, a pretty woman and proud of it, was yet conscious of her deficiencies in dress and in manners through her plain and rural early surroundings. It was interesting, and instructive, too, to watch her studying and cleverly copying, or rather, adapting Carlotta; for she took from Carlotta only that which could be fitted without visible joint into her own pattern.

Latterly, whenever I was urging upon Burbank a line of action requiring courage or a sacrifice of some one of his many insidious forms of personal vanity, I always arranged for her to be present at our conferences. And she would sit there, apparently absorbed in her sewing; but in reality she was seeing not only the surface reasons I gave him, but also those underlying and more powerful reasons which we do not utter, sometimes because we like to play the hypocrite to ourselves, again because we must give the other person a chance to play the hypocrite before himself—and us. And often I left him reluctant and trying to muster courage to refuse or finesse to evade, only to find him the next day consenting, perhaps enthusiastic. Many's the time she spared me the disagreeable necessity of being peremptory—doubly disagreeable because show of authority has ever been distasteful to me and because an order can never be so heartily executed as is an assimilated suggestion.

When I went to him a month after her death, I expected he would still be crushed as he was at the funeral. I listened with a feeling of revulsion to his stilted and, as it seemed to me, perfunctory platitudes on his "irreparable loss"—stale rhetoric about *her,* and to her most intimate friend and his! I had thought he would be imagining himself done with ambition for ever; I had feared his strongly religious nature would lead him to see a "judgment" upon him and her for having exaggerated her indisposition to gain a political point. And I had mapped out what I would say to induce him to go on. Instead, after a few of those stereotyped mortuary sentences, he shifted to politics and was presently showing me that her death had hardly interrupted his plannings for

the presidential nomination. As for the "judgment," I had forgotten that in his religion his
deity was always on his side, and his misfortunes
were always of the evil one. These deities of men
of action! Man with his god a ventriloquist puppet in his pocket, and with his conscience an old
dog Tray at his heels, needing no leading string!

However, it gave me a shock, this vivid reminder from Burbank of the slavery of ambition
—ambition, the vice of vices. For it takes its
victims' all—moral, mental, physical. And, while
other vices rarely wreck any but small men or injure more than what is within their small circles
of influence, ambition seizes only the superior and
sets them on to use their superior powers to blast
communities, states, nations, continents. Yet it is
called a virtue. And men who have sold themselves to it and for it to the last shred of manhood are esteemed and, mystery of mysteries, esteem themselves!

I had come to Burbank to manufacture him
into a President. His wife and I had together
produced an excellent raw material. Now, to
make it up into the finished product!

He pointed to the filing-cases that covered the west wall of his library from floor to ceiling, from north window to south. "I base my hope on those —next to you, of course," said he. Then with his "woeful widower" pose, he added: "They were *her* suggestions."

I looked at the filing-cases and waited for him to explain.

"When we were first married," he went on presently, "she said, 'It seems to me, if I were a public man, I should keep everything relating to myself—every speech, all that the newspapers said, every meeting and the lists of the important people who were there, notes of *all* the people I ever met anywhere, every letter or telegram or note I received. If you do, you may find after a few years that you have an enormous list of acquaintances. You've forgotten them because you meet so many, but they will not have forgotten you, who were one of the principal figures at the meeting or reception.' That's in substance what she said. And so, we began and kept it up"—he paused in his deliberate manner, compressed his lips, then added—"together."

I opened one of the filing-cases, glanced at him
for permission, took out a slip of paper under the
M's. It was covered with notes, in Mrs. Burbank's writing, of a reception given to him at the
Manufacturers' Club in St. Louis three years before. A lot of names, after each some reminders
of the standing and the personal appearance of
the man. Another slip, taken at random from the
same box, contained similar notes of a trip
through Montana eight years before.

"Wonderful!" I exclaimed, as the full value of
these accumulations loomed in my mind. "I knew
she was an extraordinary woman. Now I see that
she had genius for politics."

His expression—a peering through that eternal
pose of his—made me revise my first judgment of
his mourning. For I caught a glimpse of a real
human being, one who had loved and lost, looking grief and pride and gratitude. "If she had
left me two or three years earlier," he said in that
solemn, posing tone, "I doubt if I should have got
one step further. As it is, I may be able to go on,
though—I have lost—my staff."

What fantastic envelopes does man, after he

has been finished by Nature, wrap about himself in his efforts to improve her handiwork! Physically, even when most dressed, we are naked in comparison with the enswathings that hide our real mental and moral selves from one another—and from ourselves.

My campaign was based on the contents of those filing-cases. I learned all the places throughout the West—cities, towns, centrally-located villages—where he had been and had made an impression; and by simple and obvious means we were able to convert them into centers of "the Burbank boom." I could afterward trace to the use we made of those memoranda the direct getting of no less than one hundred and seven delegates to the national convention—and that takes no account of the vaster indirect value of so much easily worked-up, genuine, unpurchased and unpurchasable "Burbank sentiment." The man of only local prominence, whom Burbank remembered perfectly after a chance meeting years before, could have no doubt who ought to be the party's nominee for President.

The national machine of our party was then

in the custody, and supposedly in the control, of
Senator Goodrich of New Jersey. He had a reputation for Machiavellian dexterity, but I found
that he was an accident rather than an actuality.

The dominion of the great business interests over politics was the rapid growth of about
twenty years—the consolidations of business naturally producing concentrations of the business
world's political power in the hands of the few
controllers of the big railway, industrial and financial combines. Goodrich had happened to be ac-
quainted with some of the most influential of these
business "kings"; they naturally made him their
agent for the conveying of their wishes and their
bribes of one kind and another to the national
managers of both parties. They knew little of the
details of practical politics, knew only what they
needed in their businesses; and as long as they
got that, it did not interest them what was done
with the rest of the power their "campaign contributions" gave.

With such resources any man of good intelligence and discretion could have got the same results as Goodrich's. He was simply a lackey,

strutting and cutting a figure in his master's clothes and under his master's name. He was pitifully vain of his reputation as a Machiavelli and a go-between. Vanity is sometimes a source of great strength; but vanity of that sort, and about a position in which secrecy is the prime requisite, could mean only weakness.

Throughout his eight years of control of our party it had had possession of all departments of the national administration—except of the House of Representatives during the past two years. This meant the uninterrupted and unchecked reign of the interests. To treat with consideration the interests, the strong men of the country, they who must have a free hand for developing its resources, to give them privileges and immunities beyond what can be permitted the ordinary citizen or corporation—that is a course which, however offensive to abstract justice, still has, as it seems to me, a practical justice in it, and, at any rate, must be pursued so long as the masses of the voters are short-sighted, unreasoning and in nose-rings to political machines. A man's rights, whatever they may be in theory, are in practice only what he has the intelligence and the power to compel. But, for the sake of the nation, for the upholding of civilization itself, these over-powerful interests should never be given their heads, should be restrained as closely as may be to their rights—their *practical* rights. Goodrich had neither the sagacity nor the patriotism—nor the force of will, for that matter—to keep them within the limits of decency and discretion. Hence the riot of plunder and privilege which revolted and alarmed me when I came to Washington and saw politics in the country-wide, yes, history-wide, horizon of that view-point.

Probably I should have been more leisurely in bringing my presidential plans to a focus, had I not seen how great and how near was the peril to my party. It seemed to me, not indeed a perfect or even a satisfactory, but the best available, instrument for holding the balances of order as even as might be between our country's two opposing elements of disorder—the greedy plunderers and the rapidly infuriating plundered. And I saw that no time was to be lost, if the party was not to be blown to fragments. The first mutterings of the

storm were in our summary ejection from control
of the House in the midway election. If the party
were not to be dismembered, I must oust Goodrich, must defeat his plans for nominating Cromwell, must nominate Burbank instead. If I should
succeed in electing him, I reasoned that I could
through him carry out my policy of moderation
and *practical* patriotism—to yield to the powerful
few a minimum of what they could compel, to
give to the prostrate but potentially powerful
many at least enough to keep them quiet—a stom-
achful. The world may have advanced; but
patriotism still remains the art of restraining the
arrogance of full stomachs and the anger of
empty ones.

In Cromwell, Goodrich believed he had a candidate with sufficient hold upon the rank and file
of the party to enable him to carry the election by
the usual means—a big campaign fund properly
distributed in the doubtful states. I said to Senator Scarborough of Indiana soon after Cromwell's candidacy was announced: "What do you
think of Goodrich's man?"

Scarborough, though new to the Senate then,

had shown himself far and away the ablest of the opposition Senators. He had as much intellect as any of them; and he had what theorists, such as he, usually lack, skill at "grand tactics"—the management of men in the mass. His one weakness—and that, from my standpoint, a great one —was a literal belief in democratic institutions and in the inspiring but in practice pernicious principle of exact equality before the law.

"Cromwell's political sponsors," was his reply, "are two as shrewd bankers as there are in New York. I have heard it said that a fitting sign for a bank would be: 'Here we do nothing for nothing for nobody.'"

An admirable summing up of Cromwell's candidacy. And I knew that it would so appear to the country, that no matter how great a corruption fund Goodrich might throw into the campaign, we should, in that time of public exasperation, be routed if Cromwell was our standard-bearer—so utterly routed that we could not possibly get ourselves together again for eight, perhaps twelve years. There might even be a re-alignment of parties with some sort of socialism in control of one of them. If control were to be retained by the few who have the capital and the intellect to make efficient the nation's resources and energy, my projects must be put through at once.

I had accumulated a fund of five hundred thousand dollars for my "presidential flotation" —half of it contributed by Roebuck in exchange for a promise that his son-in-law should have an ambassadorship if Burbank were elected; the other half set aside by me from the "reserve" I had formed out of the year-by-year contributions of my combine. By the judicious investment of that capital I purposed to get Burbank the nomination on the first ballot—at least four hundred and sixty of the nine hundred-odd delegates.

In a national convention the delegates are, roughly speaking, about evenly divided among the three sections of the country—a third from east of the Alleghanies; a third from the West; a third from the South. It was hopeless for us to gun for delegates in the East; that was the especial bailiwick of Senator Goodrich. The most we could do there would be to keep him occupied by quietly encouraging any anti-Cromwell sentiment—and it existed a-plenty. Our real efforts were to be in the West and South.

I organized under Woodruff a corps of about thirty traveling agents. Each man knew only his own duties, knew nothing of the general plan, not even that there was a general plan. Each was a trained political worker, a personal retainer of ours. I gave them their instructions; Woodruff equipped them with the necessary cash. During the next five months they were incessantly on the go—dealing with our party's western machines where they could; setting up rival machines in promising localities where Goodrich controlled the regular machines; using money here, diplomacy there, both yonder, promises of patronage everywhere.

Such was my department of secrecy. At the head of my department of publicity I put De Milt, a sort of cousin of Burbank's and a newspaper man. He attended to the subsidizing of news agencies that supplied thousands of country papers with boiler-plate matter to fill their inside pages. He also subsidized and otherwise won over many small town organs of the party. Fur-

ther, he and three assistants wrote each week
many columns of "boom" matter, all of which
was carefully revised by Burbank himself before
it went out as "syndicate letters." If Goodrich
hadn't been ignorant of conditions west of the
Alleghanies and confident that his will was law,
he would have scented out this department of publicity of mine and so would have seen into my
"flotation." But he knew nothing beyond his
routine. I once asked him how many country
newspapers there were in the United States, and
he said: "Oh, I don't know. Perhaps three or
four thousand." Even had I enlightened him to
the extent of telling him that there were about
five times that number, he would have profited
nothing. Had he been able to see the importance
of such a fact to capable political management, he
would have learned it long before through years
of constant use of the easiest avenue into the
heart of the people.

He did not wake up to adequate action until the
fourth of that group of states whose delegations
to our national conventions were habitually
bought and sold, broke its agreement with him

and instructed its delegation to vote for Burbank. By the time he had a corps of agents in those states, Doc Woodruff had "acquired" more than a hundred delegates. Goodrich was working only through the regular machinery of the party and was fighting against a widespread feeling that Cromwell shouldn't, and probably couldn't, be elected; we, on the other hand, were manufacturing presidential sentiment for a candidate who was already popular. Nor had Goodrich much advantage over us with the regular machines anywhere except in the East.

Just as I was congratulating myself that nothing could happen to prevent our triumph at the convention, Roebuck telegraphed me to come to Chicago. I found with him in the sitting-room of his suite in the Auditorium Annex, Partridge and Granby, next to him the most important members of my combine, since they were the only ones who had interests that extended into many states. It was after an uneasy silence that Granby, the uncouth one of the three, said:

"Senator, we brought you here to tell you this Burbank nonsense has gone far enough."

XV

MUTINY

It was all I could do not to show my astonishment and sudden fury. "I don't understand," said I, in a tone which I somehow managed to keep down to tranquil inquiry.

But I did understand. It instantly came to me that the three had been brought into line for Cromwell by their powerful business associates in Wall Street, probably by the great bankers who loaned them money. Swift upon the surge of anger I had suppressed before it flamed at the surface came a surge of triumph—which I also suppressed. I had often wished, perhaps as a matter of personal pride, just this opportunity; and here it was!

"Cromwell must be nominated," said Granby in his insolent tone. He had but two tones—the insolent and the cringing. "He's safe and sound. Burbank isn't trusted in the East. And we didn't

like his conduct last year. He caters to the demagogues."

Roebuck, through his liking for me, I imagine,
rather than through refined instinct, now began to
speak, thinly disguising his orders as requests. I
waited until he had talked himself out. I waited
with the same air of calm attention until Partridge had given me his jerky variation. I waited,
still apparently calm, until the silence must have
been extremely uncomfortable to them. I waited
until Granby said sharply, "Then it is settled?"

"Yes," said I, keeping all emotion out of my
face and voice. "It is settled. Ex-Governor Burbank is to be nominated. I am at a loss to account
for this outbreak. However, I shall at once take
measures to prevent its occurring again. Good
day."

And I was gone—straight to the train. I did
not pause at Fredonia but went on to the capital.
The next morning I had the legislature and the
attorney-general at work demolishing Granby's
business in my state—for I had selected him to
make an example of, incidentally because he had
insulted me, but chiefly because he was the most

notorious of my ten, was about the greediest and cruelest "robber baron" in the West. My legislature was to revoke his charter; my attorney-general was to enforce upon him the laws I had put on the statute books against just such emergencies. And it had never entered their swollen heads that I might have taken these precautions that are in the primer of political management.

My three mutineers pursued me to the capital, missed me, were standing breathless at the door of my house near Fredonia on the morning of the third day. I refused to be seen until the afternoon of the fourth day, and then I forbade Granby. But when I descended to the reception-room he rushed at me, tried to take my hand, pouring out a stream of sickening apologies. I rang the bell. When a servant appeared, I said, "Show this man the door."

Granby turned white and, after a long look into my face, said in a broken voice to Roebuck: "For God's sake, don't go back on me, Mr. Roebuck. Do what you can for me."

As the curtain dropped behind him, I looked expectantly at Roebuck, sweating with fright for his imperiled millions. Probably his mental state can be fully appreciated only by a man who has also felt the dread of losing the wealth upon which he is wholly dependent for courage, respect and self-respect.

"Don't misunderstand me, Harvey," he began to plead, forgetting that there was anybody else to save besides himself. "I didn't mean—"

"What *did* you mean?" I interrupted, my tone ominously quiet.

"We didn't intend—" began Partridge.

"What *did* you intend?" I interrupted as quietly as before.

They looked nervously each at the other, then at me. "If you think Burbank's the man," Roebuck began again, "why, you may go ahead—"

There burst in me such a storm of anger that I dared not speak until I could control and aim the explosion. Partridge saw how, and how seriously, Roebuck had blundered. He thrust him aside and faced me. "What's the use of beating around the bush?" he said bluntly. "We've made damn fools of ourselves, Senator. We thought we had the whip. We see that we haven't. We're

mighty sorry we didn't do a little thinking before
Roebuck sent that telegram. We hope you'll let
us off as easy as you can, and we promise not to
meddle in your business again—and you can bet
your life we'll keep our promise."

"I think you will," said I.

"I am a man of my word," said he. "And so is
Roebuck."

"Oh, I don't mean that," was my answer. "I
mean, when the Granby object-lesson in the stupidity of *premature* ingratitude is complete, you
shan't be able to forget it."

They drifted gloomily in the current of their
unpleasant thoughts; then each took a turn at
wringing my hand. I invited them up to my sitting-room where we smoked and talked amicably
for a couple of hours. It would have amused the
thousands of employés and dependents over
whom these two lorded it arrogantly to have
heard with what care they weighed their timid
words, how nervous they were lest they should
give me fresh provocation. As they were leaving,
Roebuck said earnestly: "Isn't there *anything* I
can do for you, Harvey?"

"Why, yes," said I. "Give out a statement next Sunday in Chicago—for the Monday morning papers—indorsing Cromwell's candidacy. Say you and all your associates are enthusiastic for it because his election would give the large enterprises that have been the object of demagogic attack a sense of security for at least four years more."

He thought I was joking him, being unable to believe me so lacking in judgment as to fail to realize what a profound impression in Cromwell's favor such a statement from the great Roebuck would produce. I wrote and mailed him an interview with himself the following day; he gave it out as I had requested. It got me Burbank delegations in Illinois, South Dakota and Oregon the same week.

XVI

I arrived at Chicago the day before the convention and, going at once to our state headquarters in the Great Northern, shut myself in with Doc Woodruff. My door-keeper, the member of the legislature from Fredonia, ventured to interrupt with the announcement that a messenger had come from Senator Goodrich.

"Let him in," said I.

As the door-man disappeared Doc Woodruff glanced at his watch, then said with a smile: "You've been here seven minutes and a half—just time for a lookout down stairs to telephone to the Auditorium and for the messenger to drive from there here. Goodrich is on the anxious-seat, all right."

The messenger was Goodrich's handy-man, Judge Dufour. I myself have always frowned on these public exhibitions of the intimacy of judges in practical politics; but Goodrich had many small vanities—he liked his judges to hold his coat and his governors to carry his satchel. One would say that such petty weaknesses would be the undoing of a man. Fortunately, we are not as weak as our weakness but as strong as our strength; and while the universal weaknesses are shared by the strong, their strength is peculiar and rare. After Dufour had introduced himself and we had exchanged commonplaces he said: "Senator, there's a little conference of some of the leaders at headquarters and it isn't complete without you. So, Senator Goodrich has sent me over to escort you."

"Thank you—very courteous of you and of him," said I without hesitation, for I knew what was coming as soon as his name had been brought in, and my course was laid out. "But I can't leave just now. Please ask him if he won't come over —any time within the next four hours." This blandly and without a sign that I was conscious of Dufour's stupefaction—for his vanity made him believe that the god the great Dufour knelt to must be the god of gods.

There is no more important branch of the art of successful dealing with men than the etiquette of

who shall call upon whom. Many a man has in
his very hour of triumph ruined his cause with a
blunder there—by going to see some one whom
he should have compelled to come to him, or by
compelling some one to come to him when he
should have made the concession of going. I had
two reasons for thus humiliating Goodrich,
neither of them the reason he doubtless attributed
to me, the desire to feed my vanity. My first reason was his temperament; I knew his having to
come to me would make him bow before me in
spirit, as he was a tyrant, and tyrants are always
cringers. My second reason was that I thought
myself near enough to control of the convention
to be able to win control by creating the atmosphere of impending success. There is always a lot
of fellows who wait to see who is likely to win, so
that they may be on the side of the man in the
plum tree; often there are enough of these to
gain the victory for him who can lure them over
at just the right moment.

As soon as Dufour had taken his huge body
away I said to Woodruff: "Go out with your men
and gather in the office down stairs as many mem-

bers of the doubtful delegations as you can. Keep them where they'll be bound to see Goodrich come in and go out."

He rushed away, and I waited—working with the leaders of three far-western states. At the end of two hours, I won them by the spectacle of the arriving Goodrich. He came in, serene, smiling, giving me the joyously shining eyes and joyously firm hand-clasp of the politician's greeting; not an outward sign that he would like to see me tortured to death by some slow process then and there. Hypocritical preliminaries were not merely unnecessary but even highly ridiculous; yet, so great was his anger and confusion that he began with the "prospects for an old-time convention, with old-time enthusiasm and that generous rivalry which is the best sign of party health."

"I hope not, Senator," said I pleasantly. "Here, we think the fight is over—and won."

He lifted his eyebrows; but I saw his maxillary muscles twitching. "We don't figure it out just that way at headquarters," he replied oilily. "But, there's no doubt about it, your man has developed strength in the West."

"And South," said I, with deliberate intent to inflame, for I knew how he must feel about those delegates we had bought away from him.

There were teeth enough in his smile—but little else. "I think Burbank and Cromwell will be about even on the first ballot," said he. "May the best man win! We're all working for the good of the party and the country. But—I came, rather, to get your ideas about platform."

I opened a drawer in the table at which I was sitting and took out a paper. "We've embodied our ideas in this," said I, holding the paper toward him. "There's a complete platform, but we only insist on the five paragraphs immediately after the preamble."

He seemed to age as he read. "Impossible!" he finally exclaimed. "Preposterous! It would be difficult enough to get any money for *Cromwell* on such a platform, well as our conservative men know they can trust him. But for *Burbank*—you couldn't get a cent—not a damn cent! A rickety candidate on a rickety platform—that's what they'd say."

I made no answer.

"May I ask," he presently went on, "has ex-Governor Burbank seen this—this astonishing document?"

Burbank had written it. I confess when he first showed it to me, it had affected me somewhat as it was now affecting Goodrich. For, a dealer with business men as well as with public sentiment, I appreciated instantly the shock some of the phrases would give the large interests. But Burbank had not talked to me five minutes before I saw he was in the main right and that his phrases only needed a little "toning down" so that they wouldn't rasp too harshly on "conservative" ears. "Yes, Mr. Burbank has seen it," said I. "He approves it—though, of course, it does not represent his *personal* views, or his *intentions.*"

"If Mr. Burbank approves *this,*" exclaimed Goodrich, red and tossing the paper on the table, "then my gravest doubts about him are confirmed. He is an utterly unsafe man. He could not carry a single state in the East where there are any large centerings of capital or of enterprise—not even our yellow-dog states."

"He can and will carry them all," said I. "They

must go for him, because after the opposition have nominated, and have announced their platform, your people will regard him as, at any rate, much the less of two evils. We have decided on that platform because we wish to make it possible for him to carry the necessary Western states. We can't hold our rank and file out here unless we have a popular platform. The people must have their way *before* election, Senator, if the interests are to continue to have their way *after* election."

"I'll never consent to that platform," said he, rising.

"Very well," said I with a mild show of regret, rising also as if I had no wish to prolong the interview.

He brought his hand down violently upon the paper. "This," he exclaimed, "is a timely uncovering of a most amazing plot—a plot to turn our party over to demagoguery."

"To rescue it from the combination of demagoguery and plutagoguery that is wrecking it," said I without heat, "and make it again an instrument of at least sanity, perhaps of patriotism."

"We control the platform committee," he went

on, "and I can tell you now, Senator Sayler, that that there platform, nor nothing like it, will never be reported." In his agitation he went back to the grammar of his youthful surroundings.

"I regret that you will force us to a fight on the floor of the convention," I returned. "It can't but make a bad impression on the country to see two factions in the party—one for the people, the other against them."

Goodrich sat down.

"But," I went on, "at least, such a fight will insure Burbank all the delegates except perhaps the two or three hundred you directly control. You are courageous, Senator, to insist upon a count of noses on the issues we raise there."

He took up the platform again, and began to pick it to pieces phrase by phrase. That was what I wanted. Some phrases I defended, some I conceded might be altered to advantage, others I cheerfully agreed to discard altogether. Presently he had a pencil in his hand and was going over the crucial paragraphs, was making interlineations. And he grew more and more reasonable. At last I suggested that he take the platform away with him, make the changes agreed upon and such others as he might think wise, and send it back for my criticism and suggestions. He assented, and we parted on excellent terms—"harmony" in the convention was assured.

When the amended platform came back late in the afternoon, I detained Goodrich's messenger, the faithful Dufour again. It was still the Burbank platform, with no changes we could not concede. I had a copy made and gave it to Dufour, saying: "Tell the Senator I think this admirable, a great improvement. But I'll try to see him to-night and thank him."

I did not try to see him, however. I took no risk of lessening the effect created by his having to come to me. He had entered through groups of delegates from all parts of the country. He had passed out through a crowd, so well did my men employ the time his long stay with me gave them.

On the next day the platform was adopted. On the following day, amid delirious enthusiasm in the packed galleries and not a little agitation among the delegates—who, even to the "knowing ones," were as ignorant of what was really going on as private soldiers are of the general's plan of battle—amid waving of banners and crash of band and shriek of crowd Burbank was nominated on the first ballot. Our press hailed the nomination as a "splendid victory of the honest common sense of the entire party over the ultra conservatism of a faction associated in the popular mind with segregated wealth and undue enjoyment of the favors of laws and law-makers."

When I saw Burbank he took me graciously by the hand. "I thank you, Harvey," he said, "for your aid in this glorious victory of the people."

I did not realize then that his vanity was of the kind which can in an instant spring into a Redwood colossus from the shriveled stalk to which the last glare of truth has wilted it. Still his words and manner jarred on me. As our eyes met, something in mine—perhaps something he imagined he saw—made him frown in the majesty of offended pose. Then his timidity took fright and he said apologetically, "How can I repay you? After all, it is your victory."

I protested.

"Then *ours*," said he. "Yours, for us."

XVII

Now came *the* problem—to elect.

We hear much of many wonders of combination and concentration of *industrial* power which railway and telegraph have wrought. But nothing is said about what seems to me the greatest wonder of them all—how these forces have resulted in the concentration of the *political* power of upwards of twelve millions of our fifteen million voters; how the few can impose their ideas and their will upon widening circles, out and out, until all are included. The people are scattered; the powers confer, man to man, day by day. The people are divided by partizan and other prejudices; the powers are bound together by the one self-interest. The people must accept such political organizations as are provided for them; the powers pay for, and their agents make and direct, those organizations. The people are poor; the powers are rich. The people have not even offices to bestow; the powers have offices to give and lucrative employment of all kinds, and material and social advancement,—everything that the vanity or the appetite of man craves. The people punish but feebly—usually the wrong persons— and soon forget; the powers relentlessly and surely pursue those who oppose them, forgive only after the offender has surrendered unconditionally, and they never forget where it is to their interest to remember. The powers know both what they want and how to get it; the people know neither.

Back in March, when Goodrich first suspected that I had outgeneraled him, he opened negotiations with the national machine of the opposition party. He decided that, if I should succeed in nominating Burbank, he would save his masters and himself by nominating as the opposition candidate a man under their and his control, and by electing him with an enormous campaign fund.

Beckett, the subtlest and most influential of the managers of the national machine of the opposition party, submitted several names to him. He selected Henry J. Simpson, Justice of the Supreme

Court of Ohio—a slow, shy, ultra-conservative man, his brain spun full in every cell with the cobwebs of legal technicality. He was, in his way, almost as satisfactory a candidate for the interests as Cromwell would have been. For, while he was honest, of what value is honesty when combined with credulity and lack of knowledge of affairs? They knew what advisers he would select, men trained in their service and taken from their legal staffs. They knew he would shrink from anything "radical" or "disturbing"—that is, would not molest the two packs of wolves, the business and the political, at their feast upon the public. He came of a line of bigoted adherents of his party; he led a simple, retired life among sheep and cows and books asleep in the skins of sheep and cows. He wore old-fashioned rural whiskers, thickest in the throat, thinning toward the jawbone, scant about the lower lip, absent from the upper. These evidences of unfitness to cope with up-to-date corruption seemed to endear him to the masses.

As soon as those big organs of the opposition that were in the control of the powers began to talk of Simpson as an ideal candidate, I suspected what was in the wind. But I had my hands full; the most I could then do was to supply my local "left-bower," Silliman, with funds and set him to work for a candidate for his party more to my taste. It was fortunate for me that I had cured myself of the habit of worrying. For it was plain that, if Goodrich and Beckett succeeded in getting Simpson nominated by the opposition, I should have a hard fight to raise the necessary campaign money. The large interests either would finance Simpson or, should I convince them that Burbank was as good for their purposes as Simpson, would be indifferent which won.

I directed Silliman to work for Rundle of Indiana, a thoroughly honest man, in deadly earnest about half a dozen deadly wrong things, and capable of anything in furthering them—after the manner of fanatics. If he had not been in public life, he would have been a camp-meeting exhorter. Crowds liked to listen to him; the radicals and radically inclined throughout the West swore by him; he had had two terms in Congress, had got a

hundred-odd votes for the nomination for President at the last national convention of the opposition. A splendid scare-crow for the Wall Street
crowd, but difficult to nominate over Goodrich's
man Simpson in a convention of practical politicians.

In May—it was the afternoon of the very day
my mutineers got back into the harness—Woodruff asked me if I would see a man he had picked
up in a delegate-hunting trip into Indiana. "An
old pal of mine, much the better for the twelve
years' wear since I last saw him. He has always
trained with the opposition. He's a full-fledged
graduate of the Indiana school of politics, and
that's the best. It's almost all craft there—they
hate to give up money and don't use it except as a
last resort."

He brought in his man—Merriweather by
name. I liked the first look at him—keen, cynical,
indifferent. He had evidently sat in so many
games of chance of all kinds that play roused in
him only the ice-cold passion of the purely profes-
sional.

"There's been nothing doing in our state for

the last two or three years—at least nothing in my line," said he. "A rank outsider, Scarborough—"

I nodded. "Yes, I know him. He came into the Senate from your state two years ago."

"Well, he's built up a machine of his own and runs things to suit himself."

"I thought he wasn't a politician," said I.

Merriweather's bony face showed a faint grin. "The best ever," said he. "He's put the professionals out of business, without its costing him a cent. I've got tired of waiting for him to blow over."

Tired—and hungry, I thought. After half an hour of pumping I sent him away, detaining Woodruff. "What does he really think about Rundle?" I asked.

"Says he hasn't the ghost of a chance—that Scarborough'll control the Indiana delegation and that Scarborough has no more use for lunatics than for grafters."

This was not encouraging. I called Merriweather back. "Why don't you people nominate Scarborough at St. Louis?" said I.

Behind his surface of attention, I saw his mind traveling at lightning speed in search of my hidden purpose along every avenue that my suggestion opened.

"Scarborough'd be a dangerous man for you," he replied. "He's got a nasty way of reaching across party lines for votes."

I kept my face a blank.

"You've played politics only in your own state or against the Eastern crowd, these last few years," he went on, as if in answer to my thoughts. "You don't realize what a hold Scarborough's got through the entire West. He has split your party and the machine of his own in our state, and they know all about him and his doings in the states to the west. The people like a fellow that knocks out the regulars."

"A good many call him a demagogue, don't they?" said I.

"Yes—and he is, in sort of a way," replied Merriweather. "But—well, he's got a knack of telling the truth so that it doesn't scare folks. And he's managed to convince them that he isn't looking out for number one. It can't be denied that he made a good governor. For instance, he got after the monopolies, and the cost of living is twenty per cent. lower in Indiana than just across the line in Ohio."

"Then I should say that all the large interests in the country would line up against him," said I.

"Every one," said Merriweather, and an expression of understanding flitted across his face. He went on: "But it ain't much use talking about him. He couldn't get the nomination—at least, it wouldn't be easy to get it for him."

"I suppose not," said I. "That's a job for a first-class man—and they're rare." And I shook hands with him.

About a week later he returned, and tried to make a report to me. But I sent him away, treating him very formally. I appreciated that, being an experienced and capable man, he knew the wisdom of getting intimately in touch with his real employer; but, as I had my incomparable Woodruff, better far than I at the rough work of politics, there was no necessity for my entangling myself. Merriweather went to Woodruff, and Woodruff reported to me—Scarborough's friends in Indianapolis all agreed that he did not want the nomination and would not have it.

"We must force it on him," said I. "We must have Scarborough."

Immediately after Burbank's nomination, Goodrich concentrated upon nominating Judge Simpson. He had three weeks, and he worked hard and well. I think he overdid it in the editorials in our party organs under his influence in New York, Boston and other eastern cities—never a day without lugubrious screeds on the dismal outlook for Burbank if the other party should put up Simpson. But his Simpson editorials in big opposition papers undoubtedly produced an effect. I set for De Milt and his bureau of underground publicity the task of showing up, as far as it was prudent to expose intimate politics to the public, Goodrich and his crowd and their conspiracy with Beckett and his crowd to secure the opposition nomination for a man of the same offensive type as Cromwell. And I directed Woodruff to supply Silliman and Merriweather and that department of my "bi-partizan" machine with all the money they wanted. "They can't spend much to advantage at this late day except for traveling expenses," said I. "Our best plan, anyhow, is good honest missionary work with the honest men of the other party who wish to see its best man nominated."

While Goodrich's agents and Beckett's agents were industriously arranging the eastern machinery of the opposition party for Simpson, Merriweather had Silliman's men toiling in the West and South to get Rundle delegates or uninstructed delegations. And, after our conversation, he was reinforced by Woodruff and such men of his staff as could be used without suspicion. Woodruff himself could permeate like an odorless gas; you knew he was there only by the results. Nothing could be done for Rundle in his own state; but the farther away from his home our men got, the easier it was to induce—by purchase and otherwise—the politicians of his party to think well of him. This the more because they regarded Simpson as a "stuff" and a "stiff"—and they weren't far wrong.

"It may not be Scarborough, and it probably won't be Rundle," Woodruff said in his final report to me, "but it certainly won't be Simpson. He's the dead one, no matter how well he does on the first ballot."

But I would not let him give me the details— the story of shrewd and slippery plots, stratagems, surprises. "I am worn out, mind and body," said I in apology for my obvious weariness and indifference.

For six months I had been incessantly at work. The tax upon memory alone, to say nothing of the other faculties, had been crushing. Easy as political facts always were for me, I could not lightly bear the strain of keeping constantly in mind not merely the outlines, but also hundreds of the details, of the political organizations of forty-odd states with all their counties. And the tax on memory was probably the least. Then added to all my political work was business care; for while I was absorbed in politics, Ed Ramsay had badly muddled the business. Nor had I, like Burbank and Woodruff, the power to empty my mind as I touched the pillow and so to get eight hours of unbroken rest each night.

Woodruff began asking me for instructions.

But my judgment was uncertain, and my imagination barren. "Do as you think best," said I. "I must rest. I've reached my limit,"—my limit of endurance of the sights and odors and befoulings of these sewers of politics I must in person adventure in order to reach my goal. I must pause and rise to the surface for a breath of decent air or I should not have the strength to finish these menial and even vile tasks which no man can escape if he is a practical leader in the practical activities of practical life.

XVIII

A DANGEROUS PAUSE

I took train for my friend Sandys' country place near Cleveland, forbidding Woodruff or Burbank or my secretaries to communicate with me. Sandys had no interest in politics—his fortune was in real estate and, therefore, did not tempt or force him into relations with political machines.

Early in the morning after my arrival I got away from the others and, with a stag-hound who remembered me with favor from my last visit, struck into woods that had never been despoiled by man. As I tramped on and on, my mind seemed to revive, and I tried to take up the plots and schemes that had been all-important yesterday. But I could not. Instead, as any sane man must when he and nature are alone and face to face, I fell to marveling that I could burn up myself, the best of me, the best years of my one life, in such a fever of folly and fraud as this

political career of mine. I seemed to be in a lucid
interval between paroxysms of insanity. I reviewed the men and things of my world as one
recalls the absurd and repellent visions of a night-
mare. I shrank from passing from this mood of
wakefulness and reason back into the unreal reality of what had for years been my all-in-all. I
wandered hour after hour, sometimes imagining
that I was flying from the life I loathed, again
that somewhere in those cool, green, golden-light-
ed mazes I should find—my lost youth, and her.
For, how could I think of *it* without thinking of
her also? It had been lighted by her; it had gone
with her; it lived in memory, illumined by her.

The beautiful, beautiful world-that-ought-to-
be! The hideous, the horrible world-that-is!

I did not return to the house until almost din-
ner-time. "I have to go away to-morrow morning," I announced after dinner. For I felt that,
if I did not fly at once, I should lose all heart for
the task which must be finished.

"Why," protested Sandys, "you came to stay
until we all started with you for St. Louis."

"I must go," I repeated. I did not care to in-

vent an excuse; I could not give the reason. Had
I followed my impulse, I should have gone at
once, that night.

By noon the next day I had again flung myself
into the vexed political ocean whose incessant buffetings give the swimmers small chance to think
of anything beyond the next oncoming wave.

XIX

I was almost master of myself again when, a week later, I got aboard the car in which Carlotta and I were taking our friends to look on at the opposition's convention at St. Louis.

When we arrived, I went at once to confer with Merriweather in a room at the Southern Hotel which no one knew he had. "Simpson has under, rather than over, five hundred delegates," was his first item of good news. "It takes six hundred and fifty to nominate. As his sort of boom always musters its greatest strength on the first ballot, I'm putting my money two to one against him."

"And Scarborough?" I asked, wondering at my indifference to this foreshadowing of triumph.

"My men talk him to every incoming delegation. It's well known that he don't want the nomination and has forbidden his friends to vote for him and has pledged them to work against him. Then, too, the bosses and the boys don't like him—to put it mildly. But I think we're making every one feel he's the only man they can put up, with a chance to beat Burbank."

My wife and our friends and I dined at the Southern that night. As we were about to leave, the streets began to fill. And presently through the close-packed masses came at a walk an open carriage—the storm-center of a roar that almost drowned the music of the four or five bands. The electric lights made the scene bright as day.

"Who is he?" asked the woman at my side—Mrs. Sandys.

She was looking at *the* man in that carriage—there were four, but there was no mistaking him. He was seated, was giving not the slightest heed to the cheering throngs. His soft black hat was pulled well down over his brows; his handsome profile was stern, his face pale. If that crowd had been hurling curses at him and preparing to tear him limb from limb he would not have looked different. He was smooth-shaven, which made him seem younger than I knew him to be. And over him was the glamour of the world-that-

ought-to-be in which he lived and had the power
to compel others to live as long as they were under the spell of his personality.

"That," I replied to Mrs. Sandys, "is Senator
Scarborough of Indiana."

"What's he so stern about?"

"I'm sure I don't know—perhaps to hide his
joy," said I.

But I did know, and my remark was the impulsive fling of envy. He had found out, several weeks before, what a strong undercurrent
was running toward him. He was faced by a
dilemma—if he did not go to the convention, it
would be said that he had stayed away deliberately, and he would be nominated; if he went, to try
to prevent his nomination, the enthusiasm of his
admirers and followers would give the excuse for
forcing the nomination upon him. And as he sat
there, with that ominous tumult about him, he
was realizing how hard his task was to be.

His companions pushed him a passage through
the crowds on the sidewalk and in the lobby, and
he shut himself away in the upper part of the hotel. When we left, half an hour later, the people

"THAT," I REPLIED TO MRS. SANDYS, "IS SENATOR SCARBOROUGH
OF INDIANA" *p. 226*

were packed before that face of the hotel which
displayed the banner of the Indiana delegation,
were cheering Scarborough, were clamoring—
in vain—for him to show himself.

"But won't he offend them?" asked my wife.

"A crowd loves like a woman," said I. "Indifference only excites it."

"Oh, *I* never loved that way," protested Mrs.
Sandys.

"Then," said my wife, rather sourly I thought,
"you and Mr. Sandys have something to live for."

And so we talked no more politics.   There may
be American women who *really* like to talk politics, but I never happened to know one with so little sense.   It's a pity we men do not imitate our
women more closely in one respect. In season and
out of season, they never talk anything but business—woman's one business. When other things
are being discussed, they listen, or rather, pretend to listen; in reality, their minds are still
on their business, and how they shall contrive to
bring it back into the conversation with advantage to themselves.

Next day the convention adopted a wishy-

washy platform much like Burbank's—if anything, weaker. I saw Goodrich's blight upon it.
But the victory cost him dear. That night the
delegates realized what a blunder they had made
—or thought they realized it after Merriweather
and his staff had circulated among them. Few
of them had been trusted by Beckett with the
secret that, with that platform and with Simpson
as the nominee, their party would have the interests behind it, would almost certainly win. They
only saw ahead a dull campaign, and no real issue
between the parties, and their candidate, if he was
Simpson, much the less attractive personality of
the two.

The following morning the voting began; and
after seven ballots Simpson had thirty-nine votes
less than on the first ballot. "It was like a
funeral," was the verdict of my disappointed
guests that evening. A night of debate and
gloom among the politicians and other delegates,
and on the opening ballot Merriweather sprung
his trap.

The first big doubtful state in the alphabetical
list of states is Illinois. When the secretary of

the convention called for Illinois' vote, it was cast
solidly for Scarborough.

There was straightway pandemonium. It was
half an hour before any one could get a hearing.
Then Indiana was called, and Pierson, attorney
general of that state and chairman of its delegation, cast its vote as in the other ballots, for
Hitchens, its governor. From my box I was
watching Scarborough and his immediate friends
going from delegation to delegation, and I knew
what he was about. When Iowa was called and
cast its vote solidly for him I knew he had failed.

"How white he is!" said Mrs. Sandys, who was
looking at him through opera-glasses.

I borrowed them and saw that his gaze was
fixed on a box on the other side of the huge auditorium, on a woman in that box—I had only to
look at her to see which woman. She was beautiful, of that type of charm which the French sum
up in the phrase "the woman of thirty." I have
heard crowds bellow too often to be moved by
it—though the twenty or thirty thousand gathered
under that roof were outdoing the cannonade of
any thunderstorm. But that woman's look in re-

sponse to Scarborough's—there was sympathy
and understanding in it, and more, infinitely more.
He had been crushed for the moment—and I understood enough of his situation to understand
what a blow to all his plans this untimely apparent triumph was. She was showing that she too
felt the blow, but she was also sending a message
of courage to him—one of those messages that
transcend words, like music, like the perfumes of
flowers and fields, like that which fills us as we
look straight up into a clear night sky. I lowered
the glasses and looked away—I could not bear it.
For the moment I hated him—hating myself
for it.

I heard Carlotta asking a woman in the box
next ours the name of "the woman with the white
plume in the big black hat in the seventh box on
the other side."

"Mrs. Scarborough," was the answer.

"Oh, is that *she?*" exclaimed Mrs. Sandys, almost snatching her glasses from me in her eagerness. "You know who she was—John Dumont's
widow—you remember him? She must be an
unusual person to have attracted two such men."

But Scarborough was nominated now. He waved aside those who tried to take him up and bear him to the platform. He walked down the aisle alone and ascended amid a tense silence; he stood looking calmly out. His face had lost its whiteness of a few minutes before. As he stood there, big and still, a sort of embodiment of fearlessness, I wondered—and I fancy many others were wondering—whether he was about to refuse the nomination. But an instant's thought drove the wild notion from my mind. He could not strike that deadly blow at his party.

"Fellow delegates," said he—a clearer, more musical voice than his I have never heard—"I thank you for this honor. As you know, I opposed the platform you saw fit to adopt. I have nothing to retract. I do not like it. But, after all, a candidate must be his own platform. And I bring my public record as proof of my pledge—that—" he paused and the silence was tremendous. He went on, each word distinct and by itself—"if I am elected"—a long pause—"I shall obey the Constitution"—another long pause—"I shall enforce the laws!"

He was descending to the aisle before the silence was broken—a feeble, rippling applause, significant of disappointment at what seemed an anti-climax. He had merely repeated in condensed form the oath of office which a President takes at his inauguration. But somehow—no doubt, it was the magic of his voice and his manner and superb presence—those simple words kept on ringing; and all at once—full half a minute must have elapsed, a long time in such circumstances—all at once the enormous meaning of the two phrases boomed into the brains of those thousands: If this man is elected, there will be a President without fear or favor, and he will really obey the Constitution, will really enforce the laws! That little speech, though only a repetition of an oath embodied in our century-old supreme law, was a firebrand to light the torch of revolution, of revolution back toward what the republic used to be before differences of wealth divided its people into upper, middle and lower classes, before enthroned corporate combinations made equality before the law a mockery, before the development of our vast material resources restored to the intelligent and energetic few their power over the careless and purposeless many.

As the multitude realized his meaning,—I doubt if many times in all history such a sight and sound has burst upon mortal ears and eyes. For the moment I was daunted; it was impossible not to think that here was the whole people, not to feel that Scarborough had been chosen President and was about to fulfil his pledge. Daunted, yet thrilled too. For, at bottom, are we not all passionate dreamers of abstract right and justice?

Then I remembered; and I said to myself, "He has defied the interests. David has gone out against Goliath—but the Davids do not win nowadays. I can elect Burbank."

But where was the elation that thought would have set to swelling in the *me* of less than two weeks before? And then I began clearly to see that, for me at least, the prize, to be prized, must be fairly won from start to goal; and to be enjoyed, must gladden eyes that would in turn gladden me with the approval and sympathy which only a woman can give and without which a man is alone and indeed forlorn.

XX

PILGRIMS AND PATRIOTS

From St. Louis I went direct to Burbank.

His heart had been set upon a grand speech-making tour. He was fond of wandering about, showing himself to cheering crowds; and he had a deep, and by no means unwarranted, confidence in his platform magnetism. At first I had been inclined to give him his way. But the more I considered the matter, the stronger seemed to become the force of the objections—it takes a far bigger man than was Burbank at that stage of his growth not to be cheapened by "steeple-chasing for votes"; also, the coming of the candidate causes jealousy and heart-burnings over matters of precedence, reception and entertainment among the local celebrities, and so he often leaves the party lukewarm where he found it enthusiastic. Further, it uses up local campaign money that ought to be spent in hiring workers at the polls, which is the polite phrase for vote-buying as "retaining-fee" is the polite phrase for bribe.

I decided against the tour and for the highly expensive but always admirable and profitable "pilgrimage plan".

Burbank's own home was at Rivington, and I should have had him visited there, had it not been on a single-track branch-railway which could not handle without danger and discomfort the scores of thousands we were planning to carry to and from him almost daily. So, it was given out that he purposed as far as possible to withdraw from the strife of the campaign and to await the results in the dignified calm in which he wished the voters to determine it. He took—after Wood-ruff had carefully selected it—a "retired" house "in the country."

And it was in the open country. A farm garden adjoined it on the one side, a wheat field on the other, a large orchard to the rear. The broad meadow in front gave plenty of room for delegations visiting the "standard bearer of the party of patriotism" in his "rural seclusion," to hear his simple, spontaneous words of welcome. But for all the remote aspect of the place, it was only five minutes' drive and ten minutes' walk from a station through which four big railroads passed. One of the out-buildings was changed into a telegraph office from which accounts of the enthusiasm of the delegations and of his speeches could be sent to the whole country. On his desk in his little study stood a private-wire telephone that, without danger of leakage, would put him in direct communication either with my study at Fredonia or with Doc Woodruff's privatest private room in the party national headquarters at Chicago. Thus, our statesman, though he seemed to be aloof, was in the very thick of the fray; and the tens of thousands of his fellow citizens, though they seemed to come almost on their own invitation inspired by uncontrollable enthusiasm for the great statesman, were in fact free excursionists —and a very troublesome, critical, expensive lot they were. But—the public was impressed. It sits in its seat in the theater of action and believes that the play is real, and ignores and forgets the fact that there is a behind-the-scenes.

The party distributed from various centers tons of "literature." And in addition to meetings arranged by state and local committees, a series of huge demonstrations was held in the cities of every doubtful state. Besides the party's regular speakers, we hired as many "independent" orators as we could. But all these other branches of the public side of the campaign were subsidiary to the work at the "retreat." It might be called the headquarters of the rank and file of the party— those millions of "principle" voters and workers who were for Burbank because he was the standard-bearer of their party. No money, no bribes of patronage have to be given to them; but it costs several millions to raise that mass to the pitch of hot enthusiasm which will make each individual in it certain to go to the polls on election day and take his neighbors, instead of staying at home and hoping the party won't lose.

Burbank's work was, therefore, highly important. But the seat of the real campaign was Woodruff's privatest private room in the Chicago headquarters. For, there were laid and were put in the way of execution the plans for acquiring those elements that, in the doubtful states, have the balance of power between the two opposing and about evenly matched masses of "principle" voters. I just now recall a talk I had with my wife, about that time. She took no interest in politics and rarely spoke of political matters—and both of us discouraged political talk before the children. One day she said to me: "This campaign of yours and Mr. Burbank's must be costing an awful lot of money."

"A good deal," said I.

"Several millions?"

"This is a big country, and you can't stir it up politically for nothing. Why do you ask?"

"Who gives the money?" she persisted.

"The rich men—the big corporations—give most of it."

"Why?"

"Patriotism," said I. "To save the nation from our wicked opponent."

"How do Mr. Roebuck and the others get it back?" she pursued, ignoring my pleasantry.

"Get what back?"

"Why the money they advance. They aren't the men to *give* anything."

I answered with a smile only.

She lapsed into thoughtfulness. When I was

assuming that her mind had wandered off to something else she said: "The people must be very stupid—not to suspect."

"Or, the rich men and the corporations very stupid to give," I suggested.

"Do you mean that they don't get it back?" she demanded.

"Of course," said I, "their patriotism must be rewarded. We can not expect them to save the country year after year for nothing."

"I should think not!" she said, adding disgustedly, "I think politics is very silly. And men get excited about it! But *I* never listen."

Arriving at the "retreat" from the Scarborough convention, I found Burbank much perturbed because Scarborough had been nominated. He did not say so—on the contrary, he expressed in sonorous phrases his satisfaction that there was to be "a real test of strength between conservatism and radicalism." He never dropped his pose, even with me—not even with himself.

"I confess I don't share your cheerfulness," said I. "If Scarborough were a wild man, we'd have a walkover. But he isn't, and I fear he'll be

more and more attractive to the wavering voters,
to many of our own people. Party loyalty has
been overworked in the last few presidential campaigns. He'll go vote-hunting in the doubtful
states, but it won't seem undignified. He's one of
those men whose dignity comes from the inside
and can't be lost."

Burbank was unable to conceal his annoyance
—he never could bear praise of another man of
his own rank in public life. Also he showed surprise. "Why, I understood—I had been led to believe—that you—favored his nomination," was
his guarded way of telling me he knew I had a
hand in bringing it about.

"So I did," replied I. "He was your only
chance. He won't be able to get a campaign fund
of so much as a quarter of a million, and the best
workers of his party will at heart be against him.
Simpson would have had—well, Goodrich could
and would have got him enough to elect him."

Burbank's eyes twitched. "I think you're prejudiced against Senator Goodrich, Harvey," said he
in his gentlest tone. "He is first of all a loyal
party man."

"Loyal fiddlesticks!" replied I. "He is agent of the Wall Street crowd—they're his party. He's just the ordinary machine politician, with no more party feeling than—than—" I smiled— "than any other man behind the scenes."

Burbank dodged this by taking it as a jest. He always shed my frank speeches as humor. "Prejudice, prejudice, Harvey!" he said in mild reproof. "We need Goodrich, and—"

"Pardon me," I interrupted. "We do not need him. On the contrary, we must put him out of the party councils. If we don't, he may try to help Scarborough. The Senate's safe, no matter who's elected President; and Goodrich will rely on it to save his crowd. He's a mountain of vanity and the two defeats we've given him have made every atom of that vanity quiver with hatred of us."

"I wish you could have been here when he called," said Burbank. "I am sure you would have changed your mind."

"When does he resign the chairmanship of the national committee?" I asked. "He agreed to plead bad health and resign within two weeks after the convention."

Burbank gave an embarrassed cough. "Don't you think, Harvey," said he, "that, to soothe his vanity, it might be well for us—for you—to let him stay on there—nominally, of course? I know *you* care nothing for titles."

Instead of being angered by this attempt to cozen me, by this exhibition of treachery, I felt disgust and pity—how nauseating and how hopeless to try to forward one so blind to his own interests, so easily frightened into surrender to his worst enemies! But I spoke very quietly to him. "The reason you want me to be chairman—for it is you that want and need it, not I—the reason I *must* be chairman is because the machine throughout the country must know that Goodrich is out and that your friends are in. In what other way can this be accomplished?"

He did not dare try to reply.

I went on: "If he stays at the head of the national committee Scarborough will be elected."

"You are prejudiced, Harvey—"

"Please don't say that again, Governor," I interrupted coldly. "I repeat, Goodrich must give place to me, or Scarborough will be elected."

"You don't mean that you would turn against me?" came from him in a queer voice after a long pause.

"While I was in St. Louis, working to make you President," said I, "you were plotting behind my back, plotting against me and yourself."

"You were at St. Louis aiding in the nomination of the strongest candidate," he retorted, his bitterness distinct though guarded.

"Strongest—yes. But strongest with whom?"

"With the people," he replied.

"Precisely," said I. "But the people are not going to decide this election. The party lines are to be so closely drawn that money will have the deciding vote. The men who organize and direct industry and enterprise—*they* are going to decide it. And, in spite of Goodrich's traitorous efforts, the opposition has put up the man who can't get a penny from them."

In fact, I had just discovered that Scarborough had instructed Pierson, whom he had made chairman of his campaign, not to take any money from any corporation even if it was offered. But I thought it wiser to keep this from Burbank.

He sat folding a sheet of paper again and again. I let him reason it out. Finally he said: "I see your point, Harvey. But I practically promised Goodrich—practically asked him to remain—"

I waited.

"For the sake of the cause," he went on when he saw he was to get no help from me, "any and all personal sacrifices must be made. If you insist on having Goodrich's head, I will break my promise, and—"

"Pardon me again," I interrupted. My mood would not tolerate twaddle about "the cause" and "promises" from Burbank—Burbank, whose "cause," as he had just shown afresh, was himself alone, and who promised everything to everybody and kept only the most advantageous promises after he had made absolutely sure how his advantage lay. "It's all a matter of indifference to me. If you wish to retain Goodrich, do so. He must not be dismissed as a personal favor to me. The favor is to you. I do not permit any man to thimblerig his debts to me into my debts to him."

Burbank seemed deeply moved. He came up to

me and took my hand. "It is not like my friend
Sayler to use the word indifference in connection
with me," he said. And then I realized how completely the nomination had turned his head. For
his tone was that of the great man addressing his
henchman.

I did not keep my amusement out of my eyes.
"James," said I, "indifference is precisely the
word. I should welcome a chance to withdraw
from this campaign. I have been ambitious for
power, *you* want place. If you think the time has
come to dissolve partnership, say so—and trade
yourself off to Goodrich."

He was angry through and through, not so
much at my bluntness as at my having seen into
his plot to help himself at my expense—for, not
even when I showed it to him, could he see that
it was to his interest to destroy Goodrich. Moral
coward that he was, the course of conciliation always appealed to him, whether it was wise or not,
and the course of courage always frightened him.
He bit his lip and dissembled his anger. Presently
he began to pace up and down the room, his head
bent, his hands clasped behind him. After per-

haps five minutes he paused to say: "You insist on taking the place yourself, Harvey?"

I stood before him and looked down at him. "Your suspicion that I have also a personal reason is well-founded, James," said I. "I wouldn't put myself in a position where I should have to ask as a favor what I now get as a right. If I help you to the presidency, I must be master of the national machine of the party, able to use it with all its power and against *any one*—" here I looked him straight in the eye—"who shall try to build himself up at my expense. Personally, we are friends, and it has been a pleasure to me to help elevate a man I liked. But there is no friendship in affairs, except where friendship and interest point the same way. It is strange that a man of your experience should expect friendship from me at a time when you are showing that you haven't for me even the friendship of enlightened self-interest."

"Your practice is better than your theory, Harvey," said he, putting on an injured, forgiving look and using his chest tones. "A better friend never lived than you, and I know no other man who gets the absolute loyalty you get." He looked at me earnestly. "What has changed you?" he asked. "Why are you so bitter and so—so unlike your even-tempered self?"

I waved his question aside,—I had no mind to show him my uncovered coffin with its tenant who only slept, or to expose to him the feelings which the erect and fearless figure of Scarborough had set to stirring in me. "I'm careful to choose my friends from among those who can serve me and whom I can therefore serve," I said. "And that is the sentimentalism of the wise. I wish us to remain friends—therefore, I must be able to be as useful to you as you can be useful to me."

"Goodrich shall go," was the upshot of his thinking. "I'll telephone him this afternoon. Is my old friend satisfied?"

"You have done what was best for yourself," said I, with wholly good-humored raillery. And we shook hands, and I went.

I was glad to be alone where I could give way to my weariness and disgust; for I had lost all the joy of the combat. The arena of ambition had now become to me a ring where men are devoured

by the beast-in-man after hideous battles. I turned
from it, heart-sick. "If only I had less intelligence, less insight," I thought, "so that I could
cheat myself as Burbank cheats himself. Or, if
I had the relentlessness or the supreme egotism,
or whatever it is, that enables great men to tram-
ple without a qualm, to destroy without pity, to
enjoy without remorse."

XXI

My nerves began to feel as if some one were
gently sliding his fingers along their bared length
—not a pain, but as fear-inspiring as the sound
of the stealthy creep of the assassin moving up
behind to strike a sudden and mortal blow. I dismissed business and politics and went cruising on
the lakes with restful, non-political Fred Sandys.

After we had been knocking about perhaps a
week, we landed one noon at the private pier of
the Liscombes to lunch with them. As Sandys
and I strolled toward the front of the house, several people, also guests for lunch, were just descending from a long buckboard. At sight of one
of them I stopped short inside, though I mechan-
ically continued to walk toward her. I recognized
her instantly—the curve of her shoulders, the
poise of her head, and her waving jet-black hair
to confirm. And without the slightest warning
there came tumbling and roaring up in me a tor-

rent of longings, regrets; and I suddenly had a clear understanding of my absorption in this wretched game I had been playing year in and year out with hardly a glance up from the table. That wretched game with its counterfeit stakes; and the more a man wins, the poorer he is.

She seemed calm enough as she faced me. Indeed, I was not sure when she had first caught sight of me, or whether she had recognized me, until Mrs. Liscombe began to introduce us. "Oh, yes," she then interrupted, "I remember Senator Sayler very well. We used to live in the same town. We went to the same school." And with a friendly smile she gave me her hand.

What did I say? I do not know. But I am sure I gave no sign of the clamor within. I had not cultivated surface-calm all those years in vain. I talked, and she talked—but I saw only her face, splendid fulfilment of the promise of girlhood; I hardly heard her words, so greatly was her voice moving me. It was an unusually deep voice for a woman, sweet and with a curious carrying quality that made it seem stronger than it was. In figure she was delicate, but radiant of life and

health—aglow, not ablaze. She was neither tall
nor short, and was dressed simply, but in the
fashion—I heard the other women discussing her
clothes after she left. And she still had the man-
nerism that was most fascinating to me—she kept
her eyes down while she was talking or listening,
and raised them now and then with a full, slow
look at you.

When Mrs. Liscombe asked her to come to dinner the next evening with the people she was visiting, she said: "Unfortunately, I must start for
Washington in the morning. I am overhauling
my school and building an addition."

It had not occurred to me to think where she
had come from or how she happened to be there,
or of anything in the years since I was last with
her. The reminder that she had a school came as
a shock—she was so utterly unlike my notion of
the head of a school. I think she saw or felt what
was in my mind, for she went on, to me: "I've
had it six years now—the next will be the seventh."

"Do you like it?" I asked.

"Don't I look like a happy woman?"

"You do," said I, after our eyes had met. "You are."

"There were sixty girls last year—sixty-three," she went on. "Next year there will be more—about a hundred. It's like a garden, and I'm the gardener, busy from morning till night, with no time to think of anything but my plants and flowers."

She had conjured a picture that made my heart ache. I suddenly felt old and sad and lonely—a forlorn failure. "I too am a gardener," said I. "But it's a sorry lot of weeds and thistles that keeps me occupied. And in the midst of the garden is a plum tree—that bears Dead Sea fruit."

She was silent.

"You don't care for politics?" said I.

"No," she replied, and lifted and lowered her eyes in a slow glance that made me wish I had not asked. "It is, I think, gardening with weeds and thistles, as you say." Then, after a pause: "Do *you* like it?"

"Don't ask me," I said with a bitterness that made us both silent thereafter.

That evening I got Fred to land me at the nearest town. The train she must have been on had just gone. In the morning I took the express for the East. Arrived at Washington, I drove straight to her school.

A high iron fence, not obstructing the view from the country road; a long drive under arching maples and beeches; a rambling, fascinating old house upon the crest of a hill; many windows, a pillared porch, a low, very wide doorway. It seemed like her in its dark, cool, odorous beauty.

She herself was in the front hall, directing some workmen. "Why, Senator Sayler, this *is* a surprise," she said, advancing to greet me. But there was no suggestion of surprise in her tone or her look, only a friendly welcome to an acquaintance.

She led the way into the drawing-room to the left. The furniture and pictures were in ghostly draperies; everything was in confusion. We went on to a side veranda, seated ourselves. She looked inquiringly at me.

"I do not know why," was my answer. "I only know—I had to come."

She studied me calmly. I remember her look, everything about her—the embroidery on the sleeves and bosom of her blouse, the buckles on her white shoes. I remember also that there was a breeze, and how good it felt to my hot face, to my eyes burning from lack of sleep. At last she said: "Well—what do you think of my little kingdom?"

"It is yours—entirely?"

"House, gardens—everything. I paid the last of my debts in June."

"I'm contrasting it with my own," I said.

"But that isn't fair," she protested with a smile. "You must remember, I'm only a woman."

"With my own," I went on, as if she had not interrupted. "Yours is—yours, honestly got. It makes you proud, happy. Mine—" I did not finish.

She must have seen or felt how profoundly I was moved, for I presently saw her looking at me with an expression I might have resented for its pity from any other than her. "Why do you tell *me* this?" she asked.

"There is always for every one," was my an-

swer, "some person to whom he shows himself as
he is. You are that person for me because—I'm
surrounded by people who care for me for what
I can give. Even my children care to a great extent for that reason. It's the penalty for having
the power to give the material things all human
beings crave. Only two persons ever cared—cared
much for me just because I was myself. They
were my mother—and you."

She laughed in quiet raillery. "Two have
cared for you, but you have cared for only one.
And what devotion you have given him!"

"I have cared for my mother—for my children—"

"Yes—your children. I forgot them."

"And—for you."

She made what I thought a movement of impatience.

"For you," I repeated. Then: "Elizabeth, you
were right when you wrote that I was a coward."

She rose and stood—near enough to me for me
to catch her faint, elusive perfume—and gazed out
into the distance.

"In St. Louis the other day," I went on, "I

saw a man who has risen to power greater than I can ever hope to have. And he got it by marching erect in the open."

"Yet you have everything you used to want," she said dreamily.

"Yes—everything. Only to learn how worthless what I wanted was. And for this trash, this dirt, I have given—all I had that was of value."

"All?"

"All," I replied. "Your love and my own self-respect."

"Why do you think you've not been brave?" she asked after a while.

"Because I've won by playing on the weaknesses and fears of men which my own weaknesses and fears enabled me to understand."

"You have done wrong—deliberately?"

"Deliberately."

"But that good might come?"

"So I told myself."

"And good has come? I have heard that figs do grow on thistles."

"Good has come. But, I think, in spite of me, not through me."

"But now that you see," she said, turning her eyes to mine with appeal in them, and something more, I thought, "you will—you will not go on?"

"I don't know. Is there such a thing as remorse without regret?" And then my self-control went and I let her see what I had commanded myself to keep hid: "I only know clearly one thing, Elizabeth—only one thing matters. *You* are the whole world to me. You and I could— what could we not do together!"

Her color slowly rose, slowly vanished. "Was *that* what you came to tell me?" she asked.

"Yes," I answered, not flinching.

"*That* is the climax of your moralizings?"

"Yes," I answered. "And of my cowardice."

A little icy smile just changed the curve of her lips. "When I was a girl, you won my love—or took it when I gave it to you, if you prefer. And then—you threw it away. For an ambition you weren't brave enough to pursue honorably, you broke my heart."

"Yes," I answered. "But—I loved you."

"And now," she went on, "after your years of

self-indulgence, of getting what you wanted, no matter about the cost, you see me again. You find I have mended my heart, have coaxed a few flowers of happiness to bloom. You find there was something you did not destroy, something you think it will make you happier to destroy."

"Yes," I answered, "I came to try to make you as unhappy as I am. For I love you."

She drew a long breath. "Well," she said evenly, "for the first time in your life you are defeated. I learned the lesson you so thoroughly taught me. And I built the wall round my garden high and strong. You—" she smiled, a little raillery, a little scorn—"you can't break in, Harvey—nor slip in."

"No need," I said. "For I *am* in—I've always been in."

Her bosom rose and fell quickly, and her eyes shifted. But that was for an instant only. "If you were as brave as you are bold!" she scoffed.

"If I were as brave without you as I should be with you!" I replied. Then: "But you love as a woman loves—herself first, the man afterward."

"Harvey Sayler denouncing selfishness!"

"Do not sneer," I said. "For—I love you as a man loves. A poor, pale shadow of ideal love, no doubt, but a man's best, Elizabeth."

I saw that she was shaken; but even as I began to thrill with a hope so high that it was giddy with fear, she was once more straight and strong and calm.

"You have come. You have tried. You have failed," she went on after a long pause. And in spite of her efforts, that deep voice of hers was gentle and wonderfully sweet. "Now—you will return to your life, I to mine." And she moved toward the entrance to the drawing-room, I following her. We stood in silence at the front doorway waiting for my carriage to come up. I watched her—maddeningly mistress of herself.

"How can you be so cold!" I cried. "Don't you see, don't you feel, how I, who love you, suffer?"

Without a word she stretched out her beautiful, white hands, long and narrow and capable. In each of the upturned palms were four deep and bloody prints where her nails had been crushing into them.

Before I could lift my eyes to her face she was turning to rejoin her workmen. As I stood uncertain, dazed, she glanced at me with a bright smile. "Good-by again," she called. "A pleasant journey!"

"Thank you," I replied. "Good-by."

Driving toward the road gates, I looked at the house many times, from window to window, everywhere. Not a glimpse of her until I was almost at the road again. Then I saw her back— the graceful white dress, the knot of blue-black hair, the big white hat, and she directing her workmen with her closed white parasol.

XXII

I went up to New York, to find confusion and gloom at our headquarters there.

Senator Goodrich had subtly given the impression, not only to the workers but also to the newspaper men, who had given it to the public, that with his resignation the Burbank campaign had fallen to pieces. "And I fear you'll have some difficulty in getting any money at all down town," said Revell, the senior Senator from New York state, who envied and hated Goodrich and was therefore, if not for personal reasons, amiably disposed toward me. "They don't like our candidate."

"Naturally," said I. "That's why he's running and that's why he may win."

"Of course, he'll carry everything here in the East. The only doubt was in this state, but I had no difficulty in making a deal with the opposition machine as soon as they had sounded Scarborough and had found that if he should win, there'd be nothing in it for them—nothing but trouble. I judged he must have thrown them down hard, from their being so sore. How do things look out West?"

"Bad," said I. "Our farmers and workingmen have had lots of idle time these last four years. They've done too much of what they call thinking."

"Then you need money?" asked Revell, lengthening his sly, smug old face.

"We must have four millions, at least. And we must get it from those people down town."

He shook his head.

"I think not," was my careless reply. "When they wake up to the danger in Scarborough's election, the danger to business, especially to their sort of business, they'll give me twice four millions if I ask it."

"What do you wish me to do?"

"Nothing, except look after these eastern states. We'll take care of the West, and also of raising money here for our campaign during October out there."

"Can I be of any service to you in introducing you down town?" he asked.

"No, thank you," said I. "I have a few acquaintances there. I'm not going to fry any fat this trip. My fire isn't hot enough yet."

And I did not. I merely called on two of the big bankers and four heads of industrial combinations and one controller of an ocean-to-ocean railway system. I stayed a very few minutes with each, just long enough to set him thinking and inquiring what the election of Scarborough would mean to him and to his class generally. "If you'll read his speeches," said I to each, "you'll see he intends to destroy your kind of business, that he regards it as brigandage. He's honest, afraid of nothing, and an able lawyer, and he can't be fooled or fooled with. If he's elected he'll carry out his program, Senate or no Senate—and no matter what scares you people cook up in the stock market." To this they made no answer beyond delicately polite insinuations about being tired of paying for that which was theirs of right. I did not argue; it is never necessary to puncture the pretenses of men of affairs with a view to saving

them from falling into the error of forgetting
that whatever "right" may mean on Sunday, on
week days it means that which a man can compel.

I returned to Fredonia and sent Woodruff
East to direct a campaign of calamity-howling in
the eastern press, for the benefit of the New York,
Boston and Philadelphia "captains of industry."
At the end of ten days I recalled him, and sent
Roebuck to Wall Street to confirm the fears and
alarms Woodruff's campaign had aroused. And
in the West I was laying out the money I had
been able to collect from the leading men of Min-
nesota, Illinois, Ohio and western Pennsylvania
—except a quarter of a million from Howard of
New York, to whom we gave the vice-presiden-
tial nomination for that sum, and about half a
million more given by several eastern men, to
whom we promised cabinet offices and posts
abroad. I put all this money, not far from two
millions, into our "campaign of education" and
into those inpourings of delegations upon Burbank at his "rural retreat."

To attempt to combat Scarborough's popularity
with the rank and file of his own party, was hope-

less. I contented myself with restoring order and arousing enthusiasm in the main body of our partizans in the doubtful and uneasy states. So ruinous had been Goodrich's management that even at that comparatively simple task we should not have succeeded but for the fortunate fact that the great mass of partizans refuses to hear anything from the other side; they regard reasoning as disloyalty—which, curiously enough, it so often is. Then, too, few newspapers in the doubtful states printed the truth about what Scarborough and his supporters were saying and doing. The cost of this perversion of publicity to us— direct money cost, I mean—was almost nothing. The big papers and news associations were big properties, and their rich proprietors were interested in enterprises to which Scarborough's election meant disaster; a multitude of the smaller papers, normally of the opposition, were dependent upon those same enterprises for the advertising that kept them alive.

Perhaps the most far-sighted—certainly, as the event showed, the most fortunate—single stroke of my campaign was done in Illinois. That state was vital to our success; also it was one of the doubtful states where, next to his own Indiana, Scarborough's chances were best. I felt that we must put a heavy handicap on his popularity there. I had noticed that in Illinois the violently radical wing of the opposition was very strong. So I sent Merriweather to strengthen the radicals still further. I hoped to make them strong enough to put through their party's state convention a platform that would be a scarecrow to timid voters in Illinois and throughout the West; and I wished for a "wild man" as the candidate for governor, but I didn't hope it, though I told Merriweather it must be done. Curiously enough, my calculation of the probabilities was just reversed. The radicals were beaten on platform; but, thanks to a desperate effort of Merriweather's in "coaxing" rural delegates, a frothing, wild-eyed, political crank got the nomination. And he never spoke during the campaign that he didn't drive voters away from his ticket—and, therefore, from Scarborough. And our machine there sacrificed the local interests to the general by nominating a popular and not insincere reformer.

When Roebuck and I descended upon Wall Street on October sixteenth, three weeks before election, I had everything in readiness for my final and real campaign.

Throughout the doubtful states, Woodruff was in touch with local machine leaders of Scarborough's party, with corruptible labor and fraternal order leaders, with every element that would for a cash price deliver a body of voters on election day. Also he had arranged in those states for the "right sort" of election officers at upward of five hundred polling places, at least half of them places where several hundred votes could be shifted without danger or suspicion. Also, Burbank and our corps of "spellbinders" had succeeded beyond my hopes in rousing partizan passion—but here again part of the credit belongs to Woodruff. Never before had there been so many free barbecues, distributions of free uniforms to well-financed Burbank and Howard Campaign Clubs, and arrangings of those expensive parades in which the average citizen delights. The wise Woodruff spent nearly one-third of my "education" money in this way.

One morning I found him laughing over the bill for a grand Burbank rally at Indianapolis—about thirty-five thousand dollars, as I remember the·figures.

"What amuses you?" said I.

"I was thinking what fools the people are, never to ask themselves where all the money for these free shows comes from, and why those who give are willing to give so much, and how they get it back. What an ass the public is!"

"Fortunately," said I.

"For us," said he.

"And for itself," I rejoined.

"Perhaps," he admitted. "It was born to be plucked, and I suppose our crowd does do the plucking more scientifically than less experienced hands would."

"I prefer to put it another way," said I. "Let's say that we save it from a worse plucking."

"That *is* better," said Doc. For, on his way up in the world, he was rapidly developing what could, and should, be called conscience.

I looked at him and once more had a qualm like shame before his moral superiority to me.

We were plodding along on about the same moral level; but he had ascended to that level, while I had descended to it. There were politicians posing as pure before the world and even in the party's behind-the-scene, who would have sneered at Doc's "conscience." Yet, to my notion, they, who started high and from whatever sophistry of motive trailed down into the mire, are lower far than they who began deep in the mire and have been struggling bravely toward the surface. I know a man who was born in the slums, was a pickpocket at eight years of age, was a boss at forty-five, administering justice according to his lights. I know a man who was born what he calls a gentleman and who, at forty-five, sold himself for the "honors" of a high office. And once, after he had shaken hands with that boss, he looked at me, furtively made a wry face, and wiped his hand with his pocket handkerchief!

The other part of our work of preparation—getting the Wall Street whales in condition for the "fat-frying"—was also finished. The Wall Street Roebuck and I adventured was in a state of quake from fear of the election of "the scourge of God," as our subsidized socialist and extreme radical papers had dubbed Scarborough—and what invaluable campaign material their praise of him did make for us!

Roebuck and I went from office to office among the great of commerce, industry and finance. We were received with politeness, deferential politeness, everywhere. But not a penny could we get. Everywhere the same answer: "We can not see our way to contributing just yet. But if you will call early next week—say Monday or Tuesday—" four or five days away—"we'll let you know what we can do." The most ardent eagerness to placate us, to keep us in good humor; but not a cent—until Monday or Tuesday.

When I heard "Monday or Tuesday" for the third time, my suspicions were rousing. When I heard it for the fifth time, I understood. Wall Street was negotiating with the other side, and would know the result by Monday, or at the latest Tuesday.

XXIII

IN WHICH A MOUSE HELPS A LION

I did not dare communicate my suspicions to my "dear friend" Roebuck. As it was, with each refusal I had seen his confidence in me sink; if he should get an inkling how near to utter disaster I and my candidate were, he would be upon me like a tiger upon its trainer when he slips. I reasoned out my course while we were descending from the fifth "king's" office to our cab: If the negotiations with the opposition should be successful, I should not get a cent; if they should fail, Wall Street would be frantic to get its contributions into my hand; therefore, the only sane thing to do was to go West, and make such preparations as I could against the worst.

"Let's go back to the Holland," said I to Roebuck, in a weary, bored tone. "These people are a waste of time. I'll start home to-night, and when they see in the morning papers that I've left for good, they may come to their senses. But they'll have to hunt me out. I'll not go near them again. And when they come dragging themselves to you, don't forget how they've treated us to-day."

Roebuck was silent, glancing furtively at me now and then, not knowing what to think. "How is it possible to win without them?" he finally said. "This demagogue Scarborough has set the people crazy. I can't imagine what possesses these men of property with interests throughout the country. They are inviting ruin."

I smiled. "My dear Roebuck," I replied, "do you suppose I'm the man to put all my eggs into one basket—and that basket Wall Street?"

And I refused to talk any more politics with him. We dined together, I calm and in the best of spirits; we went to a musical farce, and he watched me glumly as I showed my lightness of heart. Then I went alone, at midnight, to the Chicago Express sleeper—to lie awake all night staring at the phantoms of ruin that moved in dire panorama before me. In every great affair there is a crisis at which one must stake all upon a single throw. I had staked all upon Wall Street.

Without its contributions, Woodruff's arrangements could not be carried out.

When I descended at the Fredonia station I
found De Milt waiting for me.   He had news
that was indeed news.   I shall give it here more
consecutively than my impatience for the event
permitted him to give it to me.

About ten days before, a paragraph in one of
Burbank's "pilgrimage" speeches had been twisted
by the reporter so that it seemed a personal attack
upon Scarborough.   As Burbank was a stickler
for the etiquette of campaigning, he not only sent
out a denial and a correction but also directed De
Milt to go to Scarborough's home at Saint X, Indiana, and convey the explanation in a personal
message.   De Milt arrived at Saint X at eight in
the evening.   As he was leaving the parlor car he
saw a man emerge from its drawing-room, make
a hasty descent to the platform, hurriedly engage
a station hack and drive away.   De Milt had an
amazing memory for identities—something far
rarer than memory merely for faces.   He was
convinced he knew that man; and being shrewd

and quick of thought, he jumped into a trap and
told the driver to follow the hack which was just
disappearing. A few minutes' driving and he
saw it turn in at a gateway.

"Whose place is that?" he asked.

"The old Gardiner homestead," was the
answer. "President Scarborough lives there."

De Milt did not discuss this rather premature
entitling of Senator Scarborough. He said:
"Oh—I've made a mistake," descended and sent
his trap away. Scarborough's house was quiet,
not a soul about, lights in only a few windows.
De Milt strolled in at the open gates and, keeping
out of view, made a detour of the gardens, the
"lay" of which he could see by the starlight. He
was soon in line with the front door—his man was
parleying with a servant. "Evidently he's not
expected," thought my chief of publicity.

Soon his man entered. De Milt, keeping in the
shadows, moved round the house until he was
close under open windows from which came light
and men's voices. Peering through a bush he
saw at a table-desk a man whom he recognized as
Senator Scarborough. Seated opposite him,

with a very uneasy, deprecating expression on his face, was John Thwing, president of the Atlantic and Western System, and Senator Goodrich's brother-in-law.

De Milt could not hear what Thwing was saying, so careful was that experienced voice to reach only the ears for whom its insinuating subtleties were intended. But he saw a puzzled look come into Scarborough's face, heard him say: "I don't think I understand you, John."

Thwing unconsciously raised his voice in his reply, and De Milt caught—"satisfactory assurances from you that these alarming views and intentions attributed to you are false, and they'll be glad to exert themselves to elect you."

Scarborough smiled. "Impossible," he said. "Very few of them would support *me* in any circumstances."

"You are mistaken, Hampden," was Thwing's answer. "On the contrary, they will—"

Scarborough interrupted with an impatient motion of his head. "Impossible!" he repeated. "But in any case, why should they send you to me? My speeches speak for themselves. Surely no intelligent man could fancy that my election would mean harm to any legitimate business, great or small, East or West. You've known me for twenty years, Thwing. You needn't come to me for permission to reassure your friends—such of them as you can *honestly* reassure."

"I have been reassuring them," Thwing answered. "I tell them that you are about the last man in the world to permit mob rule."

"Precisely," said Scarborough. "I purpose to continue to do what I can to break up the mob that is being led on by demagogues disguised as captains of industry and advance agents of prosperity—led on to pillage the resources of the country, its riches and its character."

This ought to have put Thwing on his guard. But, convinced that the gods he worshiped must be the gods of all men, whatever they might profess, he held to his purpose.

"Still, you don't quite follow me," he persisted. "You've said some very disquieting things against some of my friends—of course, they understand that the exigencies of campaigning, the necessity of rousing the party spirit, the—"

Thwing stopped short; De Milt held his breath. Scarborough was leaning forward, was holding Thwing's eyes with one of those looks that grip. "Do you mean," said he, "that, if I'll assure these friends of yours that I don't mean what I say, they'll buy me the presidency?"

"My dear Hampden," expostulated Thwing, "nothing of the sort.   Simply that the campaign fund which Burbank must get to be elected won't go to him, but will be at the disposal of your national committee.   My friends, naturally, won't support their enemies."

De Milt, watching Scarborough, saw him lower his head, his face flushing deeply.

"Believe me, Hampden," continued Thwing, "without our support Burbank is beaten, and you are triumphantly elected—not otherwise.   But you know politics; I needn't tell you.   You know that the presidency depends upon getting the doubtful element in the doubtful states."

Scarborough stood, and, without lifting his eyes, said in a voice very different from his strong, clear tones of a few minutes before: "I suppose in this day no one is beyond the reach of insult.   I have thought I was. I see I have been mistaken. And it is a man who has known me twenty years and has called me friend, who has taught me the deep meaning of the word shame. The servant will show you the door." And he left Thwing alone in the room.

I had made De Milt give me the point of his story as soon as I saw its drift. While he was going over it in detail, I was thinking out all the bearings of Scarborough's refusal upon my plans.

"Has Senator Goodrich seen Governor Burbank yet?" I asked De Milt in a casual tone, when he had told how he escaped unobserved in Thwing's wake and delivered Burbank's message the next morning.

"I believe he's to see him by appointment to-morrow," replied De Milt.

So my suspicion was well-founded. Goodrich, informed of his brother-in-law's failure, was posting to make peace on whatever terms he could honeyfugle out of my conciliation-mad candidate.

A few minutes later I shut myself in with the long-distance telephone and roused Burbank from bed and from sleep. "I am coming by the first train to-morrow," I said. "I thought you'd be glad to know that I've made satisfactory arrangements in New York—unexpectedly satisfactory."

"That's good—excellent," came the reply. I noted an instant change of tone which told me that Burbank had got, by some underground route, news of my failure in New York and had been preparing to give Goodrich a cordial reception.

"If Goodrich comes, James," I went on, "don't see him till I've seen you."

A pause, then in a strained voice: "But I've given him an appointment at nine to-morrow."

"Put him off till noon. I'll be there at eleven. It's—imperative." That last word with an accent I did not like to use, but knew how to use—and when.

Another pause, then: "Very well, Harvey. But we must be careful about him. De Milt has told you how dangerous he is, hasn't he?"

"Yes—how dangerous he tried to be." I was about to add that Goodrich was a fool to permit any one to go to such a man as Scarborough with such a proposition; but I bethought me of Burbank's acute moral sensitiveness and how it would be rasped by the implication of his opponent's moral superiority. "We're past the last danger, James. That's all. Sleep sound. Good night."

"Good night, old man," was his reply in his pose's tone for affection. But I could imagine him posing there in his night shirt, the anger against me snapping in his eyes.

On the train the next morning, De Milt, who had evidently been doing a little thinking, said, "I hope you won't let it out to Cousin James that I told you Goodrich was coming to see him."

"Certainly not," I replied, not losing the opportunity to win over to myself one so near to my political ward. "I'm deeply obliged to you for telling me." And presently I went on: "By the way, has anything been done for you for your brilliant work at Saint X?"

"Oh, that's all right," he said, "I guess Cousin James'll look after me—unless he forgets about it." "Cousin James" had always had the habit of taking favors for granted unless reward was pressed for; and since he had become a presidential candidate, he was inclining more than ever to look on a favor done him as a high privilege which was its own reward.

I made no immediate reply to De Milt; but just before we reached the capital, I gave him a cheque for five thousand dollars.   "A little expression of gratitude from the party," said I.   "Your reward will come later."   From that hour he was mine, for he knew now by personal experience that "the boys" were right in calling me appreciative.

It is better to ignore a debt than to pay with words.

XXIV

Burbank had grown like a fungus in his own esteem.

The adulation of the free excursionists I had poured in upon him, the eulogies in the newspapers, the flatteries of those about him, eager to make themselves "solid" with the man who might soon have the shaking of the huge, richly laden presidential boughs of the plum tree—this combination of assaults upon sanity was too strong for a man with such vanity as his, a traitor within. He had convinced his last prudent doubt that he was indeed a "child of destiny." He was resentful lest I might possibly think myself more important than he to the success of the campaign. And his resentment was deepened by the probably incessant reminders of his common sense that all this vast machine, public and secret, could have been set in motion just as effectively for any one of a score of "statesmen" conspicuous in the party.

I saw through his labored cordiality; and it depressed me again—started me down toward those depths of self-condemnation from which I had been held up for a few days by the excitement of the swiftly thronging events and by the necessity of putting my whole mind upon moves for my game.

"I am heartily glad you were successful," he began when we were alone. "That takes a weight off my mind."

"You misunderstood me, I see," said I. "I haven't got anything from those people in New York as yet. But within a week they'll be begging me to take whatever I need. Thwing's report will put them in a panic."

His face fell. "Then I must be especially courteous to Goodrich," he said, after thinking intently. "Your hopes might be disappointed."

"Not the slightest danger," was my prompt assurance. "And if you take my advice, you will ask Goodrich how his agent found Senator Scarborough's health, and then order him out of this

house.   Why harbor a deadly snake that can be
of no use to you?"

"But you seem to forget, Harvey, that he is the
master of at least the eastern wing of the party.
And you must now see that he will stop at nothing, unless he is pacified."

"He is the fetch-and-carry of an impudent and
cowardly crowd in Wall Street," I retorted, "that
is all.   When they find he can no longer do their
errands, they'll throw him over and come to us.
And we can have them on our own terms."

We argued, with growing irritation on both
sides, and after an hour or so, I saw that he was
hopelessly under the spell of his pettiness and his
moral cowardice.   He had convinced himself that
I was jealous of Goodrich and would sacrifice
anything to gratify my hate.   And Goodrich's
sending an agent to Scarborough had only made
him the more formidable in Burbank's eyes.   As
I looked in upon his mind and watched its weak,
foolish little workings, my irritation subsided.
"Do as you think best," said I wearily.   "But when
he presents the mortgage you are going to give
him on your presidency, remember my warning."

He laughed this off, feeling my point only in
his vanity, not at all in his judgment. "And how
will *you* receive him, Harvey?   He will be sure
to come to you next—must, as you are in charge
of my campaign."

"I'll tell him straight out that I'll have nothing
to do with him," said I blandly. "The Wall
Street submission to the party must be brought
to me by some other ambassador.   I'll not help
him to fool his masters and to hide it from them
that he has lost control."

I could have insisted, could have destroyed
Goodrich—for Burbank would not have dared disobey me.   But the campaign, politics in general,
life itself, filled me with disgust, a paralyzing disgust that made me almost lose confidence in my
theory of practical life.

"What's the use?" I said to myself.   "Let Burbank keep his adder.   Let it sting him.   If it so
much as shoots a fang at me, I can crush it."

And so, Burbank lifted up Goodrich and gave
hostages to him; and Goodrich, warned that I
would not deal with him, made some excuse or
other to his masters for sending Senator Revell to

me. "See Woodruff," said I to Revell, for I was in no mood for such business. "He knows best what we need."

"They give up too damn cheerfully," Woodruff said to me, when I saw him a week or ten days later, and he gave me an account of the negotiations. "I suspect they've paid more before."

"They have," said I. "In two campaigns where they had to elect against hard times."

"But I've a notion," he warned me, "that our candidate has promised them something privately."

"No doubt," I replied, as indifferently as I felt.

I had intended to make some speeches—I had always kept the public side of my career in the foreground, and in this campaign my enforced prominence as director of the machine was causing the public to dwell too much on the real nature of my political activity. But I could not bring myself to it. Instead, I set out for home to spend the time with my children and to do by telephone, as I easily could, such directing of Woodruff as might be necessary.

My daughter Frances was driving me from the

Fredonia station. A man darted in front of the horses, flung up his arms and began to shriek curses at me. If she had not been a skilful driver, we should both have been thrown from the cart. As it was, the horses ran several miles before she got them under control, I sitting inactive, because I knew how it would hurt her pride if I should interfere.

When the horses were quiet, she gave me an impetuous kiss that more than repaid me for the strain on my nerves. "You are the dearest papa that ever was!" she said. Then—"Who was he? He looked like a crazy man!"

"No doubt he is," was my reply. And I began complimenting her on her skill with horses, chiefly to prevent her pressing me about the man. I had heard, and had done, so much lying that I had a horror of it, and tried to make my children absolutely truthful—my boy Ed used to think up and do mischief just for the pleasure of pleasing me by confessing. To make my example effective, I was always strictly truthful with them. I did not wish to tell her who the man was; but I instantly recognized, through the drunken dishevelment, my mutineer. Granby—less than a year before one of the magnates of the state. My orders about him had been swiftly and literally obeyed. Deserted by his associates, blacklisted at the banks, beset by his creditors, harassed by the attorney general, his assets chained with injunctions, his liabilities given triple fangs, he went bankrupt, took to drink, became a sot and a barroom lounger. His dominant passion was hatred of me; he discharged the rambling and frantic story of his wrongs upon whoever would listen. And here he was in Fredonia!

I had one of my secretaries telephone the police to look after him; they reported that he had disappeared.

The next morning but one, my daughter and I went for an early walk. At the turn of the main drive just beyond view from the lodge, she exclaimed, "Oh, father, *oh!*" and clung to me. Something—like a scarecrow, but not a scarecrow —swung from a limb overhanging the drive. The face was distorted and swollen; the arms and legs were drawn up in sickening crookedness. Before I saw, I knew it was Granby.

I took Frances home, then returned, passing the
swaying horror far on the other side of the road.
I got the lodge-keeper, and he and I went back together. I had them telephone from the lodge for
the coroner and personally saw to it that the
corpse should be reported as found in the open
woods a long distance from my place. But Granby had left a message "to the public" in his room
at the hotel: "Senator Sayler ruined me and
drove me to death. I have gone to hang myself
in his park. Down with monopoly!" In spite of
my efforts, this was published throughout the
country—though not in Fredonia. Such of the
big opposition papers as were not under our control sent reporters and raked out the whole story;
and it was blown up hugely and told everywhere.
Our organs retold it, giving the true color and
perspective; but my blundering attempt to avoid
publicity had put me in too bad a light.

It was the irony of fate—my power thus ludi-
crously thwarted by a triviality. Within twenty-
four hours I realized the danger to our campaign. I sent Woodruff post-haste to the widow.
He gave her convincing assurances that she and

her children were to be lifted from the slough of poverty into which Granby's drunkenness had thrust them. And in return she wrote at his dictation and issued an apparently uninspired public statement, exonerating me from all blame for her husband's reverses, and saying that he had been acting strangely for over a year and had been insane for several months. In brief, I did everything suggested by sincere regret and such skill at influencing public opinion as I had and commanded. But not until my reports began to show the good effects of the million dollars Woodruff put into the last week of the campaign, did I begin to hope again.

Another hope brightened toward confidence when, on the Saturday before election, I sprung my carefully matured scheme for stiffening those of our partizans who were wavering. The Scarborough speakers had, with powerful effect, been taunting us with our huge campaign fund, daring us to disclose its sources. On that Sunday morning, when it was too late for the opposition to discount me, I boldly threw open *a* set of campaign ledgers which showed that our fund was just under a million dollars, with the only large subscription, the hundred thousand which I myself had given. Tens of thousands of our partizans, longing for an excuse for staying with us, returned cheering to the ranks—enough of them in the doubtful states, we believed, to restore the floating vote to its usual balance of power.

Each horse of my team had taken a turn at doing dangerous, even menacing, threshing about; but both were now quietly pulling in the harness, Partizanship as docile as Plutocracy. The betting odds were six to five against us, but we of the "inside" began to plunge on Burbank and Howard.

XXV

AN HOUR OF EMOTION

It was after midnight of election day before
we knew the result, so close were the two most
important doubtful states.

Scarborough had swept the rural districts and
the small towns. But we had beaten him in the
cities where the machines and other purchasable
organizations were powerful. His state gave him
forty-two thousand plurality, Burbank carried
his own state by less than ten thousand—and in
twenty-four years our majority there in presidential campaigns had never before been less than
forty thousand.

By half-past one, the whole capital city knew
that Burbank had won. And they flocked and
swarmed out the road to his modest "retreat,"
until perhaps thirty thousand people were shouting, blowing horns, singing, sending up rockets
and Roman candles, burning red fire, lighting
bonfires in and near the grounds. I had come

down from Fredonia to be in instant touch with Burbank and the whole national machine, should there arise at the last minute necessity for bold and swift action. When Burbank finally yielded to the mob and showed himself on his porch with us, his immediate associates, about him, I for the first time unreservedly admired him. For the man inside seemed at last to swell until the presidential pose he had so long worn prematurely was filled to a perfect fit. And in what he said as well as in the way he said it there was an unexpected dignity and breadth and force. "I have made him President," I thought, "and it looks as if the presidency had made him a man."

After he finished, Croffut spoke, and Senator Berwick of Illinois. Then rose a few calls for me. They were drowned in a chorus of hoots, toots and hisses. Burbank cast a quick glance of apprehension at me—again that hidden conviction of my vanity, this time shown in dread lest it should goad me into hating him. I smiled reassuringly at him—and I can say in all honesty that the smile came from the bottom of my heart. An hour later, as I bade him good night, I said:

"I believe the man and the opportunity have met, Mr. President. God bless you."

Perhaps it was the unusualness of my speaking with feeling that caused the tears to start in his eyes. "Thank you, Harvey," he replied, clasping my hand in both his. "I realize now the grave responsibility. I need the help of every friend—the *true* help of every *true* friend. And I know what I owe to you just as clearly as if *she* were here to remind me."

I was too moved to venture a reply. Woodruff and I drove to the hotel together—the crowd hissing me wherever it recognized me. Woodruff looked first on one side then on the other, muttering at them. "The fools!" he said to me, with his abrupt, cool laugh. "Just like them, isn't it? Cheering the puppet, hissing its proprietor."

I made no answer—what did it matter? Not for Burbank's position and opportunity, as in that hour of emotion they appeared even to us who knew politics from behind the scenes, not for the reality of what the sounding title of President seems to mean, would I have changed with him, would I have paid the degrading price he had

"I HAVE MADE HIM PRESIDENT," I THOUGHT, "AND IT LOOKS AS
IF THE PRESIDENCY HAD MADE HIM A MAN" *p. 293*

paid. I preferred my own position—if I had bowed the knee, at least it was not to men. As for hisses, I saw in them a certain instinctive tribute to my power. The mob cheers its servant, hisses its master.

"Doc," said I, "do you want to go to the Senate instead of Croffut?"

By the flames on the torches on either side I saw his amazement. "Me?" he exclaimed. "Why, you forget I've got a past."

"I do," said I, "and so does every one else. All we know is that you've got a future."

He drew in his breath hard and leaned back into the corner where the shadow hid him. At last he said in a quiet earnest voice: "You've given me self-respect, Senator. I can only say—I'll see that you never regret it."

I was hissed roundly at the hotel entrance, between cheers for Croffut and Berwick, and even for Woodruff. But I went to bed in the most cheerful, hopeful humor I had known since the day Scarborough was nominated. "At any rate" —so I was thinking—"my President, with my help, will be a man."

XXVI

"ONLY AN OLD JOKE"

On the train going home, I was nearer to castle-building than at any time since my boyhood castles collapsed under the rude blows of practical life.

My paths have not always been straight and open, said I to myself; like all others who have won in the conditions of this world of man still thrall to the brute, I have had to use the code of the jungle. In climbing I have had to stoop, at times to crawl. But, now that I have reached the top, I shall stand erect. I shall show that the sordidness of the struggle has not unfitted me to use the victory. True, there are the many and heavy political debts I've had to contract in getting Burbank the presidency; and as we must have a second term to round out our work, we shall be compelled to make some further compromises. We must still deal with men on the terms which human nature exacts. But in the main we can

and we will do what is just and right, what helps
to realize the dreams of the men and women who
founded our country—the men and women like
my father and mother.

And my mother's grave, beside my father's
and among the graves of my sisters and my
grandparents, rose before me. And I recalled the
pledge I had made there, in the boyish beginnings
of my manhood and my career. "My chance and
Burbank's," said I, "comes just in time. We are
now at the age where reputation is fixed; and
our children are growing up and will soon begin
to judge us and be judged from us."

Years of patient sowing, thought I, and at last
the harvest! And what a harvest it will be! For
under the teachings of experience I have sown
not starlight and moonshine, but seeds.

The next morning I could not rise; it was six
weeks before I was able to leave my bed. During
that savage illness I met each and every one of
the reckless drafts I had been drawing against my
reserve vitality. Four times the doctors gave me
up; once even Frances lost hope. When I was
getting well she confessed to me how she had

warned God that He need never expect to hear from her again if her prayer for me were not answered—and I saw she rather suspected that her threat was not unassociated with my recovery.

Eight weeks out of touch with affairs, and they the crucial eight weeks of all my years of thought and action! At last the harvest, indeed; and I was reaping what I had sown.

In the second week of January I revolted against the doctors and nurses and had my political secretary, Wheelock, telephone for Woodruff—the legislature had elected him to the Senate three days before. When he had sat with me long enough to realize that I could bear bad news, he said: "Goodrich and Burbank have formed a combination against you."

"How do you know?" said I, showing no surprise, and feeling none.

"Because"—he laughed—"I was in it. At least, they thought so until they had let me be safely elected. As nearly as I can make it out, they began to plot about ten days after you fell sick. At first they had it on the slate to do me up, too. But—the day after Christmas—Burbank sent for me—"

"Wait a minute," I interrupted. And I began to think. It was on Christmas day that Burbank telephoned for the first time in nearly three weeks, inquiring about my condition. I remembered their telling me how minute his questionings were. And I had thought his solicitude was proof of his friendship! Instead, he had been inquiring to make sure about the reports in the papers that I was certain to recover, in order that he might shift the factors in his plot accordingly. "When did you say Burbank sent for you?" I asked.

"On Christmas day," Woodruff replied.

I laughed; he looked at me inquiringly. "Nothing," said I. "Only an old joke—as old as human nature. Go on."

"Christmas day," he continued; "I didn't get to him until next morning. I can't figure out just why they invited me into their combine."

But I could figure it out, easily. If I had died, my power would have disintegrated and Woodruff would have been of no use to them. When

they were sure I was going to live, they had to
have him because he might be able to assassinate
me, certainly could so cripple me that I would—
as they reasoned—be helpless under their assaults.
But it wasn't necessary to tell Woodruff this, I
thought.

"Well," said I, "and what happened?"

"Burbank gave me a dose of his 'great and gracious way'—you ought to see the 'side' he puts on
now!—and turned me over to Goodrich. He had
been mighty careful not to give himself away any
further than that. Then Goodrich talked to me
for three solid hours, showing me it was my duty
to the party as well as to myself to join him and
Burbank in eliminating the one disturber of harmony—that meant you."

"And didn't they tell you they'd destroy you if
you didn't?"

"Oh, that of course," he answered indifferently.

"Well, what did you do?"

"Played with 'em till I was elected. Then I
dropped Goodrich a line. 'You can go to hell,' I
wrote. 'I travel only with men'."

"Very imprudent," was my comment.

"Yes," he admitted, "but I had to do something to get the dirt off my hands."

"So Burbank has gone over to Goodrich!" I went on presently, as much to myself as to him.

"I always knew he was one of those chaps you have to keep scared to keep straight," said Woodruff. "They think your politeness indicates fear and your friendship fright. Besides, he's got a delusion that his popularity carried the West for him and that you and I did him only damage." Woodruff interrupted himself to laugh. "A friend of mine," he resumed, "was on the train with Scarborough when he went East to the meeting of Congress last month. He tells me it was like a President-elect on the way to be inaugurated. The people turned out at every crossroads, even beyond the Alleghanies. And Burbank knows it. If he wasn't clean daft about himself he'd realize that if it hadn't been for you—well, I'd hate to say how badly he'd have got left. But then, if it hadn't been for you, he'd never have been governor. He was a dead one, and you hauled him out of the tomb."

True enough. But what did it matter now?

"He's going to get a horrible jolt before many months," Woodruff went on. "I can see you after him."

"You forget. He's President," I answered. "He's beyond our reach."

"Not when he wants a renomination," insisted Woodruff.

"He can get that without us—*if*," I said. "You must remember we've made him a fetish with our rank and file. And he's something of a fetish with the country, now that he's President. No, we can't destroy him—can't even injure him. He'll have to do that himself, if it's done. Besides—"

I did not finish. I did not care to confess that since Frances and I saw Granby swinging from that tree in my grounds I had neither heart nor stomach for the relentless side of the game. Indeed, whether from calculation or from sentimentality or from both—or, from a certain sympathy and fellow feeling for all kinds of weakness—I have never pursued those who have played me false, except when exemplary punishment was imperative.

"Well—" Woodruff looked bitterly disappointed. "I guess you're right." He brightened. "I forgot Goodrich for a minute. Burbank'll do himself up through that—I'd have to be in a saloon to feel free to use the language that describes him."

"I fear he will," I said. And it was not a hypocrisy—for I did not, and could not, feel anger toward him. Had I not cut this staff deliberately because it was crooked? What more natural than that it should give way under me as soon as I leaned upon it?

"Your sickness certainly couldn't have come at an unluckier time," Woodruff observed just before he left.

"I'm not sure of that," was my reply. "It would have been useless to have found him out sooner. And if he had hidden himself until later, he might have done us some serious mischief."

As he was the President-elect, to go to him uninvited would have been infringement of his dignity as well as of my pride. A few days later I wrote him, thanking him for his messages and inquiries during my illness and saying that I was once more taking part in affairs. He did not reply by calling me up on the telephone, as he would

have done in the cordial, intimate years preceding
his grandeur. Instead he sent a telegram of con-
gratulation, following it with a note. He urged
me to go South, as I had planned, and to stay until I was fully restored. "I shall deny myself the
pleasure of seeing you until you return." That
sentence put off our meeting indefinitely—I could
see him smiling at its adroitness as he wrote it.

But he made his state of mind even clearer. His
custom had been to begin his notes "Dear Harvey," or "Dear Sayler," and to end them "James"
or "Burbank." This note began "My dear Senator"; it ended, "Yours sincerely, James E. Burbank." As I stared at these phrases my blood
steamed in my brain. Had he spat in my face my
fury would have been less, far less. "So!" I
thought in the first gush of anger, "you feel that
you have been using me, that you have no further
use for me. You have decided to take the advice
of those idiotic independent newspapers and
'wash your hands of the corruptionist who almost defeated you'."

To make war upon him was in wisdom impossible—even had I wished. And when anger flowed

away and pity and contempt succeeded, I really
did not wish to war upon him. But there was
Goodrich—the real corruptionist, the wrecker of
my plans and hopes, the menace to the future of
the party. I sent for Woodruff and together we
mapped out a campaign against the senior senator from New Jersey in all the newspapers we
could control or influence. I gave him a free hand
to use—with his unfailing discretion, of course—
all the facts we had accumulated to Goodrich's
discredit. I put at his disposal a hundred thousand dollars. As every available dollar of the
party funds had been used in the campaign, I advanced this money from my own pocket.

And I went cheerfully away to Palm Beach,
there to watch at my ease the rain of shot and
shell upon my enemy.

XXVII

A DOMESTIC DISCORD

After a month in the South, I was well again—younger in feeling, and in looks, than I had been for ten years. Carlotta and the children, except "Junior" who was in college, had gone to Washington when I went to Florida. I found her abed with a nervous attack from the double strain of the knowledge that Junior had eloped with an "impossible" woman he had met, I shall not say where, and of the effort of keeping the calamity from me until she was sure he had really entangled himself hopelessly.

She was now sitting among her pillows, telling the whole story. "If he only hadn't married her!" she ended.

This struck me as ludicrous—a good woman citing to her son's discredit the fact that he had goodness' own ideals of honor.

"What are you laughing at?" she demanded.

I was about to tell her I was hopeful of the boy

chiefly because he had thus shown the splendid courage that more than redeems folly. But I refrained. I had never been able to make Carlotta understand me or my ideas, and I had long been weary of the resentful silences or angry tirades which mental and temperamental misunderstandings produce.

"Courage never gets into a man unless it's born there," said I. "Folly is born into us all and can be weeded out."

"What can be expected?" she went on after trying in vain to connect my remark with our conversation. "A boy needs a father. You've been so busy with your infamous politics that you've given him scarcely a thought."

Painfully true, throughout; but it was one of those criticisms we can hardly endure even when we make it upon ourselves. I was silent.

"I've no patience with men!" she went on. "They're always meddling with things that would get along better without them, and letting their own patch run to weeds."

Unanswerable. I held my peace.

"What are you going to do about it, Harvey?

How *can* you be so calm? Isn't there *anything* that would rouse you?"

"I'm too busy thinking what to do to waste any energy in blowing off steam," was my answer in my conciliatory tone.

"But there's nothing we *can* do," she retorted, with increasing anger, which vented itself toward me because the true culprit, fate, was not within reach.

"Precisely," I agreed. "Nothing."

"That creature won't let him come to see me."

"And you musn't see him when he sends for you," said I. "He'll come as soon as his money gives out. She'll see that he does."

"But you aren't going to cut him off!"

"Just that," said I.

A long silence, then I added in answer to her expression: "And *you* must not let him have a cent, either."

In a gust of anger, probably at my having read her thoughts, she blurted out: "One would think it was *your* money."

I had seen that thought in her eyes, had watched her hold it back behind her set teeth, many times in our married years. And I now thanked my stars I had had the prudence to get ready for the inevitable moment when she would speak it. But at the same time I could not restrain a flush of shame. "It *is* my money," I forced myself to say. "Ask your brother. He'll tell you what I've forbidden him to tell before—that I have twice rescued you and him from bankruptcy."

"With our own money," she retorted, hating herself for saying it, but goaded on by a devil that lived in her temper and had got control many a time, though never before when I happened to be the one with whom she was at outs.

"No—with my own," I replied tranquilly.

"*Your* own!" she sneered. "Every dollar you have has come through what you got by marrying me—through what you married me for. Where would you be if you hadn't married me? You know very well. You'd still be fighting poverty as a small lawyer in Pulaski, married to Betty Crosby or whatever her name was." And she burst into hysterical tears. At last she was showing me the secrets that had been tearing at her, was showing me her heart where they had torn it.

"Probably," said I in my usual tone, when she was calm enough to hear me. "So, that's what you brood over?"

"Yes," she sobbed. "I've hated you and myself. Why don't you tell me it isn't so? I'll believe it—I don't want to hear the truth. I know you don't love me, Harvey. But just say you don't love *her*."

"What kind of middle-aged, maudlin moonshine is this, anyway?" said I. "Let's go back to Junior. We've passed the time of life when people can talk sentimentality without being ridiculous."

"That's true of me, Harvey," she said miserably, "but not of you. You don't look a day over forty—you're still a young man, while I—"

She did not need to complete the sentence. I sat on the bed beside her and patted her vaguely. She took my hand and kissed it. And I said—I tried to say it gently, tenderly, sincerely: "People who've been together, as you and I have, see each other always as at first, they say."

She kissed my hand gratefully again. "Forgive me for what I said," she murmured. "You know I didn't think it, really. I've got such a

nasty disposition and I felt so down, and—that
was the only thing I could find to throw at you."

"Please—*please!*" I protested. "Forgive isn't
a word that I'd have the right to use to any one."

"But I must—"

"Now, *I've* known for years," I went on, "that
you were in love with that other man when I
asked you to marry me. I might have taunted you
with it, might have told you how I've saved him
from going to jail for passing worthless checks."

This delighted her—this jealousy so long and
so carefully hidden. Under cover of her delight
I escaped from the witness-stand. And the dis-
covery that evening by Doc Woodruff that my
son's ensnarer had a husband living put her in
high good humor. "If he'd only come home,"
said she, adding: "Though, now I feel that he's
perfectly safe with her."

"Yes—let them alone," I replied. "He has at
least one kind of sense—a sense of honor. And
I suspect and hope that he has at bottom common
sense too. Let him find her out for himself. Then,
he'll be done with her, and her kind, for good."

"I must marry him off as soon as possible,"

said Carlotta. "I'll look about for some nice, quiet young girl with character and looks and domestic tastes." She laughed a little bitterly. "You men can profit by experience and it ruins us women."

"Unjust," said I, "but injustice and stupidity are the ground plan of life."

We had not long to wait. The lady, as soon as Junior reached the end of his cash, tried to open negotiations. Failing and becoming convinced that he had been cast off by his parents, she threw aside her mask. One straight look into her real countenance was enough for the boy. He fled shuddering—but not to me as I had expected. Instead, he got a place as a clerk in Chicago.

"Why not let him shift for himself a while?" suggested Woodruff, who couldn't have taken more trouble about the affair if the boy had been his own. "A man never knows whether his feet were made to stand on and walk with, unless he's been down to his uppers."

"I think the boy's got his grandmother in him," said I. "Let's give him a chance."

"He'll make a career for himself yet—like his father's," said Woodruff.

That, with the sincerest enthusiasm. But instinctively I looked at him for signs of sarcasm. And then I wondered how many "successful" men would, in the same circumstances, have had the same curiously significant instinct.

XXVIII

It was now less than a month before inauguration. Daily the papers gave probable selections
for the high posts under the approaching administration; and, while many of them were attributed to my influence, Roebuck's son as ambassador to Russia was the only one I even approved of.
As payments for the services of the plutocracy
they were unnecessary and foolishly lavish; as
preparations for a renomination and reëlection,
the two guiding factors in every plan of a President-elect, they were preposterous. They were
first steps toward an administration that would
make Scarborough's triumph inevitable, in spite
of his handicap of idealism.

I sent Woodruff west to find out what Burbank was doing about the places I had pledged—
all of them less "honorable" but more lucrative
offices which party workers covet. He returned
in a few days with the news that, according to the

best information he could get through his spies in
Burbank's *entourage,* all our pledges would be
broken; the Sayler-Burbank machine was to be
made over into a Goodrich-Burbank.

I saw that I could not much longer delay action. But I resolved to put it off until the very
last minute, meanwhile trying to force Burbank
to send for me. My cannonade upon Goodrich in
six thousand newspapers, great and small,
throughout the West and South, had been reinforced by the bulk of the opposition press. I could
not believe it was to be without influence upon
the timid Burbank, even though he knew who was
back of the attack, and precisely how I was directing it. I was relying—as I afterward learned, not
in vain—upon my faithful De Milt to bring to
"Cousin James'" attention the outburst of public sentiment against his guide, philosopher and
friend, the Wall Street fetch-and-carry.

I had fixed on February fifteenth as the date on
which I would telegraph a formal demand for an
interview. On February eleventh, he surrendered—he wired, asking me to come. I took a
chance; I wired back a polite request to be excused

as I had urgent business in Chicago. And twenty-four hours later I passed within thirty miles of Rivington on my way to Chicago with Carlotta—we were going to see Junior, hugely proud of himself and his twenty-seven dollars a week. At the Auditorium a telegram waited from Burbank: ˙ He hoped I would come as soon as I could; the matters he wished to discuss were most important.

Toward noon of the third day thereafter we were greeting each other—he with an attempt at his old-time cordiality, I without concealment of at least the coldness I felt. But my manner apparently, and probably, escaped his notice. He was now blind and drunk with the incense that had been whirling about him in dense clouds for three months; he was incapable of doubting the bliss of any human being he was gracious to. He shut me in with him and began confiding the plans he and Goodrich had made—cabinet places, foreign posts, and so forth. His voice, lingering and luxuriating upon the titles—"my ambassador to his Brittanic Majesty," "my ambassador to the German Emperor," and so on—amused and a little, but only a little, astonished me; I had always known that he was a through-and-through snob. For nearly an hour I watched his ingenuous, childish delight in bathing himself in himself, the wonderful fountain of all these honors. At last he finished, laid down his list, took off his nose-glasses. "Well, Harvey, what do you think?" he asked, and waited with sparkling eyes for my enthusiastic approval.

"I see Goodrich drove a hard bargain," said I. "Yet he came on his knees, if you had but realized it."

Burbank's color mounted. "What do you mean, Sayler?" he inquired, the faint beginnings of the insulted god in his tone and manner.

"You asked my opinion," I answered, "I'm giving it. I don't recall a single name that isn't obviously a Goodrich suggestion. Even the Roebuck appointment—"

"Sayler," he interrupted, in a forbearing tone, "I wish you would not remind me so often of your prejudice against Senator Goodrich. It is unworthy of you. But for my tact—pardon my frankness—your prejudice would have driven him away, and with him a support he controls—"

I showed my amusement.

"Don't smile, Sayler," he protested with some anger in his smooth, heavy voice. "You are not the only strong man in the party. And I venture to take advantage of our long friendship to speak plainly to you. I wish to see a united party. One of my reasons for sending for you was to tell you how greatly I am distressed and chagrined by the attacks on Senator Goodrich in our papers."

"Did you have any other reason for sending for me?" said I very quietly.

"That was the principal one," he confessed.

"Oh!" I exclaimed.

"What do you mean, Sayler?"

"I thought possibly you might also have wished to tell me how unjust you thought the attacks on me in the eastern papers, and to assure me that they had only strengthened our friendship."

He was silent.

I rose, threw my overcoat on my arm, took up my hat.

"Wait a moment, please," he said. "I have al-

ways found you very impartial in your judgments
—your clear judgment has been of the highest
usefulness to me many times."

"Thank you," I said. "You are most kind—
most generous."

"So," he went on, not dreaming that he might
find sarcasm if he searched for it, "I hope you
appreciate why I have refrained from seeing you,
as I wished. I know, Sayler, your friendship was
loyal. I know you did during the campaign what
you thought wisest and best. But I feel that you
must see now what a grave mistake you made.
Don't misunderstand me, Harvey. I do not hold
it against you. But you must see, no doubt you
do see, that it would not be fair for me, it would
not be in keeping with the dignity of the great
office with which the people have intrusted me, to
seem to lend my approval."

I looked straight at him until his gaze fell.
Then I said, my voice even lower than usual: "If
you will look at the election figures carefully you
will find written upon them a very interesting fact.
That fact is: In all the doubtful states—the ones
that elected you—Scarborough swept everything

where our party has heretofore been strongest; you were elected by carrying districts where our party has always been weakest. *And in those districts, James, our money was spent—as you well know."*

I waited for this to cut through his enswaddlings of self-complacence, waited until I saw its acid eating into him. Then I went on: "I hope you will never again deceive yourself, or let your enemies deceive you. As to your plans—the plans for Goodrich and his crowd—I have nothing to say. My only concern is to have Woodruff's matters—his pledges—attended to. That I must insist upon."

He lowered his brows in a heavy frown.

"I have your assent?" I insisted.

"Really, Harvey,"—there was an astonishing change from the complacent, superior voice of a few minutes before,—"I'll do what I can—but—the responsibilities—the duties of—of my position—"

"You are going to *take* the office, James," said I. "You can't cheat the men who *gave* it to you."

He did not answer.

"I pledged my word," I went on. "You gave the promises. I indorsed for you. The debts *must* be met." Never before had I enjoyed using that ugliest of words.

"You ask me to bring myself into unpopularity with the entire country," he pleaded. "Several of the men on your list are ex-convicts. Others are about to be indicted for election frauds. Many are men utterly without character—"

"They did *your* work, James," said I. "I guarantee that in no case will the unpleasant consequences to you be more than a few disagreeable but soon forgotten newspaper articles. You haggle over these trifles, and—why, look at your cabinet list! There are two names on it—two of the four Goodrich men—that will cost you blasts of public anger—perhaps the renomination."

"Is *this* my friend Harvey Sayler?" he exclaimed, grief and pain in that face which had been used by him for thirty years as the sculptor uses the molding clay.

"It is," I answered calmly. "And never more your friend than now, when you have ceased to be a friend to him—and to yourself."

"Then do not ask me to share the infamy of those wretches," he pleaded.

"They are our allies and helpers," I said, "wretches only as I and all of us in practical politics are wretches. Difference of degree, perhaps; but not of kind. And, James, if our promises to these invaluable fellow workers of ours are not kept, kept to the uttermost, you will compel me and my group of Senators to oppose and defeat your most important nominations. And I shall myself, publicly, from the floor of the Senate, show up these Goodrich nominees of yours as creatures of corrupt corporations and monopolies." I said this without heat; every word of it fell cold as arctic ice upon his passion.

A long pause, then: "Your promises shall be kept," he assented with great dignity of manner; "not because you threaten, Harvey, but because I value your friendship beyond anything and everything. And I may add I am sorry, profoundly sorry, my selections for the important places do not please you."

"I think of your future," I said. "You *talk* of friendship—"

"No, no, Harvey," he protested, with a vehe-
mence of reassurance that struck me as amusing.

"And," I went on, "it is in friendship, James,
that I warn you not to fill all your crucial places
with creatures of the Goodrich crowd. They will
rule your administration, they will drive you, in
spite of yourself, on and on, from excess to excess. You will put the middle West irrevocably
against you. You will make even the East doubtful. You are paying, paying with your whole
future, for that which is already yours. If you
lose your hold on the people, the money-crowd
will have none of you. If you keep the people,
the money-crowd will be your very humble servant."

I happened just then to glance past him at a
picture on the wall over his chair. It was a crayon
portrait of his wife, made from an enlarged photo-
graph—a poor piece of work, almost ludicrous in
its distortions of proportion and perspective. But
it touched me the more because it was such a humble thing, reminiscent of her and his and my lowly
beginnings. And an appeal seemed to go straight
to my heart from those eyes that had so often

been raised from the sewing in sympathetic understanding of the things I was struggling to make her husband see.

I pointed to the picture; he slowly turned round in his chair until he too was looking at it. "What would *she* say, Burbank," I asked, "if she were with us now?"

And then I went on to analyze his outlined administration, to show him in detail why I thought it would ruin him, to suggest men who were as good party men as the Goodrich crowd and would be a credit to him and a help. And he listened with his old-time expression, looking up at his dead wife's picture all the while. "You must be *popular*, at any cost," I ended. "The industrial crowd will stay with the party, no matter what we do. As long as Scarborough is in control on the other side, we are their only hope. And so, we are free to seek popularity—and we must regain it or we're done for. Money won't save us when we've lost our grip on the rank and file. The presidency can't be bought again for *you*. If it must be bought next time, another figure-head will have to be used."

"I can't tell you how grateful I am," was his conclusion after I had put my whole mind before him and he and I had discussed it. "But there are certain pledges to Goodrich—"

"Break them," said I. "To keep them is catastrophe."

I knew the pledges he had in the foreground of his thoughts—a St. Louis understrapper of the New York financial crowd for Secretary of the Treasury; for Attorney General a lawyer who knew nothing of politics or public sentiment or indeed of anything but how to instruct corporations in law-breaking and law-dodging.

He thought a long time. When he answered it was with a shake of the head. "Too late, I'm afraid, Harvey. I've asked the men and they've accepted. That was a most untimely illness of yours. I'll see what can be done. It's a grave step to offend several of the most conspicuous men in the party."

"Not so serious as to offend the party itself," I replied. "Money is a great power in politics, but partizanship is a greater."

"I'll think it over," was the most he had the

courage to concede. "I must look at all sides, you know. But, whatever I decide, I thank you for your candor."

We separated, the best friends in the world, I trying to recover some few of the high hopes of him that had filled me on election night. "He's weak and timid," I said to myself, "but at bottom he must have a longing to be President in fact as well as in name. Even the meanest slave longs to be a man."

I should have excepted the self-enslaved slaves of ambition. Of all bondmen, they alone, I believe, not only do not wish freedom, but also are ever plotting how they may add to their chains.

XXIX

A LETTER FROM THE DEAD

I was living alone at the Willard.

Soon after the death of Burbank's wife, his sister and brother-in-law, the Gracies, had come with their three children to live with him and to look after his boy and girl. Trouble between his family and mine, originating in some impertinences of the oldest Gracie girl, spread from the children to the grown people until, when he went into the White House, he and I were the only two on speaking terms. I see now that this situation had large influence on me in holding aloof and waiting always for overtures from him. At the time I thought, as no doubt he thought also, that the quarrel was beneath the notice of men.

At any rate my family decided not to come to Washington during his first winter in the White House. I lived alone at the Willard. One afternoon toward the end of February I returned there from the Senate and found Woodruff, bad news in his face. "What is it?" I asked indifferently, for I assumed it was some political tangle.

"Your wife—was taken—very ill—very suddenly," he said. His eyes told me the rest.

If I had ever asked myself how this news would affect me, I should have answered that it would give me a sensation of relief. But, instead of relief, I felt the stunning blow of a wave of sorrow which has never wholly receded. Not because I loved her—that I never did. Not because she was the mother of my children—my likes and dislikes are direct and personal. Not because she was my wife—that bond had been galling. Not because I was fond of her—she had one of those cold, angry natures that forbid affection. No; I was overwhelmed because she and I had been intimates, with all the closest interests of life in common, with the whole world, even my children whom I loved passionately, outside that circle which fate had drawn around us two. I imagine this is not uncommon among married people,— this unhealable break in their routine of association when one departs. No doubt it often passes with the unthinking for love belatedly discovered.

"She did not suffer," said Woodruff gently. "It was heart disease. She had just come in from a ride with your oldest daughter. They were resting and talking in high spirits by the library fire. And then—the end came—like putting out the light."

Heart disease! Often I had noted the irregular beat of her heart—a throb, a long pause, a flutter, a short pause, a throb. And I could remember that more than once the sound had been followed by the shadowy appearance, in the door of my mind, of one of those black thoughts which try to tempt hope but only make it hide in shame and dread. Now, the memory of those occasions tormented me into accusing myself of having wished her gone. But it was not so.

She had told me she had heart trouble; but she had confided to no one that she knew it might bring on the end at any moment. She left a letter, sealed and addressed to me:

Harvey—

I shall never have the courage to tell you, yet I feel you ought to know. I think every one attributes to every one else less shrewdness than he possesses. I know you have

never given me the credit of seeing that you did not love
me. And you were so kind and considerate and so patient
with my moods that no doubt I should have been deceived
had I not known what love is. I think, to have loved and
to have been loved develops in a woman a sort of sixth
sense—sensitiveness to love. And that had been developed
in me, and when it never responded to your efforts to deceive me, I knew you did not love me.

Well, neither did I love you, though I was able to hide
it from you. And it has often irritated me that you were so
unobservant. You know now the cause of many of my difficult moods, which have seemed causeless.

I admired you from the first time we met. I have liked
you, I have been proud of you, I would not have been the
wife of any other man in the world, I would not have had
any other father for my children. But I have kept on loving
the man I loved before I met you.

Why? I don't know. I despised him for his weaknesses.
I should never have married him, though mother and Ed
both feared I would. I think I loved him because I knew he
loved me. That is the way it is with women—they seldom
love independently. Men like to love; women like to be
loved. And, poor, unworthy creature that he was, still he
would have died for me, though God had denied him the
strength to live for me. But all that God gave him—the
power to love—he gave me. And so he was different in my
eyes from what he was in any one's else in the world. And
I loved him.

I don't tell you this because I feel regret or remorse. I
don't; there never was a wife truer than I, for I put him

completely aside. I tell you, because I want you to remember me right after I'm gone, Harvey dear. You may remember how I was silly and jealous of you, and think I am mistaken about my own feelings. But jealousy doesn't mean love. When people really love, I think it's seldom that they're jealous. What makes people jealous usually is suspecting the other person of having the same sort of secret they have themselves. It hurt my vanity that you didn't love me; and it stung me to think you cared for some one else, just as I did.

I want you to remember me gently. And somehow I think that, after you've read this, you will, even if you did love some one else. If you ever see this at all, Harvey—and I may tear it up some day on impulse—but if you ever do see it, I shall be dead, and we shall both be free. And I want you to come to me and look at me and—"

It ended thus abruptly. No doubt she had intended to open the envelope and finish it—but, what more was there to say?

I think she must have been content with the thoughts that were in my mind as I looked down at her lying in death's inscrutable calm. I had one of my secretaries hunt out the man she had loved—a sad, stranded wreck of a man he had become; but since that day he has been sheltered at least from the worst of the buffetings to which his incapacity for life exposed him.

There was a time when I despised incapables; then I pitied them; but latterly I have felt for them the sympathetic sense of brotherhood. Are we not all incapables? Differing only in degree, and how slightly there, if we look at ourselves without vanity; like practice-sketches put upon the slate by Nature's learning hand and impatiently sponged away.

XXX

After the funeral I lingered at our Fredonia place. There was the estate to settle; my two daughters had now no one to look after them; Junior must be started right at learning the business of which he would soon be the head, as his uncle had shown himself far too easy-going for large executive responsibility. So, I stayed on, doing just enough to keep a face of plausibility upon my pretexts for not returning to Washington. The fact was that Carlotta's death had deepened my mood of distaste into disgust. It had set me to brooding over the futility and pettiness of my activities in politics, of all activities of whatever kind. I watched Ed and my children resuming the routine of their lives, swiftly adjusting themselves to the loss of one who had been so dear to them and apparently so necessary to their happiness. The cry of "man overboard," a few ripples, a few tears; the sailing on, with the surface

333

of the water smooth again and the faces keen and bright.

Woodruff wrote, urging; then he sent telegram after telegram. Still I procrastinated; for all the effect his letters and telegrams had upon me, I might as well have left them unopened. My final answer was: "Act as you would if I were dead."

Probably, what had given my pessimism its somberest tone was the attitude of the public toward Burbank's high appointments. I had confidently predicted that filling all the high offices with men who had no interest but "the interests," men who were notoriously the agents and servants of the great "campaign contributors," would cause a public outcry that could not be ignored. The opposition press did make perfunctory criticisms; but nowhere was there a sign that the people were really angered.

I got the clue to this mystery from my gardener, who prided himself on being strenuously of the opposition party. "What do you think of the new administration?" said I when I came upon him one morning at the rhododendron beds.

"Much better than I allowed," said he.   "Burbank's got good men around him."

"You approve of his Cabinet?"

"Of course, they're all strong party men.   I
like a good party man.   I like a man that has con-
victions and principles, and stands up for 'em."

"Your newspapers say some pretty severe
things about those men."

"So I read," said he, "but you know how that
is, Mr. Sayler.   They've got to pound 'em to
please the party.   But nobody believes much he
sees in the newspapers.   Whenever I read an item
about things I happen to know, it's all wrong.
And I guess they don't get it any nearer right
about the things I don't happen to know.   Now,
all this here talk of there being so many million-
aires—I don't take no kind of stock in it."

"No?" said I.

"Of course, some's poor and some's rich—that's
got to be.   But I think it's all newspaper lies
about these here big fortunes and about all the
leading men in politics being corrupt.   I know it
ain't so about the leading men in *my* party, and I

reckon there ain't no more truth in it about the
leading men of your'n. I was saying to my wife
last night, 'It's all newspaper lies,' says I, 'just
like the story they printed about Mrs. Timmins
eloping with Maria Wilmerding's husband, when
she had only went over to Rabbit Forks to visit
her married daughter.' No, they can't fool me—
them papers."

"That's one way of looking at it," said I.

"It's horse sense," said he.

And I have no doubt that to the average citizen,
leading a small, quiet life and dealing with affairs
in corner-grocery retail, the stupendous facts of
accumulations of wealth and wholesale, far-and-
wide purchases of the politicians, the vast system of bribery, with bribes adapted to every taste
and conscience, seem impossibilities, romanc-
ings of partizanship and envy and sensationalism.
Nor can he understand the way superior men play
the great games, the heartlessness of ambition, the
cynicism of political and commercial prostitution,
the sense of superiority to the legal and moral
codes which comes to most men with success.

Your average citizen is a hero-worshiper too.

He knows his own and his neighbor's weaknesses, but he gapes up at the great with glamoured eyes, and listens to their smooth plausibilities as to the reading of the Gospel from the pulpit. He belongs to the large mass of those who believe, not to the small class of those who question. But for the rivalries and jealousies of superior men which have kept them always divided into two parties, the ins and the outs, I imagine the masses would have remained for ever sunk in the most hopeless, if the most delightful, slavery—that in which the slave accepts his lowliness as a divine ordinance and looks up to his oppressors and plunderers as hero-leaders. And no doubt, so long as the exuberant riches of our country enable the triumphant class to "take care of" all the hungry who have intellect enough to make themselves dangerous, we shall have no change—except occasional spasms whenever a large number of unplaced intelligent hungry are forcing the full and fat to make room for them. How long will this be?

If our education did not merely feed prejudices instead of removing them, I should say not long. As it is, I expect to "leave the world as wicked and as foolish as I found it." At any rate, until the millenium, I shall continue to play the game under the rules of human nature—instead of under the rules of human ideals, as does my esteemed friend Scarborough. And I claim that we practical men are as true and useful servants of our country and of our fellow men as he. If men like him are the light, men like us are the lantern that shields it from the alternating winds of rapacity and resentment.

But, in running on about myself, I have got away from my point, which was how slight and even flimsy a pretense of fairness will shelter a man in high place—and therefore a Burbank. "He will fool the people as easily as he fools himself," said I. And more than ever it seemed to me that I must keep out of the game of his administration. My necessity of party regularity made it impossible for me to oppose him; my equal necessity of not outraging my sense of the wise, not to speak of the decent, made it impossible for me to abet him.

At last Woodruff came in person. When his name was brought to me, I regretted that I could not follow my strong impulse to refuse to see him. But at sight of his big strong body and big strong face, with its typically American careless good humor—the cool head, the warm heart, the amused eyes and lips that could also harden into sternness of resolution—at sight of this old friend and companion-in-arms, my mood began to lift and I felt him stirring in it like sunshine attacking a fog. "I know what you've come to say," I began, "but don't say it. I shall keep to my tent for the present."

"Then you won't have a tent to keep to," retorted he.

"Very well," said I. "My private affairs will give me all the occupation I need."

He laughed. "The general resigns from the command of the army to play with a box of lead soldiers."

"That sounds well," said I. "But the better the analogy, the worse the logic. I am going out of the business of making and working off gold bricks and green goods—and that's no analogy."

"Then you must be going to kill yourself," he replied. "For that's life."

"Public life—active life," said I. "Here, there
are other things."   And I looked toward my two
daughters, whose laughter reached us from their
pony-cart just rounding a distant curve in the
drive.

His gaze followed mine and he watched the two
children until they were out of sight, watched
them with the saddest, hungriest look in his eyes.
"Guess you're right," he said gruffly.

After a silence I asked: "What's the news?"

A quizzical smile just curled his lips, and it
broadened into a laugh as he saw my own rather
shamefaced smile of understanding. "Seems to
me," said he, "that I read somewhere once how a
king, perhaps it was an emperor, so hankered for
the quiet joys that he got off the throne and retired to a monastery—and then established lines
of post-horses from his old capital to bring him
the news every half-hour or so.   I reckon he'd
have taken his job back if he could have got it."

"I reckon," said I.

"Well," said he, "the news is that they're about
to oust you from the chairmanship of the national
committee and from control in this state."

"Really?" said I, in an indifferent tone—though I felt anything but indifferent.

"Really," said he. "Burbank is throwing out our people throughout the country and is putting Goodrich men in place of 'em—wherever our fellows won't turn traitor. And they've got hold of Roebuck. He's giving a dinner at the Auditorium to-morrow night. It's a dinner of eleven covers. I think you can guess who ten of 'em are for. The eleventh is for Dominick!"

That was enough. I grasped the situation instantly. The one weak spot in my control of my state was my having left the city bosses their local power, instead of myself ruling the cities from the state capital. Why had I done this? Perhaps the bottom reason was that I shrank from permitting any part of the machine for which I was directly responsible to be financed by collections from vice and crime. I admit that the distinction between corporate privilege and plunder and the pickings and stealings and prostitutions of individuals is more apparent than real. I admit that the kinds of vice and crime I tolerated are far more harmful than the other sorts

which are petty and make loathed outcasts of
their wretched practitioners. Still, I was snob
or Pharisee or Puritan enough to feel and to act
upon the imaginary distinction. And so, I had
left the city bosses locally independent—for,
without the revenues and other aids from vice
and crime, what city political machine could be
kept up?

"Dominick!" I exclaimed.

"Exactly!" said Woodruff. "Now, Mr. Sayler, the point is just here. I don't blame you for
wanting to get out. If I had any other game, I'd
get out myself. But what's to become of us—
of all your friends, not only in this state but
throughout the country? Are you going to stand
by and see them slaughtered and not lift a finger
to help 'em?"

There was no answering him. Yet the spur of
vanity, which clipped into me at thought of myself thrown down and out by these cheap in-
grates and scoundrels, had almost instantly
ceased to sting; and my sense of weary disgust
had returned. If I went into the battle again,
what work faced me? The same old monotonous

round. To outflank Burbank and Goodrich by
tricks as old as war and politics, and effective
only because human stupidity is infinite and un-
teachable. To beat down and whip back into the
ranks again these bandits of commerce disguised
as respectable, church-going, law-upholding men
of property—and to do this by the same old
methods of terror and force.

"You can't leave us in the lurch," said Doc.
"And the game promises to be interesting once
more. I don't like racing on the flat. It's the
hurdles that make the fun."

I pictured myself again a circus horse, going
round and round the ring, jumping the same old
hurdles at the same old intervals. "Take my
place, Doc," said I.

He shook his head. "I'm a good second," said
he, "but a rotten bad first."

It was true enough. He mysteriously lacked
that mysterious something which, when a man
happens to have been born with it, makes other
men yield him the command—give it to him,
force it on him, if he hangs back.

"What do you want me to do?" I asked.

"That dinner to-morrow night is in Suite L. Go to it—that's the shortest way to put Roebuck and Dominick out of business. Face 'em and they'll skulk."

"It's a risk," said I. I saw at once that he was right, but I was in a reluctant humor.

"Not a bit of it," was his confident reply. "I had a horse that was crazy—would run away on any old provocation. But no matter how busy he was at kicking up the dust and the dashboard, you could always halt him by ringing a bell once. He'd been in the street-car service. That's the way it is with men, especially strong men, that have been broken to the bell. They hear it ring and they can't resist. Go up and ring the bell."

"Go ring it yourself," said I.

"You're the bell," said he.

XXXI

HARVEY SAYLER, SWINEHERD

At a little after eight the following night, I was in Chicago, was knocking at Suite L in the Auditorium Hotel; I was hearing sounds from within that indicated that the dinner was under way. The door swung back and there stood old Roebuck himself, napkin in hand, his shriveling old face showing that his dollar sense was taking up the strength which his other senses were losing. He was saying cordially, "Ah, Croffut, you are late—"

Then his dim eyes saw me; he pulled himself up like a train when the air-brakes are clapped on.

"They told me at the office that you were at dinner," said I in the tone of one who has unintentionally blundered. "As I was looking for dinner, I rather hoped you'd ask me to join you. But I see that—"

"Come right in," he said smoothly, but gray

as a sheep. "You'll find some old friends of
yours. We're taking advantage of the convention of western manufacturers to have a little re-
union."

I now had a full view of the table. There was
a silence that made the creaking of starched
evening shirt-bosoms noisy as those men drew
long stealthy breaths when breathing became imperative. All my "clients" and Dominick—he at
Roebuck's right. At Roebuck's left there was a
vacant chair. "Shall I sit here?" said I easily.

"That place was reserved—was for—but—"
stammered Roebuck.

"For Granby's ghost?" said I pleasantly.

His big lips writhed. And as my glance of
greeting to these old friends of mine traveled
down one side of the table and up the other, it
might have been setting those faces on fire, so
brightly did they flare. It was hard for me to
keep my disgust beneath the surface. Those
"gentlemen" assembled there were among the
"leading citizens" of my state; and Roebuck was
famous on both sides of the Atlantic as a king
of commerce and a philanthropist. Yet, every

one of those brains was busy most of its hours with assassin-like plottings—and for what purpose? For ends so petty, so gross and stupid that it was inconceivable how intelligence could waste life upon them, not to speak of the utter depravity and lack of manliness. Liars, cheats, bribers; and flaunting the fruits of infamy as honors, as titles to respect, as gifts from Almighty God! And here they were, assembled now for silly plottings against the man whose only offense in their eyes was that he was saving them from themselves—was preventing them from killing the goose that would cheerfully keep on laying golden eggs for the privilege of remaining alive. It was pitiful. It was nauseating. I felt my degradation in stooping to such company.

I spoke to Dominick last. To my surprise he squarely returned my gaze. His eyes were twinkling, as the eyes of a pig seem to be, if you look straight into its face when it lifts its snout from a full trough. Presently he could contain the huge volume of his mirth no longer. It came roaring from him in a great coarse torrent, shak-

ing his vast bulk and the chair that sustained it,
swelling the veins in his face, resounding
through the silent room while the waiters literally stood aghast. At last he found breath to
ejaculate: "Well, I'll be good and—damned!"

This gale ripped from the others and whirled
away their cloaks of surface-composure. Naked,
they suggested a lot of rats in a trap—Dominick
jeering at them and anticipating the pleasure of
watching me torment them. I choked back the
surge of repulsion and said to Roebuck: "Then
where *shall* I sit?"

Roebuck looked, almost wildly, toward the
foot of the table. He longed to have me as far
from him as possible. Partridge, at the foot of
the table, cried out—in alarm: "Make room for
the Senator between you and Mr. Dominick, Roebuck! He ought to be as near the head of the table as possible."

"No matter where Senator Sayler sits, it's the
head of the table," said Roebuck. His commonplace of courtesy indicated, not recovered self-
control, but the cunning of his rampant instinct
of self-preservation—that cunning which men

so often exhibit in desperate straits, thereby winning credit for cool courage.

"We're a merry company," said I, as we sat.
This, with a glance at Dominick heaving in the
subsiding storm of his mirth. My remark set him
off again. I glanced at his place to see if he had
abandoned his former inflexible rule of total abstinence. There stood his invariable pot of tea.
Clearly, it was not drink that enabled him to enjoy a situation which, as it seemed to me, was
fully as unattractive for him as for his fellows.

Soon the door opened and in strode Croffut;
handsome, picturesque, with his pose of dashing,
brave manhood, which always got the crowds
into the mood for the frenzy his oratory conjured. Croffut seemed to me to put the climax
upon this despicable company—Croffut, one of
the great orators of the party, so adored by the
people that, but for our overwhelming superiority
in the state, I should never have dared eject him
from office. Since I ejected him he had not
spoken to me. Dominick looked at him, said in a
voice that would have flared even the warm
ashes of manhood into a furious blaze: "Go

and shake hands with Senator Sayler, Croffut, and sit down."

Croffut advanced, smiling. "I am fit for my company," thought I as I let him clasp my hand.

"Better tilt Granby's ghost out of that chair, Croffut," said Dominick, as the ex-Senator was seating himself. And in his animal exuberance of delight at his joke and at the whole situation he clapped Roebuck on the shoulder.

Roebuck shrank and winced. Moral humiliation he could shed as an armor-plated turret sheds musket-balls. But a physical humiliation, especially with spectators, sank in and sank deep. Instantly, alarmed lest Dominick had seen and understood, he smiled and said: "That's a vigorous arm of yours, Mr. Dominick."

"Not bad for a man of sixty," said Dominick.

I ate because to eat was a necessary part of my pose of absolute calmness; but I had to force down the food. It seemed to me to embody the banquet there set before my mental appetite. I found I had no stomach for that banquet. It takes the coarse palate of youth or the depraved palate of a more debauched manhood than mine

to enjoy such a feast. Yet, less than a year before, I had enjoyed, had delighted in, a far less
strenuous contest with these mutineers. As I sat
holding down my gorge and acting as if I were
at ease, I suddenly wondered what Elizabeth
Crosby would think of me if she could see. And
then I saw her, with a reality of imagining that
startled me—it was as if she were in the doorway; and her eyes lifted to mine in that slow,
steady, searching gaze of hers.

I suppose, if a soldier thrusting his saber into
the bowels of his enemy on the battle-field were
suddenly to see before him his mother or the
good and gentle wife or daughter he loved, he
would drop the saber and fly to hide himself like
a murderer. So, I, overwhelmed, said to myself: "I can not go on! Let these wretches wallow in their own vileness. I shall not wallow
with them. I am no swineherd!"

As I was debating how to escape and what one
of the many other ways of saving my friends
and lieutenants I should adopt, Dominick
touched me on the arm. "A word with you, Senator," said he.

He glanced at the others as if he were debating whether he should order them from the table while he talked with me. If he had ordered it, they would have gone. But restrained, perhaps by his crude though reverent sense of convention, he rose and led the way over to a corner.

"I want to tell you, Senator, that as soon as I got on to what this here push was plottin', I wired you askin' an appointment. You'll find the telegram at your house when you go home. I don't stand for no foulin'. I play the game straight. I came because I thought you'd want the party to be represented at such a getherin'."

I saw that he had come to the dinner, doubtful whether any enterprise against me, promising enough for him to risk embarking, could be launched; as soon as I entered the room he, like the rat when the cat interrupted the rat-and-mouse convention to discuss belling it, unceremoniously led the way to safety. But this was not one of those few occasions on which it is wise to show a man that his lies do not fool you. "I am glad to hear you say these things, Dominick," said I. "I am glad you are loyal to the party."

"You can trust me, Senator," said he earnestly.

"I can trust your common sense," said I. And I proceeded to grasp this lucky chance to get away. "I am leaving," I went on, "as soon as the coffee is served. I shall look to you to send these gentlemen home in a proper frame of mind toward the party."

His eyes glistened. Except his growing fortune, nothing delighted him so much as a chance to "rough-house" his eminently respectable "pals." He felt toward them that quaint mixture of envy, contempt and a desire to fight which fills a gamin at sight of a fashionably dressed boy. He put out his big hand and dampened mine with it. "You can count on me, Senator," he said gratefully. "I'll trim 'em, comb and tail-feathers."

"Don't overlook their spurs," said I.

"They ain't got none," said he, "except those you lend 'em."

We returned to a table palled by sullen dread —dread of me, anger against Dominick who, in the courage of his ignorance of the convention-alities which restrained them, had taken the short, straight cut to me and peace. And, as veterans in the no-quarter warfare of ambition, they knew I had granted him peace on no less terms than their heads.

They had all, even Roebuck, been drinking freely in the effort to counteract the depression. But the champagne seemed only to aggravate their gloom except in the case of young Jamieson. He had just succeeded, through the death of his father, to the privilege of levying upon the people of eleven counties by means of trolley franchises which the legislature had granted his father in perpetuity in return for financial services to "the party." It is, by the way, an interesting illustration of the human being's lack of thinking power that a legislature could not give away a small gold-mine belonging to the public to any man for even a brief term of years without causing a revolution, but could and does give away far more valuable privileges to plunder and to tax, and give them away for ever, without causing any real stir. However—young Jamieson's liquor, acting upon a mind that had not had enough experience to appreciate the meaning of the situation, drove him on to insolent taunts and boasts, addressed to his neighbors but intended for me. I ignored him and, when the coffee was served, rose to depart.

Roebuck urged me to stay, followed me to the coat-room, took my coat away from the servant and helped me with it. "I want to see you the first thing in the morning, Harvey," said he.

"I'll call you up, if I have time," said I.

We came out of the cloak-room, his arm linked in mine, and crossed the corner of the dining-room toward the outside door. Jamieson threw up his arm and fluttered his hand in an impertinent gesture of farewell. "So long, Senator Swollenhead," he cried in a thick voice. "We'll teach you a lesson in how to treat gentlemen."

The last word—gentlemen—was just clearing his mouth when Dominick's tea-pot, flung with all the force of the ex-prize-fighter's big muscles and big body, landed in the midst of his broad white shirt-bosom. And with the tea-pot Dominick hurled his favorite epithet from his garbage barrel of language. With a yell Jamieson crashed over backward; his flying legs, caught by the table, tilted it; his convulsive kicks sent it over, and half the diners, including Dominick, were floored under it.

All this in a snap of the fingers. And with the disappearance of the physical semblance of a company of civilized men engaged in dining in civilized fashion, the last thin veneer over hate and fury was scraped away. Curses and growling roars made a repulsive mess of sound over that repulsive mess of unmasked, half-drunken, wholly infuriated brutes. There is shrewd, sly wisdom snugly tucked away under the fable of the cat changed into a queen and how she sprang from her throne at sight of a mouse to pursue it on all fours. The best of us are, after all, animals changed into men by the spell of reason; and in some circumstances, it doesn't take much of a blow to dissolve that spell.

For those men in those circumstances, that blow proved sufficient. Partridge extricated himself, ran round the table and kicked Jamieson in the head—partly in punishment, perhaps, and because he needed just that vent for his rage, but chiefly to get credit with me, for he glanced toward me as he did it. Men, sprawling and squirming side by side on the floor, lashed out with feet and fists, striking each other and adding to the wild dishevelment. The candles set fire to the table-cloth and before the blaze was extinguished burned several in the hair and mustaches.

Dominick, roaring with laughter, came to Roebuck and me standing at the door, both dazed at this magic shift of a "gentlemen's" dinner into a bear-pit. "Granby's ghost is raisin' hell," said he.

But I had no impulse to laugh or to gloat. "Good night," said I to Roebuck and hastened away.

It was the end of the attempt to mine the foundations of my power. But I did not neglect its plain warning. As soon as the legislature assembled, I publicly and strongly advocated the appointment of a joint committee impartially to investigate all the cities of the state, those ruled by my own party no less than those ruled by the opposition. The committee was appointed and did its work so thoroughly that there was a popular clamor for the taking away of the charters of the cities and for ruling them from the state capital. It is hardly necessary to say that my legislature and governor yielded to this clamor. And so the semi-independent petty princes, the urban bosses, lost their independence and passed under my control; and the "collections" which had gone directly to them reached them by way of Woodruff as grants from my machine, instead of as revenues of their own right.

Before this securing of my home power was complete, I had my counter-attack upon the Burbank-Goodrich combine well under way. Immediately on my return to Fredonia from the disastrous dinner, I sent for the attorney general of the state, Ferguson. He was an ideal combination of man and politician. He held to the standards of private morality as nearly as it is possible for a man in active public life to hold to them—far more nearly than most men dare or, after they have become inured, care, to hold. He always maintained with me a firm but tactful independence; he saw the necessity for the sordid side of politics, but he was careful personally to keep clear of smutched or besmutching work. He had as keen an instinct for popularity as a bee has for blossoms; he knew how to do or to direct unpopular things on dark nights with a dark lantern, how to do or to direct popular things in full uniform on a white horse. I have never ordered any man to a task that was not morally congenial; and I was careful to respect Ferguson's notion of self-respect. I sent for him now, and outlined my plan—to bring suits, both civil and criminal, in the Federal courts in the name of the state, against Roebuck and his associates of the Power Trust.

When he had heard, he said: "Yes, Mr. Sayler, we can break up the Power Trust, can cause the indictment and conviction of Mr. Roebuck. I can prevent the United States Attorney General from playing any of the usual tricks and defending the men whom the people think he is vigorously prosecuting. But—"

"But?" said I encouragingly.

"Is this on the level? If I undertake these prosecutions, shall I be allowed to push them *honestly?* Or will there be a private settlement as soon as Roebuck and his crowd see their danger?"

"No matter what happens," I replied, "you shall prosecute at least the civil suits to the end. I give you my word for that."

He thanked me warmly, for he appreciated that I was bestowing upon him an enormous opportunity for national fame.

"And you?" said I. "If you succeed in this prosecution, will you remain in the public service or will you accept the offers the interests will make, and remove to New York and become a rich corporation lawyer?"

He reflected before answering. "That depends," said he. "If *you* are going to stay on in control in this state, I shall stick to public life, for I believe you will let me have what I call a career. But, if you are going to get out and leave me at the mercy of those fellows, I certainly shan't stay where they can fool the people into turning on me."

"I shall stay on," said I; "and after me, there will be Woodruff—unless, of course, there's some sort of cataclysm."

"A man must take chances," he answered. "I'll take that chance."

We called Woodruff into the consultation. Although he was not a lawyer, he had a talent for taking a situation by the head and tail and stretching it out and holding it so that every crease and wrinkle in it could be seen. And this made him valuable at any conference.

In January we had our big battery loaded, aimed and primed. We unmasked it, and Ferguson fired. I had expected the other side to act stupidly, but I had not hoped for such stupidity as they exhibited. Burbank's year of bathing in presidential flatteries and of fawning on and cringing to the multi-millionaires and their agents hedging him around, had so wrought upon him that he had wholly lost his point of view. And he let his Attorney General pooh-pooh the proceedings,—this in face of the great popular excitement and enthusiasm. It was not until Roebuck's lawyers got far enough into the case against him to see his danger that the administration stopped flying in the teeth of the cyclone of public sentiment and began to pretend enthusiasm, while secretly plotting the mistrial of Ferguson's cases. And not until the United States Attorney General—a vain Goodrich creature whose talents were crippled by his contempt for "the rabble" and "demagoguery"—not until he had it forced upon him that Ferguson could not be counter-mined, did they begin to treat with me for peace.

I shall not retail the negotiations. The upshot was that I let the administration drop the criminal cases against Roebuck in return for the restoration of my power in the national committee of the party to the smallest ejected postmaster in the farthest state. The civil action was pressed by Ferguson with all his skill as a lawyer and a popularity-seeking politician; and he won triumphantly in the Supreme Court—the lower Federal Court with its Power Trust judge had added to his triumph by deciding against him.

Roebuck was, therefore, under the necessity of going through the customary forms of outward obedience to the Supreme Court's order to him to dissolve. He had to get at huge expense, and to carry out at huger, a plan of reorganization.

Though he was glad enough to escape thus lightly, he dissembled his content and grumbled so loudly that Burbank's fears were roused and arrangements were made to placate him. The scheme adopted was, I believe, suggested by Vice-President Howard, as shrewd and cynical a rascal as ever lived in the mire without getting smutch or splash upon his fine linen of respectability.

For several years there had been a strong popular demand for a revision of the tariff. The party had promised to yield, but had put off redeeming its promise. Now, there arose a necessity for revising the tariff in the interest of "the interests." Some of the schedules were too low; others protected articles which the interests wanted as free raw materials; a few could be abolished without offending any large interests and with the effect of punishing some small ones that had been niggard in contributing to the "campaign fund" which maintains the standing army of political workers and augments it whenever a battle is on. Accordingly, a revision of the tariff was in progress. To soothe Roebuck, they gave him a tariff schedule that would enable him to collect each year more than the total of the extraordinary expenses to which I had put him. Roebuck "forgave" me; and I really forgave Burbank.

But I washed my hands of his administration. Not only did I actually stand aloof but also I disassociated myself from it in the public mind. When the crash should come, as come it must with such men at the helm, I wished to be in a position successfully to take full charge for the work of repair.

XXXII

A GLANCE BEHIND THE MASK OF GRANDEUR

Not until late in the spring of his second year did Burbank find a trace of gall in his wine.

From the night of his election parasites and plunderers and agents of plunderers had imprisoned him in the usual presidential fool's paradise. The organs of the interests and their Congressional henchmen praised everything he did; I and my group of Congressmen and my newspapers, as loyal partizans, bent first of all upon regularity, were silent where we did not praise also. But the second year of a President's first term is the beginning of frank, if guarded, criticism of him from his own side. For it is practically his last year of venturing to exercise any real official power. The selection of delegates to the party's national convention, to which a President must submit himself for leave to re-submit himself to the people, is well under way before the end of his third year; and direct and active preparations for it must begin long in advance.

Late in that second spring Burbank made a tour of the country, to give the people the pleasure of seeing their great man, to give himself the pleasure of their admiration, and to help on the Congressional campaign, the result of which would be the preliminary popular verdict upon his administration. The thinness of the crowds, the feebleness of the enthusiasm, the newspaper sneers and flings at that oratory once hailed as a model of dignity and eloquence—even he could not accept the smooth explanations of his flatterers. And in November came the party's memorable overwhelming defeat—reducing our majority in the Senate from twenty to six, and substituting for our majority of ninety-three in the House an opposition majority of sixty-seven.

I talked with him early in January and was amazed that, while he appreciated the public anger against the party, he still believed himself personally popular. "There is a lull in prosperity," said he, "and the people are peevish."

Soon, however, by a sort of endosmosis to which the densest vanity is somewhat subject, the truth began to seep through and to penetrate into him.

He became friendlier to me, solicitous toward spring—but he clung none the less tightly to Goodrich. The full awakening came in his third summer when the press and the politicians of the party began openly to discuss the next year's nomination and to speak of him as if he were out of the running. He was spending the hot months on the Jersey coast, the flatterers still swarming about him and still assiduous, but their flatteries falling upon ever deafer ears as his mind rivetted upon the hair-suspended sword. In early September he invited me to visit him—my first invitation of that kind in two years and a half. We had three interviews before he could nerve himself to brush aside the barriers between him and me.

"I am about to get together my friends with a view to next year," said he through an uneasy smile. "What do you think of the prospects?"

"What do your friends say?" I asked.

"Oh, of course, I am assured of a renomination—" He paused, and his look at me made
the confident affirmation a dubious question.

"Yes?" said I.

"And—don't you think my record has made
me strong?" he went on nervously.

"Strong—with whom?" said I.

He was silent. Finally he laid his hand on
my knee—we were taking the air on the ocean
drive. "Harvey," he said, "I can count on you?"

I shook my head. "I shall take no part in
the next campaign," I said. "I shall resign the
chairmanship."

"But I have selected you as my chairman. I
have insisted on you. I can't trust any one else.
I need others, I use others, but I trust only you."

I shook my head. "I shall resign," I repeated.
"What's the matter—won't Goodrich take the
place?"

He looked away. "I have not seriously
thought of any one but you," he said reproachfully.

I happened to know that the place had been offered to Goodrich and that he had declined it,

protesting that I, a Western man, must not be disturbed when the West was vital to the party's success. "My resolution is fixed," said I.

A long silence, then: "Sayler, have you heard anything of an attempt to defeat me for the nomination?"

"Goodrich has decided to nominate Governor Ridgeway of Illinois," said I.

He blanched and had to moisten his dry, wrinkled lips several times before he could speak. "A report of that nature reached me last Thursday," he went on. "For some time I have been perplexed by the Ridgeway talk in many of our organs. I have questioned Goodrich about it— and—I must say—his explanations are not—not wholly satisfactory."

I glanced at him and had instantly to glance away, so plainly was I showing my pity. He was not hiding himself from me now. He looked old and tired and sick—not mere sickness of body, but that mortal sickness of the mind and heart which kills a man, often years before his body dies.

"I have come to the conclusion that you were

right about Goodrich, Sayler. I am glad that I took your advice and never trusted him. I think you and I together will be too strong for him."

"You are going to seek a renomination?" I asked.

He looked at me in genuine astonishment. "It is impossible that the party should refuse me," he said.

I was silent.

"Be frank with me, Sayler," he exclaimed at last. "Be frank. Be my friend, your own old self."

"As frank and as friendly as you have been?" said I, rather to remind myself than to reproach him. For I was afraid of the reviving feeling of former years—the liking for his personal charms and virtues, the forbearance toward that weakness which he could no more change than he could change the color of his eyes. His moral descent had put no clear markings upon his pose. On the contrary, he had grown in dignity through the custom of deference. The people passing us looked admiration at him, had a new sense of the elevation of the presidential office.

Often it takes the trained and searching eye to detect in the majestic façade the evidences that the palace has degenerated into a rookery for pariahs.

"I have done what I thought for the best," he answered, never more direct and manly in manner. "I have always been afraid, been on guard, lest my personal fondness for you should betray me into yielding to you when I ought not. Perhaps I have erred at times, have leaned backward in my anxiety to be fair. But I had and have no fear of your not understanding. Our friendship is too long established, too well-founded." And I do not doubt that he believed himself; the capacity for self-deception is rarely short of the demands upon it.

"It's unfortunate—" I began. I was going to say it was unfortunate that no such anxieties had ever restrained him from yielding to Goodrich. But I hadn't the heart. Instead, I finished my sentence with: "However, it's idle to hold a post-mortem on this case. The cause of death is unimportant. The fact of it is sufficient. No doubt you did the best you could, Mr. President."

My manner was that of finality. It forbade

further discussion. He abandoned the finesse of negotiation.

"Harvey, I ask you, as a personal favor, to help me through this crisis," he said. "I ask you, my friend and my dead wife's friend."

No depth too low, no sentiment too sacred! Anger whirled up in me against this miserable, short-sighted self-seeker who had brought to a climax of spoliation my plans to guide the strong in developing the resources of the country. And I turned upon him, intending to overwhelm him with the truth about his treachery, about his attempts to destroy me. For I was now safe from his and Goodrich's vengeance—they had destroyed themselves with the people and with the party. But a glance at him and—how could I strike a man stretched in agony upon his deathbed? "If I could help you, I would," said I.

"You—you and I together can get a convention that will nominate me," he urged, hope and fear jostling each other to look pleadingly at me from his eyes.

"Possibly," I said. "But—of what use would that be?"

He sank back in the carriage, yellow-white and with trembling hands and eyelids. "Then you don't think I could be elected?" he asked in a broken, breathless way.

For answer I could only shake my head. "No matter who is the nominee," I went on after a moment, "our party can't win." I half-yielded to the impulse of sentimentality and turned to him appealingly. "James," said I, "why don't you—right away—before the country sees you are to be denied a renomination—publicly announce that you won't take it in any circumstances? Why don't you devote the rest of your term to regaining your lost—popularity? Every day has its throngs of opportunities for the man in the White House. Break boldly and openly with Goodrich and his crowd."

I saw and read the change in his face. My advice about the nomination straightway closed his mind against me; at the mention of Goodrich, his old notion of my jealousy revived. And I saw, too, that contact with and use of and subservience to corruption had so corrupted him that he no longer had any faith in any method not corrupt.   All in an instant I realized the full folly of what I was doing.   I felt confident that by pursuing the line I had indicated he could so change the situation in the next few months that he would make it impossible for them to refuse to renominate him, might make it possible for him to be elected.   But even if he had the wisdom to listen, where would he get the courage and the steadfastness to act?   I gave him up finally and for ever.

A man may lose his own character and still survive, and even go far.   But if he lose belief in character as a force, he is damned.   He could not survive in a community of scoundrels.

Burbank sat motionless and with closed eyes, for a long time.   I watched the people in the throng of carriages—hundreds of faces all turned toward him, all showing that mingled admiration, envy and awe which humanity gives its exalted great.   "The President!   The President!" I heard every few yards in excited undertones. And hats were lifting, and once a crowd of enthusiastic partizans raised a cheer.

"The President!" I thought, with mournful irony. And I glanced at him.

Suddenly he was transformed by an expression the most frightful I have ever seen. It was the look of a despairing, weak, vicious thing, cornered, giving battle for its life—like a fox at bay before a pack of huge dogs. It was not Burbank —no, *he* was wholly unlike that. It was Burbank's ambition, interrupted at its meal by the relentless, sure-aiming hunter, Fate.

"For God's sake, Burbank!" I exclaimed. "All these people are watching us."

"To hell with them!" he ground out. "I tell you, Sayler, I *will* be nominated! And elected too, by God! I will not be thrown aside like an emptied orange-skin. I will show them that I am President."

Those words, said by some men, in some tones, would have thrilled me. Said by him and in that tone and with that look, they made me shudder and shrink. Neither of us spoke again. When he dropped me at my hotel we touched hands and smiled formally for appearances before the gap-

ing, peeping, peering crowd. And as he drove
away, how they cheered him—the man risen high
above eighty millions, alone on the mountain-
peak, in the glorious sunshine of success. The
President!

The next seven months were months of turmoil in the party and in the country—a turmoil of which I was a silent spectator, conspicuous by my silence. Burbank, the deepest
passions of his nature rampant, had burst
through the meshes of partizanship and the
meshes of social and personal intimacies in
which he, as a "good party man" and as the
father of children with social aspirations and
as the worshiper of wealth and respectability,
was entangled and bound down; with the desperate courage that comes from fear of destruction, he was trying to save himself.

But his only available instruments were all
either Goodrich men or other kinds of machine-
men; they owed nothing to him, they had
nothing to fear from him—a falling king is
a fallen king. Every project he devised for
striking down his traitor friends and making

himself popular was subtly turned by his Cabinet or by the Senate or by the press or by all three into something futile and ridiculous or contemptible. It was a complete demonstration of the silliness of the fiction that the President could be an autocrat if he chose. Even had Burbank seen through the fawnings and the flatteries of the traitors round him, and dismissed his Cabinet, whatever men he might have put into it would not have attached themselves to his lost cause, but would have used their positions to ingratiate themselves with the power that had used and exhausted and discarded him.

He had the wisdom, or the timidity, to proceed always with caution and safe legality and so to avoid impeachment and degradation. His chief attempts were, naturally, upon monopoly; they were slyly balked by his sly Attorney General, and their failure was called by the press, and was believed by the people, the cause of the hard times which were just beginning to be acute. What made him such an easy victim to his lieutenants was not their craft, but the fact that he had lost his sense of right and wrong. A man of affairs may not, indeed will not, always steer by that compass; but he must have it aboard. Without it he can not know how far off the course he is, or how to get back to it. No ship ever reached any port except that of failure and disgrace, unless it, in spite of all its tackings before the cross-winds of practical life, kept in the main to the compass and to the course.

His last stagger was—or seemed to be—an attempt to involve us in a war with Germany. I say "seemed to be" because I hesitate to ascribe a project as infamous to him, even when unbalanced by despair. The first ugly despatch he ordered his Goodrich Secretary of State to send, *somehow* leaked to the newspapers before it could be put into cipher for transmission. It was not sent—for from the press of the entire country rose a clamor against "deliberate provocation of a nation with which we are, and wish to remain, at peace." He repudiated the despatch and dismissed the Secretary of State in disgrace to disgrace—the one stroke in his fight against

Goodrich in which he got the advantage. But that advantage was too small, too doubtful and too late.

His name was not presented to the convention.

XXXIII

A "SPASM OF VIRTUE"

I forced upon Goodrich my place as chairman
of the national committee and went abroad with
my daughters. We stayed there until Scarborough was inaugurated. He had got his nomination from a convention of men who hated and
feared him, but who dared not flout the people
and fling away victory; he had got his election because the defections from our ranks in the doubtful states far outbalanced Goodrich's extensive
purchases there with the huge campaign-fund of
the interests. The wheel-horse, Partizanship, had
broken down, and the leader, Plutocracy, could
not draw the chariot to victory alone.

As soon as the election was over, our people
began to cable me to come home and take charge.
But I waited until Woodruff and my other faithful lieutenants had thoroughly convinced all the
officers of the machine how desperate its plight
was, and that I alone could repair and restore,

and that I could do it only if absolute control
were given me. When the ship reached quaran-
tine Woodruff came aboard; and, not having
seen him in many months, I was able to see, and
was startled by, the contrast between the Doc
Woodruff I had met on the train more years before than I cared to cast up, and the United
States Senator Woodruff, high in the councils of
the party and high in the esteem of its partizans
among the people. He was saying: "You can
have anything you want, Senator," and so on.
But I was thinking of him, of the vicissitudes of
politics, of the unending struggle of the foul
stream to purify itself, to sink or to saturate its
mud. For we ought not to forget that if the
clear water is saturated with mud, also the mud
is saturated with clear water.

A week or so after I resumed the chairmanship, Scarborough invited me to lunch alone with
him at the White House. When I had seen him,
four years before, just after his defeat, he was
in high spirits and looked a youth. Now it depressed me, but gave me no surprise, to find him
worn, and overcast by that tragic sadness which

canopies every one of the seats of the mighty.
"I fear, Mr. President," said I, "you are finding
the men who will help you to carry out your
ideas as rare as I once warned you they were."

"Not rare," was his answer, "but hard to get
at through the throngs of Baal-worshipers that
have descended upon me and are trying to hedge
me in."

"Fortunately, you are free from political and
social entanglements," said I, with ironic intent.

He laughed with only a slightly concealed bitterness. "From political entanglements—yes,"
said he. "But not from social toils. Ever since
I have been in national life, my wife and I have
held ourselves socially aloof, because those with
whom we would naturally and even inevitably
associate would be precisely those who would
some day beset me for immunities and favors.
And how can one hold to a course of any sort of
justice, if doing so means assailing all one's
friends and their friends and relatives? For who
are the offenders? They are of the rich, of the
successful, of the clever, of the socially agreeable
and charming. And how can one enforce justice

against one's dinner companions—and in favor
of whom? Of the people, voiceless, distant, un-
known to one. Personal friendship on the one
side; on the other, an abstraction."

"I should not class you among those likely to
yield many inches to the social bribe," said I.

"That is pleasant, but not candid," replied he
with his simple directness. "No man of your experience could fail to know that the social bribe
is the arch-corrupter, the one briber whom it is
not in human nature to resist. But, as I was
saying, to my amazement, in spite of my wife's
precautions and mine, I find myself beset—and
with what devilish insidiousness! When I refuse, simply to save myself from flagrant treachery to my obligations of duty, I find myself seeming, even to my wife and to myself, churlish and
priggish; Pharisaical, in the loathsome attitude
of a moral *poseur*. Common honesty, in presence of this social bribe, takes on the sneaking
seeming of rottenest hypocrisy. It is indeed hard
to get through and to get at the men I want and
need, and must and will have."

"Impossible," said I. "And if you could get

at them, and if the Senate would let you put them where they seem to you to belong, the temptation would be too much for them. They too would soon become Baal-worshipers, the more assiduous for their long abstinence."

"Some," he admitted, "perhaps most. But at least a few would stand the test—and just one such would repay and justify all the labor of all the search. The trouble with you pessimists is that you don't take our ancestry into account. Man isn't a falling angel, but a rising animal. So, every impulse toward the decent, every gleam of light, is a tremendous gain. The wonder isn't the bad but the good, isn't that we are so imperfect, but that in such a few thousand years we've got so far—so far *up*. I know you and I have in the main the same purpose—where is there a man who'd like to think the world the worse for his having lived? But we work by different means. You believe the best results can be got through that in man which he has inherited from the past—by balancing passion against passion, by offsetting appetite with appetite. I hope for results from that in the man of to-day which is the seed, the prophecy, of the man who is to be."

"Your method has had one recent and very striking *apparent* success," said I. "But—the spasm of virtue will pass."

"Certainly," he replied, "and so too will the succeeding spasm of reaction. Also, your party must improve itself—and mine too—as the result of this spasm of virtue."

"For a time," I admitted. "I envy you your courage and hope. But I can't share in them. You will serve four stormy years; you will retire with friends less devoted and enemies more bitter; you will be misunderstood, maligned; and there's only a remote possibility that your vindication will come before you are too old to be offered a second term. And the harvest from the best you sow will be ruined in some flood of reaction."

"No," he answered. "It will be reaped. The evil I do, all evil, passes. The good will be reaped. Nothing good is lost."

"And if it is reaped," I rejoined, "the reaping

will not come until long, long after you are a
mere name in history."

Even as I spoke my doubts I was wishing I
had kept them to myself; for, thought I, there's
no poorer business than shooting at the beautiful
soaring bird of illusion. But he was looking at
me without seeing me. His expression suggested
the throwing open of the blinds hiding a man's
inmost self.

"If a man," said he absently, "fixes his mind
not on making friends or defeating enemies, not
on elections or on history, but just on avoiding
from day to day, from act to act, the condemna-
tion of his own self-respect—" The blinds closed
as suddenly as they had opened—he had become
conscious that some one was looking in. And I
was wishing again that I had kept my doubts
to myself; for I now saw that what I had thought
a bright bird of illusion was in fact the lost star
which lighted my own youth.

Happy the man who, through strength or
through luck, guides his whole life by the star
of his youth. Happy, but how rare!

XXXIV

"LET US HELP EACH OTHER"

In the following September I took my daughters to Elizabeth. She looked earnestly, first at Frances, tall and slim and fancying herself a woman grown, then at Ellen, short and round and struggling with the giggling age. "We shall like each other, I'm sure," was her verdict. "We'll get on well together." And Frances smiled, and Ellen nodded. They evidently thought so, too.

"I want you to teach them your art," said I, when they were gone to settle themselves and she and I were alone.

"My art?"

"The art of being one's self. I am sick of men and women who hide their real selves behind a pose of what they want others to think them."

"Most of our troubles come from that, don't they?"

"All mine did," said I. "I am at the age when the very word age begins to jar on the ear, and the net result of my years of effort is—I have convinced other people that I am somebody at the cost of convincing myself that I am nobody."

"No, you are master," she said.

"As a lion-tamer is master of his lions. He gives all his thought to them, who think only of their appetites. And his whole reward is that with his life in his hand he can sometimes cow them through a few worthless little tricks." I looked round the attractive reception-room of the school. "I wish you'd take *me* in, too," I ended.

She flushed a little, then shook her head, her eyes twinkling. "This is not a reformatory," said she. And we both laughed.

As I did not speak or look away, but continued to smile at her, she became uneasy, glanced round as if seeking an avenue of retreat.

"Yes—I mean just that, Elizabeth," I admitted, and my tone explained the words.

She clasped her hands and started up.

"In me—in every one," I went on, "there's a beast and a man. Just now—with me—the man is uppermost. And he wants to stay uppermost. Elizabeth—will you—help him?"

She lowered her head until I could see only the splendor of her thick hair, sparkling like black quartz.

"Will you—dear? Won't you—dear?"

Suddenly she gave me both her hands. "Let us help each other," she said. And slowly she lifted her glance to mine; and never before had I felt the full glory of those eyes, the full melody of that deep voice.

And so, I end as I began, as life begins and ends—with a woman. In a woman's arms we enter life; in a woman's arms we get the courage and strength to bear it; in a woman's arms we leave it. And as for the span between—the business, profession, career—how colorless, how meaningless it would be but for her!

THE END

THE MUCKRAKERS

*A series of American novels of Muckraking,
Propaganda, and Social Protest*

EDWARD BELLAMY
Equality
ARTHUR BULLARD
Comrade Yetta
CHARLES W. CHESNUTT
The Colonel's Dream
WINSTON CHURCHILL
Mr. Crewe's Career
JAMES FENIMORE COOPER
The Ways of the Hour
ERNEST H. CROSBY
Captain Jinks, Hero
REBECCA HARDING DAVIS
Waiting for the Verdict
IGNATIUS DONNELLY
The Golden Bottle
MARY EASTMAN
Aunt Phillis's Cabin; or, Southern Life as It Is
HAMLIN GARLAND
A Member of the Third House
ROBERT GRANT
The Orchid
SARAH J. HALE
Liberia: or Mr. Peyton's Experiments
ROBERT HERRICK
The Common Lot
RICHARD HILDRETH
The Slave; or Memoirs of Archy Moore
JOSIAH G. HOLLAND
Sevenoaks
JAMES M. HOPPER & FRED R. BECHDOLT
9009
FREDERIC C. HOWE
Confessions of a Monopolist
SYLVESTER JUDD
Margaret
REGINALD W. KAUFFMAN
The House of Bondage